THE MERMAID'S CALL

a&b

THE MERMAID'S CALL

KATHERINE STANSFIELD

Allison & Busby Limited
11 Wardour Mews
London W1F 8AN
allisonandbusby.com

First published in Great Britain by Allison & Busby in 2019.

A CIP catalogue record for this book is available from
the British Library.

First Edition

ISBN 978-0-7490-2382-9

Typeset in 11/16 pt Adobe Garamond Pro by
Allison & Busby Ltd.

The paper used for this Allison & Busby publication
has been produced from trees that have been legally sourced
from well-managed and credibly certified forests.

Printed and bound by
CPI Group (UK) Ltd, Croydon, CR0 4YY

For Beth and Rose

ONE

The girl's scream woke me.

I was used to such starts by then, so I didn't reach for the candlestick ready to brain a stranger come to harm us. I did what I had done so often since the girl had come into my life. I pushed off the blankets and gathered the sweating weight of her into my arms, sat her up but held her down, against me. That was the best way. I had learnt that over many nights of screams and sobs and words in a way of talking I still didn't know. She had given up her German words when she was awake, but when she was asleep it was German that was her scream tongue. Only in sleep did she make any noise about what had happened to her.

'There now,' I said, and rocked her, though she was no small creature for that, and she was strong, too. Her sleeping body fought me, but I held on, rode it out with her. As I did too often.

She smelt of the harbour, where she had been all day amongst the crab pots. Salt and fish and something else. The ham hock we'd had for our supper. There was her day in her red, clammy skin, in her thick hair brown as the caulk of the boats she loved to watch. This poor girl in my arms. I pressed my cheek against hers.

I told her it was done now. She was safe, my girl. My poor girl.

Mathilda.

To speak true, we owed the girl debts, we being Anna Drake and me, and I wanted to repay her, truly I did.

Mathilda thrashed and I held tighter, but it was no good. I could feel the muscles in her neck tighten and then her head was shaking. I tried to prise open her lips. On my fingers, a warm wet. Even without the light I knew what it was. Tonight's dreams were bad.

'Anna!' I shouted. She'd have heard the screams already, her room being next to ours, and put the pillow over her head. 'Anna, please!'

I fought Mathilda's wild arms and with a thump we tumbled to the floor. My hip was dull with pain but at least now I could get her on her side so she wouldn't choke on her blood, and then the door opened and there was light.

'There's only so much of this Mrs Yeo will put up with,' Anna said, setting down her candle.

'Never mind that – Mathilda's going to bite her tongue clean off!'

'Where's the bar?'

'On the window ledge,' I said. 'No – the other side.'

The whites of Mathilda's eyes rolled, there was sweat above her lip, and I thought of the pony I had seen drown in the marsh. A long time ago. Another life.

'Quick! Hold her arms.'

Anna scrambled onto the bed next to me and her robe grazed my hand – a slink of cool, fine silk. She pinned Mathilda's arms behind her back and I got two fingers into the corner of the girl's mouth, as my father had done to horses to make them take the bit. The clamp of Mathilda's jaw eased for a heartbeat and I slipped the small bar of much-chewed wood we kept for such purpose between her teeth. All at once she ceased her jerks and thrashes

8

and went limp as if dead in my lap. The bar of wood rolled free of her mouth and landed on the floorboard with a wet tap. It left a smear of blood.

For a moment neither Anna nor I spoke, just watched the still-sleeping girl and let the work of our own panic ease from us. It was Anna who broke the silence. It often was.

'To see what Mathilda saw,' she said, and tucked a strand of Mathilda's hair behind her ear. 'And she's so young. It's been more than six months now. Will she ever be free of it?'

I thought of my own terrors. They'd been with me far longer than Mathilda had had hers. I knew she wouldn't be free for a fair time to come, if at all, but what use was it to say? Anna didn't like me to speak of my losses. There was nothing to be done but to keep eating bread and breathing and going to sleep.

'Let's get her back in bed before she catches a chill,' Anna said.

Together we hauled the sleeping Mathilda to her feet and then onto the bed. She was shivering now as her sweat cooled, so Anna fetched her blanket and added it to the one I shared with Mathilda.

'Is it too early to get up or too late to go back to sleep?' Anna said.

I pushed aside the curtain. The harbour of Boscastle was still dark save for a lamp burning here and there on the boats with night business.

'Neither,' I said. 'Mathilda has woken us in the true middle of the night.'

Anna gave a little smile. 'That must be some kind of talent. How to sleep after that? You go back to bed, Shilly. I'll see—'

'We'll light the fire, will we?'

'I suppose we—'

'And I'll get the paper.' I was making for the door before she had a chance to say no, Shilly, it's too late, no, Shilly, you'll never learn. No, Shilly, I don't love you.

'Shilly, wait.'

'You promised you'd teach me, Anna, and it's been months and I'm still so slow. I'll light the fire and make the tea, and there's some of Mrs Yeo's cake. Not much left, but you can have my—'

'Your hands, Shilly. Look.'

I looked. My palms were bloodied.

'Let me fetch a cloth,' Anna said. 'I doubt our landlord will welcome blood upstairs as well as down.'

She was speaking of the butcher's shop. Our rooms were above it.

Anna took the candle and I followed her into the little room she liked to call a parlour but that was more than it earned. Two rickety chairs and a stool. A table that sagged. A patch of damp by the window, shaped like a swan. Still, it was ours, for now at least. I held up my palms to keep the blood from touching anything.

'You look like a martyr in a painting,' Anna said.

'A what?'

'Someone who dies for others.' She set to cleaning my hands with a wet cloth. The fire was glowing embers and all the room was kind to me in that moment. Anna, holding my hands.

'Murdered?' I said, but soft as embers turning over. Like *murdered* was a good word.

'I suppose you could say that. But not the kind of murders we concern ourselves with.'

'We haven't concerned ourselves with many of late,' I said.

It was a poor thing to say. Her hands stilled.

'There's only a bit left,' she said. 'There – your thumb. You can do the rest. I'll stir up the fire.'

And she let go of my hands and turned away, only for the poker, only bending low to the grate but I felt the loss of her keenly. It was between us always. What had been once – me and Anna had lain together. What might be again? When we had first come to Boscastle I said to myself, Shilly, if you wait. If you wait and let her see you're not doing the bad things any more. That you are good and work hard at your reading. If you just wait. My God but it was hard not to touch her, to tell her. Some days I wanted to claw my skin from my face it was so hard.

'What about this cake, then?' she said, and I nodded and that was that. Our life together.

For now.

TWO

I went to the little room next to the parlour where we kept our few plates and cups and the teapot. Mrs Yeo, our landlady, had brought us the seed cake the day before. Anna had said we should keep some for another day, make it last, and that I couldn't fathom, for we had money now, plenty of it. We could eat fresh cakes every day, eat them until we were sick and still have money for more.

Our riches were thanks to Mathilda. She had *in hair i tance*. That was the money of the dead, gifted to Mathilda because she'd been a lady before she met us, in a place called *ger man ee*. Anna said that was far from here, so far that people spoke a different tongue. It was *across the sea*. I liked the song of that. *Ger man ee, a cross the sea*. Mathilda had come to Cornwall for a sad purpose, and found only more sadness here, for in the woods where she'd made her home there was darkness waiting for her – people who wished to do her harm, and she the sweetest creature I had ever known, who wanted only to be loved.

It was a bad business, and Anna and I had saved her from this. Afterwards, when it was over, Anna said Mathilda should give us her money, that it wouldn't be spending but saving, for

Anna and I were detectives. We were to start the agency and Anna said Mathilda was an *in ves tor* and she would get *returns*. I didn't know what that meant but Mathilda did, and she'd agreed to Anna's plan. I had many new words all to do with money since meeting Mathilda. One thing I did know, I wasn't poor now. I didn't have to go back to milking cows, which was my work previous and hateful.

But now I asked myself if my thinking was wrong, for even with Mathilda's money, Anna was all for being careful with our spending. Too careful. I poked the leftover seed cake. It was dry. Some things were better enjoyed at once. There was too much went stale in life.

I took what was left of the cake to the parlour, which was now a room of light for Anna had gathered our candle ends and set them round the table we used for lessons. My heart turned over with joy at the sight of the papers. My papers. For writing and for reading.

Life had changed much since I had first met Anna Drake. That meeting was close on a year before this though I was not wise about the keeping of time so it was her that told me of dates and such. She had come to the moor, where I was living then. It was a bad reason that had brought her – the death of someone I had loved. But goodness had come from it. She had taken me from that place where I had no one, nothing, and given me a new life. Had we done the same for Mathilda? Anna Drake was a great collector of women.

'I'll leave the door open,' I said, 'to hear Mathilda's screams.'

'How restful,' Anna said. 'Reading first, then cake. Where did we get to?'

I sat at the table and looked over the pages I had written. That *I* had written! I had taken to reading easier than writing, truth be told. My writing was not careful, and the ink was devious in getting places it had no business being, where there were no words. But on this page now before me there were words in the middle of the whiteness, and I had made them with my own hand. And Anna's help, of course. That was the bargain we had struck. If I could keep from the drink, she would help me learn reading and writing.

I put my finger under the first word at the top. '*To day.*' I stopped and looked at her.

'Keep going.' She wrapped herself tighter in her silk robe and settled back in her chair.

'*To day ma tild da and shi lie saw three boats.*' My finger plodded along the page as Anna had told me to do when reading, and she was my teacher so I did everything she said. '*The su san. The me rry ma . . . ma . . .*' My mouth was hardening tallow.

'Merry Maiden,' Anna said.

'*Me rry may den.*'

'Good. And the next—'

We both stiffened at a noise from the room where Mathilda lay. A moan. The bed creaking beneath her. I waited for the scream, but nothing more came. As if we were one body, Anna and I let our shoulders slump.

'Would that we were merrier ourselves,' she said.

'I wouldn't want to be the Merry Maidens proper,' I said.

'Why not?'

'Well, they're girls turned to stone. For dancing on the Sabbath. You can't be very merry if you've moor stone for a body.'

'A fair point,' Anna said.

This pleased me for it meant I was being useful. Anna was a detective and she had asked me to join her in this, to be a detective alongside her. It was a word I hadn't got to spelling yet. It was tricksy enough to say, and I was still finding my way with the

14

work. Some days it was better than milking cows, but others it was worse. Much worse.

'Shilly?' She was staring at me, her thin features made narrower still with worry. 'You were muttering again.'

'I wasn't.'

'Are you feeling it, the need to—'

'No! No, Anna, I promise.'

She put her hand on mine. I took it, but too quick, too eager to press it against my lips. She pulled away. She had loved me once. I had made her cry out with the goodness of my hands and of my mouth.

'I know you're trying,' she said, 'and I know the effort it must be.'

'Then why can't we—'

'You didn't tell me the third boat.'

'What?' I said.

'The third boat you saw today. You're keeping your end of the bargain, Shilly, so I must keep mine.'

'Yes,' I managed to whisper, and tried to send from my thoughts the memory of her sharp hip bones and the taut skin between them. My finger sought the last words in the line I had written. '*The per ince of Way uls.*'

'Very good,' she said.

'Very slow, you mean.' I helped myself to cake.

'You're too hard on yourself, Shilly. These things take time.'

'How long did it take you to learn writing?' I said.

That set her thinking. Her long thin nose, her thin bloodless lips, were tight with considering. I heard the sound I knew to be her thinking sound, just soft, on the edge of hearing. The *tap tap* of her false teeth knocking about. You had to know it to hear it, and I did know it for we spent much time together thinking, Anna Drake and I. That was our work. There were other things I'd rather be doing with her. Wait, Shilly. Wait.

'I don't know,' she said. 'I don't remember learning.'

'That's because you were young,' I said. 'I don't remember learning the things I learnt then.'

'Such as?'

'How much water pigs drink in summer. Where the blackberries grew best.'

And how to slip free my father's fists I thought but didn't say.

What I did say was, 'Who taught *you* to write?'

Anna picked up the poker and stirred the fire though it was burning fine enough. She didn't like questions about herself but that didn't mean I wouldn't ask them. Working together meant knowing each other. That was hard going with Anna Drake. Harder than writing. She was easier being her other selves, the ones fashioned from wigs and paints and clothes with padding sewn inside to give her new bodies. When she was stripped back like this, her own cropped yellow hair showing, she was more a stranger. And a little-seen one at that, for Anna Drake was only like this first thing in the morning or late at night for that was when others wouldn't see her. These were the best times to turn detective on *her*, when she had no one to hide behind.

'The butcher and his wife who took you in,' I said, to help her, 'when you were left on their doorstep. The first butcher's shop you lived in, not this one. It was them that taught you writing?'

She nodded.

'And then you went to school,' I said.

Her breath had shortened. Her cheeks were pink. 'My mother – my adoptive mother, she . . . Well, she didn't enjoy good health. She liked to have me with her, so there was no mention of school. You and I have that in common, Shilly.'

'What was the matter with her?'

'This cake is rather dry. Some tea, I think.'

16

And that was the end of that *in ves tig ay shun*.

She stood up. 'I'll make the tea. You write a new line.'

'What about?'

'Whatever takes your fancy,' she said. 'What happened after you saw the boats. The weather. Remember what we talked about – say the words aloud before you write them down. Your mouth must make each sound separately.'

She hung the kettle over the fire and went to fetch the teapot. I thought about what to put. There were so many things I wanted to write down, words to own there on the page in my own poor hand, but I wrote so slow and badly that none of them ever got there. I decided to write a line I had been practising – *my name is Shilly Williams. I am nineteen years of age.*

The first part wasn't true but that didn't matter. Anna was all for false names. I wasn't even sure *she* was really called Anna Drake but I'd stopped asking her about that for it made no difference and I had to call her something. The second part, about my age, was as true as I could know, not having any family left to ask and being none too certain of the truth when my father had signed me into service at the farm the year before.

That was where I had met Anna, and then together we escaped. We met Mathilda after that, in the woods, and we had a terrible time, Mathilda the worst of it, for people had tried to kill her – a stranger, it was, that first tried to take Mathilda's life, and then someone who shouldn't have been a stranger to my poor, sweet girl. And the birds there, in the woods . . . I shook such thinking away. If I let myself remember that time, then I'd be as wretched as poor Mathilda, biting off my tongue. Anna would have two of us to care for and wouldn't have any time for detecting, if a case should come to the door. We had got away from the woods and the birds and all the hatred at last. We had escaped, the three of us, and now we were in Boscastle which was a good place and we had no need of escaping.

But we did need some work. Anna said we did, to live on, even though we had five hundred pounds from Mathilda. That was hard to fathom. Five hundred sounded plenty to me.

'The notice is still in the newspaper?' I asked Anna while we waited for the kettle to boil.

She nodded.

'And it's the same one as before, that you showed me?' I said.

'It is. Mathilda did a fine job of it.'

'You mean her drawing?'

'It's more draughtsmanship, Shilly. It means—Never mind.'

The notice was placed when we had first come to Boscastle, before I had started my reading proper, so I hadn't been able to tell the letters then, but I had seen the smart lines Mathilda had put around Anna's words.

'Much good the advertisement is doing us, though,' Anna said. 'Not a case to speak of.'

'That's not true. There was the woman up Trequite Farm.'

Anna made a noise of scorn. 'That? You can hardly call that a case, Shilly. A farmer with shocking breath and a lazy eye thinks his much younger wife is possessed by a demon that makes her walk in her sleep. The only devil tempting that woman was lust for the cowhand in the barn.'

'Her husband did pay us for finding that out, though,' I said, remembering his tears as he handed me the coins. Were they from relief there were no devils on his land, or sadness at his wife betraying him? Either way, it was hard to see him weep.

'Well yes, all right,' Anna said. 'Ten shillings for a night's observation and a few traps. Not bad as a rate, but I suspect we wouldn't even have had *that* work if it weren't for Mrs Yeo taking pity on us and telling the delusional farmer we could help.'

'Mrs Yeo is very kindly.'

The kettle whistled so I lifted it from the fire with the cloth we kept close by for such a purpose. It was a scrap from Anna's travelling case and I knew it to be the pattern of one of Mrs Williams' dresses. My dresses when I was that lovely creature, for Anna wasn't the only one who wore disguises. I was often in them myself.

'Do you think it's because of who we are?' I said. 'Not being men.'

'Hmm?'

'That it's because we're women we haven't had many cases, and so we can't move to a better place with a sign over the door like you said we would have. A sign painted by Mathilda.'

Anna stirred the tea with some viciousness, then clamped the lid on the pot.

'I think it must be the same trouble you had before,' I said. 'In Scotland, when the men wouldn't have you.'

'It was Scotland *Yard*, Shilly. That's where the new detective force is housed. And you might be right. I hold out no hope that north Cornwall will be any more enlightened than the streets of London, but still . . .'

I patted her hand. 'Still, we must try. It's what we're good at, and it's better work than milking cows.'

Anna smiled. 'I don't doubt it.'

'And after all,' I said, and looked at her askance, 'we're not always women, are we?'

And now she blushed. 'Quite so, Shilly.'

'Pass me your cup, then. We'll drink to better times, shall we?'

'We shall. Or at least the continuing kindness of landladies.'

'To Mrs Yeo,' I said, and raised my cup.

Anna clanked me and we sipped.

'Mrs Yeo might not be so kindly when we can no longer pay for a roof over our heads,' Anna muttered, taking her pipe from the shelf above the fire.

'We'll have to go and work in the shop downstairs, then,' I said. 'You must know your way around a meat hook, Anna, you growing up in a butcher's.' I grinned, for I was playing the game along with her. Such talk of no rent could only be foolishness. We had all the money in the world since meeting Mathilda.

I cleared my throat. 'I know you say we must save the money Mathilda has given us—'

'That she has *invested*, Shilly.'

'All right, invested, for the agency.' The smell of her tobacco made my nose prickle. 'But we can use it to live on, can't we? And it's more than enough.'

But Anna wouldn't meet my eye and I saw she hadn't been making a game of our rent. And that made my stomach drop to a cold, dark place, because we had been so careful with money, saving, that we should have most of it left. Shouldn't we?

'These seeds . . .' Anna took out her little row of false teeth and poked at them with the stem of her pipe.

I said nothing. She had shown me again that she was still the one who had the business of our earning and our spending, though she had said we were to be partners in the business of detection.

A piece of wood dropped against the fire's grate. From the harbour, a faraway shout and then a man's laugh. And still I waited.

'It's fine, Shilly,' she said at last. 'I'm just looking to the future, that's all. Mathilda won't get much for her investment if we only have unfaithful farmers' wives to deal with.' A black speck flew from her false teeth and shot across the room. 'There! Got it. That would have kept me awake all night. Speaking of which.' She got up and stretched. 'I'm going to try to get some sleep.'

She put her hand on my shoulder. No squeeze, no stroke. But her hand there, for two breaths. Then she was gone.

I stayed in the parlour for the fire to burn out for I was uneasy. The patch of damp on the wall looked to have grown, the swan shape fattened to a goose. I'd become so used to the damp being there I had stopped thinking of it as a bad thing, that we were living poor. But now, with Anna saying we'd have no money for rent, I saw the damp anew. And I asked myself, Shilly, why are you three living this way when you have Mathilda's five hundred pounds?

Because Anna says we must. And why is that?

Surely the money was all right? It had only been six months since we'd come to Boscastle and we'd been so careful. I was used to thrift – my life before Anna had meant I'd had to be. But Anna herself . . . Who knew how she was with money? If she could be trusted. I still knew so little about Anna Drake.

Apart from that I loved her.

THREE

Mrs Yeo woke me, banging the door at the bottom of our stairs.

'Only me, my dears!' she called out.

She said that every morning when she brought the breakfasts, as if we might think someone else had come to visit. But no one had called on us in Boscastle, even with the advert in the paper.

The door to the parlour was flung open by Mrs Yeo's ample hip and she carried in the plates of bread and bacon.

'Going to be a dirty one today,' she said. 'Weather's turned. Miss Mathilda will need to take care on the harbour wall, what with the wind.' She set the plates down.

She was tall, unlike her stooped husband the butcher, and strong, too, for she worked in the shop, hauling the joints and using the cleaver. Her arms were thick as the hams she cured.

'I think spring's given up on us this year,' I said. I was cold and stiff having slept in the chair and my bones went *click click click* as I stood.

'I fear you might be right, but here's something to warm you, Mrs Williams.'

'Hm?'

Mrs Yeo was holding something out to me. A letter. She was all eagerness, her face lit with excitement.

'It must surely be about a crime! I said to my husband, it'll be a murder. Mark my words. A dreadful one. And our ladies will find the truth of it! A letter for them can only mean one thing.'

She pressed it into my hands, but I as soon wanted to push it away for it *stung* me. There was no other word for it. The letter was prickly in my hands. Mrs Yeo had seemed to feel nothing like this. To her it was just paper. But I could feel the words inside and they were sharp. The writing on the outside was not so curly as to be hard to read. It said *Mrs Williams*. This was the name I had taken but so few people knew me by it that the letter had to be for Anna, not for me.

'You're not going to open it?' Mrs Yeo said, unable to hide her disappointment.

'I—'

Anna herself came in then. She yawned good morning to Mrs Yeo, and that gave me the chance to drop the letter onto Anna's chair. It was for her. But I would know what stung.

Mrs Yeo had realised there would be no news of murder for the moment, so she took her leave, disappointed. She was back to the weather's likely course as she went down the stairs. We were in for a bad day to come.

Anna saw the letter on the chair and snatched it up. She tore it open and began to read but she didn't need to read out loud to understand it, as I did, so I couldn't hear the words. I looked at the paper over her shoulder, but the writing was too close together. If I could put my finger beneath the words and go slow—

Anna saw me and folded the pages.

I waited for her to speak, to say something of this letter that was an uncommon thing in our lives, but she didn't. The only sound was the clack of her false teeth, which I knew to be her thinking sound. It had been the strange song of all our detecting so far.

Mathilda came in then, her face pale and her hair tangled as a furze bush. She looked younger than her sixteen years. She looked a child.

'How are you feeling?' I asked her.

'Tired, a little.'

She never spoke of her terrors after bad nights, and we never asked her. What good would it do? I told her to have some bacon before it went cold.

'Mrs Yeo, she say the weather will be bad?' Mathilda asked. 'We cannot go to the harbour?' In her way of speaking there was some echo of her German voice. The way she put her words together, and the gaps sometimes. The words that weren't there. I had the same when writing, reaching for a word I knew but how to catch it, get it down in ink?

'There might be work for us to do today instead,' I said, and then to Anna, 'Have we got a case?'

'A case . . .' Anna looked at the fire. Her fingers closed over the letter, made the pages crumple.

'Yes, Anna. That's what we do, isn't it? Have cases and do the solving of them. Or have you forgot yourself since going to bed? Have some little folk been and changed you, like they do with babes?'

That made Mathilda laugh, at least, but Anna . . . She still stared at the fire.

'Here, Shilly. You pass this.' Mathilda handed me a laden plate and I placed it in Anna's lap.

But when I tried to take the pages from her so that she could eat, she snatched them back and was all at once herself again.

'You don't want me to see it?' I said. 'Why?'

'It's nothing, Shilly. Have we some butter left from yesterday?'

Mathilda said she would fetch it.

'I should have let Mrs Yeo give me the letter as she'd wished,' I muttered. 'I *am* Mrs Williams, after all.'

'Only in name,' Anna said, which hurt me.

Mathilda came back with the butter and we fell to eating, the only sound the shifting of the fire, the clinking of our knives. But there wasn't the peace that was custom between us most mornings. This morning was different.

It was true what Anna said. Mrs Williams was a name that Anna had given me, for of the two of us, Anna had been Mrs Williams first. Now *I* used that name and the story of that woman, who was a *fic shun* – that was the word Anna used. It meant lying.

I had Mrs Williams' long red curls to wear, and her little black hat. She had a dress of purple mourning too, for Mrs Williams had lost a husband. But only sometime was he lost. Sometimes he appeared too – another of Anna's selves.

I had met *Mr* Williams. That was Anna too, of course, though I hadn't learnt that until later, to my great surprise, and then I had wondered, as I still wondered, if there had ever been a *real* Mr Williams, in London, where Anna had lived before. The letter come that morning wasn't thick, which meant there could only be a little paper inside the packet. But the way it had stung me – that was because the letter had to have come from her other life. Her life before me. London. It was calling her back. I wondered who had loved her there. Who she had loved.

But my wonder was bad and made me think bad thoughts of drowning such people in the Thames, which was a river Anna spoke of sometimes, of the bodies thrown in its waters and found by men in boats with hooks. I told myself, hadn't Anna stayed with me here in Cornwall? She hadn't gone back to London. There could be no one there for her now.

A touch on my hand made me jump.

'You are not hungry?' Mathilda said, her eyes wide with concern, the lovely girl.

I saw I hadn't eaten a scrap, though my fork held meat.

I forced myself to eat. Mathilda had enough worries. She didn't need me to add to them. But I'd made up my mind. My name was Mrs Williams now, so it was only right I should read the letter. It might take me a good length of time, but I was getting better, and Anna kept saying I had to practise and so I stretched out my fingers, along the arm of the chair, a little further, reached in. The dryness of the paper, a slick of bacon fat thinning it.

Quick as a blink Anna threw the letter on the fire, then turned to me with a smile on her face I didn't know. A smile brittle as the first ice of autumn. If I touched it, it would shatter.

'Honestly, Shilly, it was nothing. Nothing at all!'

And she laughed, a high strange laugh, and then I knew something terrible had happened. But what it was, she wouldn't tell me.

FOUR

My thoughts at the letter coming were bad so I said I would go out. Mathilda said she would come too, that we would go to the harbour together. But I wasn't good company, I could feel it. Could feel the sting of the letter, still, in my hands that had touched it. Mathilda's face was all sorrow at being left behind. Anna didn't even turn round when I said I was going.

The wind was a fierce creature today, fiercer than I had known it since we had come to Boscastle. The street with the butcher's shop sloped down to the water, and the houses flanking my path sloped likewise. The wind blew the cloying smell of meat away and coated me with fish instead. That was a much better smell. When I had first come to Boscastle, the air had tasted so much of fish I couldn't think how it would be to live here and swallow it every day. And now I was doing it, and I found I liked it. It was the same with the sea, this change in me.

The harbour came in sight. It was two walls that made it, and they didn't quite meet, one set a little back from the other. Almost touching, as if reaching, but that gap between. Like Anna and me. How to bring us closer to one another when we seemed as unyielding as these moor stone walls built into the sea? I turned away from them. Walked on alone.

Anna had asked me to work with her for I could see the parts of the world she couldn't. The parts that were hard to see for they had to be looked at askance. They were dark and strange, rooted deep in the earth where by rights they should remain. They were long ago deaths and deaths still to come. They were devils and unquiet souls. Where Anna saw the cuts a knife made in a young girl's throat, could tell the kind of knife it was, I felt the dead girl's anger like a hot brand on my own breast. When Anna saw things that could be touched and smelt, I saw beneath them.

This talent had been gifted me by my first love, though there were days it felt more like a curse, for the things I saw were frightening and hard to fathom, and there was nothing I could do about them by myself. Only see, only weep. I needed Anna to help me understand, and Anna needed me to help her put all the pieces together. Then we could have things like suspects and motives and all of that detecting business.

But Anna couldn't help with my worst fears, for if I could see the darkness in other people, and in the places where they lived, did that not mean I was a dark creature likewise? Some beast, like the ones the chapel preachers said should be cast out? This thinking left me jittery.

I found I had stopped and was at the inn by the bridge, the Wellington, where I tried so hard *not* to be. Every day I tried. I hadn't touched a drop since we had come to Boscastle, and it was all for Anna. She was right to keep me from it, I knew, for it did me no good, but my hands were ashake all the same.

I scrambled up the cliff path. I would not be again as I had been before.

The wind grew fiercer the higher I climbed but I pushed into it to drive out the devil that plagued me. Up up up, walking into the clouds. My hair got free of its knot and streamed around me so I could not see where to put my feet, but the path guided me.

A crash, a boom, and I saw that I'd come to the top of the cliff and the sea was a way away below, surging a white fury that was like the inside of my head. I scraped my hair from my eyes and forced it back into a knot. Some order here, Shilly. Take some care of your poor self.

And then I saw her.

A woman in the water right below me, in all that mess of waves and drag-about. She must have fallen from the very spot where I now stood. How could I fetch help before she went under? I was cursed to watch her die, and watch her I had to, for what unkindness it was to leave a person to die alone when you could be with them and see their final breath, see them go to wherever it was we went. I couldn't look away. And it was so watching I saw that she *didn't* go under and drown. Her head and her arms stayed clear above, and she moved *with* the waves rather than fight them.

She was swimming.

I could tell she *was* a woman from that distance by her long yellow hair that trailed behind her, and by her breasts, which were bare. What would the fishermen make of such a catch if they should pull up their nets and find her inside? They would be lucky souls, that I did know, for she was a fine creature.

Now that I didn't fear she was drowning I could watch her in peace, admire the way she spread her hands and carved the water, how her skin gleamed, how her legs pushed her forward, as if they were one bit of body. I wondered if she was something for Anna and I. If this was our next case, finding us, and me glimpsing it early, as sometimes happened.

Anna had told me I might see such things as this now that I'd given up the drink. A strange long word she said, *hal oo sin a chuns*. Seeing things that weren't there. I said, Anna, you told me that happened when I *had* a drink. Now you're saying it'll happen when I don't. You can't have it both ways. I might as well have a drink if I'm to see such things anyway. Where's the difference? And she had lifted her eyes to heaven and wondered if there was any hope for me.

But I knew there was hope for me as I stood on the cliff above Boscastle harbour and stared at that fine creature in the water below me, for who *wouldn't* want to see such a thing? I had all the hope in the world.

The wind gusted and I stumbled forward, leaving the path to go closer to the edge of the cliff, and as I righted myself there was a voice, a call. But the wind drowned it. Or snatched the words away. Or the wind was the call and the call was in the sea, with the woman. A burst of it again, and I wanted to hear more so I stepped forward, into the wind and the words that spun around me. I closed my eyes and tried to listen. It was just there, and not there, and there again. Another step, then one more.

My feet slid out from under me and I fell heavily against one of the rocks that lay between the path and the cliff edge, and all at once I came to my senses and thought of Anna's long word, and Anna herself. I hadn't gone without a drop for six months just so I could fall into the sea and drown, even if there was a beautiful thing down there.

I crawled to the safety of the path. I didn't look back. The rain helped quieten the woman's noise.

It rained all night, and the wind—

The wind was a woman's voice that called me to the cliff edge.

FIVE

My sleep was dark, churned like the rough sea I had spied from the cliff top. And in those waves a woman, swimming. She was ahead of me. I reached for her, tried to catch her feet but she got away. And then I saw that her feet had somehow raked my fingers, torn the flesh in lines, as if her feet were barbed, or set with teeth. My hands were little rivers of blood. It was because Mathilda had been dreaming again and we'd had to use the bar to keep her from biting off her tongue, but that couldn't be right because I could hear Mathilda, and how could she shout with the bar between her teeth? Perhaps the bar was in *my* mouth, and it was *my* tongue's blood on my hands. Mathilda's voice clanged through the waters of my sleep. But she didn't seek to comfort me, as I comforted her when her night terrors came.

'You have no right—'

The waves surged, the water bubbled past my ears, and there was another voice. Lower, seeking to make peace. Anna.

I couldn't hear what Anna said but it seemed to do no good for Mathilda's voice was getting louder.

'. . . *mine*, Anna. You take this decision with no thought for me or for Shilly.'

My name brought me to the surface. The swimmer was gone. There was only shouting.

They were in the parlour, each as far from the other as was possible in that small room – Anna in her chair by the fire, Mathilda at the window where the rain was still loud against the glass.

Anna looked small, crumpled in the chair as if chilled to the bone, though the fire crackled merrily enough. She was about to speak, but then she saw me in the doorway and her thin lips clamped shut.

'You two could wake the pigs hanging in the cold room,' I said, but neither of them saw the mirth there. 'What's the matter? Mathilda?'

Mathilda whirled round. 'Tell her, Anna. Tell her what has happened. Is not too late.' There was anger in her voice but pleading too. I could hear her desire for all to be well, for there to be no breach between us. We who were all she had in the world now.

Anna looked at me and shrugged. 'It's nothing, Shilly. A misunderstanding.'

'Is really that?' Mathilda asked her. 'You swear, Anna?'

'Of course!' Anna said. 'You mustn't worry.'

Mathilda gave a great sigh, as if she'd been holding her breath. 'You will write to them, yes? At once, to tell them is not possible what is asked, because—'

'Of course, of course.' Anna reached for the poker, and as she leant forward I saw a scrap of something on her chair, something cream. A folded sheet of paper, busy with writing. Before I could reach for it her backside had returned to the chair and the letter was lost. When had another one come? And who did Mathilda want Anna to write to?

Anna had told Mathilda not to worry but I was awash with it as I stood in the dimly lit parlour, the day's light only just beginning to reach us and made thin by the rain. The room was the same as it always was – the two chairs, the stool, the patch of damp – but it was made strange.

I tried to speak but my mouth was dry. 'Anna . . .'

Did she hear me? I put my hand on her shoulder. She waited too long to turn and look at me, and when she did—

A bang made us all jump. It was the door at the bottom of the stairs, then there were feet rushing up and Mrs Yeo's voice.

''Tis only me, my dears.'

Mathilda was all at once busy. She grabbed a shawl from where it hung over the door and set to raking her hair with her fingers.

'Let me brush it for you,' I said. 'It's tangled, look, from sleeping.'

But she slipped from me like the swimming woman had slipped free in my dreams, and then Mrs Yeo was there, all a smile.

'You're here! My husband said you would be, what with the weather, but you never know, and how unfortunate if you *had* decided to go visiting today, just as someone came asking for you!'

Anna had stood up at Mrs Yeo's arrival but now she went trembly and dropped back into her chair.

'Who is it that's come, Mrs Yeo?' Her voice was barely a whisper, but Mrs Yeo didn't seem to notice the fear which was writ large to me.

'Oh, he's in a state, Miss Drake. Chilled to the bone. I've put him next to our fire and told my girls to mind their manners, for he is a sea captain, after all.'

'A sea captain?' Anna's shoulders softened. 'Thank heavens . . . To see us? Whatever for?'

'About the body,' Mrs Yeo said. 'A man's been found dead.'

Mathilda left the room.

I called for her to stop, to wait, but she wouldn't, and that was not the usual way of things between us, for we were great friends, Mathilda and I. When I reached the landing, she was already down the stairs and near out the door to the courtyard.

I called her again and she stopped, at last.

'You can't be going out in all this rain!' I said.

'I must. I must go to think. With no one. Is *outrage*, what Anna does.' She closed her eyes for a moment and gave a short huff, then put her shawl over her head.

'Tell me what happened. What were you and Anna rowing about?'

'It is not her fault. I see that. But she has problem, Shilly. Bad problem. And it will be our problem too.' Mathilda's hand was on the door.

'What are you talking about? What problem?'

'Anna must be strong. If she is strong then we—'

Anna herself called then, called me from the parlour. I looked over to see her frantic waving in the doorway. Telling me I must come that instant to hear what Mrs Yeo was saying. I was caught between them, the pair of women in my life – Anna and Mathilda. Some dark thing had passed between them. Which of them to go to, which of them to choose in that instant on the landing?

When I looked back at the stairs, Mathilda had gone. In my shilly-shallying I'd made my choice. With a heavy heart I turned and went back to the parlour. Mathilda was worried, and now so was I. But in another way we were different, for Mathilda was angry too.

In the parlour, Mrs Yeo bubbled like a stream.

'He says he must see you now, and it was all I could do to make him wait in my cottage while I came over here. I thought I should do that, to be proper, given that you party are *professionals*.'

With this last word Mrs Yeo beamed and I wondered if our rent was low as it was because she liked having detectives living close by. Even those without many cases.

'Quite right, Mrs Yeo,' Anna said. 'I appreciate your thoughtfulness. Please let the captain know we'd be pleased to receive him. Oh – his name?'

At this Mrs Yeo bit her lip. 'You know, he did tell me, but I couldn't catch it, funny sound that it was, and I didn't like to ask again and him think me rude.'

Anna patted her arm. 'No matter.'

Mrs Yeo left us then, joy in her step as she went to fetch this captain who had come to us about death. That was the lot of a detective, I had learnt in my few months of the work. We were in the business of loss.

'Now, how does our visitor find us?' Anna glanced round the parlour.

With her caught before me like that, I asked the question that had been taking shape inside me.

'When Mrs Yeo said a man had come to see us, who were you thinking had come?'

'I don't know what you mean. I know no one here, Shilly.'

'And yet you were afraid.'

'You're mistaken.'

'I could see it on your face, Anna! You don't have to lie to me. Is it something to do with the letters?'

'That again. I told you, it was nothing.' She twisted from my hands and looked harsh at the furniture. 'This isn't quite the impression I would wish to make, but there we are. It won't be this way forever.'

'And why is it this way now? Why do you make us so mean with spending, Anna?'

'We haven't time for this now, Shilly.' She set one of the chairs so it stood before the damp patch. 'You'll take the stool.'

'I thought as much.'

'Why do you sound so low? We have a case, at last!' She looked me over as she had looked over the furniture, then smoothed my hair neater and rubbed something from my cheek. 'This is what we've been waiting for.'

'I suppose,' I said. 'But Mathilda. What were you two arguing about?'

'Arguing? You're mistaken, Shilly. We were discussing our plans for setting up the agency. As an investor, Mathilda has a right to be party to our decisions.'

'*Our* decisions? I didn't know we'd made any.'

'Not that we've been in much of a position to move forward. But now!'

And she kissed me, and I forgot all my worries about letters and rows and murders.

Until the drowned man walked into the room.

SIX

He was soaked. Not just his clothes but his skin, too, I was sure of
it, for the water seemed to pour from him, even though Mrs Yeo
said she'd made him wait by her fire. His broad face was coarse with
stubble. This made him seem grey, and his skin was grey, all of it that
I could see – his cheeks, his hands, the snatch of his throat where his
stock had come untied and now hung limp about his neck.

He surely had come to us from the bottom of the sea. I
whispered as much to Anna while our guest took off his coat and
sat down.

Her eyes widened. 'You think him—'

'A spirit, yes.'

'He looks corporeal enough to me,' she said. 'Do spirits wear coats?'

'We must be sure not to touch him.'

'Why ever not?' she whispered.

'Touch a man who walked after drowning? There's bound to
be a curse in that.'

'Shilly . . . He's simply wet from the rain. It is pouring, after all.'

She turned to take the man's coat and hang it near the fire.
Drops of water slid down his sleeves and pooled beneath his chair.

We both saw the same creature before us, but we each saw him different. That was our way of working together. We would soon know which of us saw the truth this time.

He had taken off his hat but didn't seem to know what to do with it. Anna eased it from his hands, but his eyes were darting here and there, not seeing us or the parlour.

Anna took the chair next to him. 'I'm afraid you find us in rather reduced circumstances, Captain . . .'

'Ians. Frederick Ians.'

No wonder Mrs Yeo hadn't caught his name. It was a strange one to my ears. His voice held only a faint warmth of my home. He was of Cornwall, but from long ago. Where had he been since? He was old – in his late fifties, I guessed. His long nose was set low on his broad face, almost as if it was trying to escape into his mouth. Though he looked like a dead man himself that morning in our parlour he was a well-dressed one, with a good coat of wool, his shirt embroidered at the cuffs. An ink stain on the shirt, though, and a stale smell to him.

Anna introduced me as Mrs Williams and her as Miss Drake, and asked if he would like tea.

He waved this offer away. Beads of water spun from his hands. 'Your landlady has seen to my every comfort.' He looked anything *but* comfortable as he dripped onto the floor. 'Forgive me, but I am surprised to find you . . .' He gestured at us, at our middles, but I could guess why that was.

'To find us . . . above a butcher's?' Anna said. 'Understandable, Captain. But I would assure you it is only—'

He coughed. 'Of the fairer sex.'

Anna stiffened beside me. This was the problem Anna knew from trying to be a detective in London, and it had followed her to Cornwall. I suffered from it too.

'The advertisement, the name,' the captain said, 'it gave no indication.' He pulled from his pocket a crumpled bit of newspaper. 'Williams and Williams Investigations. No mention of the . . . *specialist* nature of your enterprise.'

'I can assure you, Captain Ians,' Anna said coldly, 'that Mrs Williams and I are in no way hindered in our endeavours due to our sex. In fact, we are often able to move more easily than men, to pass in plain sight, for we are ignored, *dismissed*.' She said this last word with some disgust, for hadn't this man just done this very thing?

'If someone doesn't see *us*, we see *them* all the better,' I said. Anna shot me a quick smile, and I knew the effort it cost her to be civil, to stop herself picking up the poker and braining this man come to say we could not do the work because we were women. Work that kept us fed and housed and safe from having to turn to men for our keep. Work that kept us together.

'And if we should need to be seen,' Anna said, 'to make men see us. Well. There are ways. I trust that puts an end to any doubts you may have?'

'Forgive me,' the captain said. 'I have spoken out of turn. It is the lack of sleep. I am not myself. This is why I have come, and I am grateful to have found you. Would that you can take this burden from me. Tell me, do you believe in the power of dreams?' He looked at each of us in turn.

'I do,' I said, thinking of Mathilda's night terrors. Thinking of my own. 'They can show the truth of things that have happened. Things we can't see when awake.'

'And the future, Mrs Williams? Do you believe that dreams can show what's still to pass?'

His hands were shaking. I would have fetched him a drop of something for his nerves but we had none in our rooms, of course.

'Why have you come to see us, Captain?' Anna said gently.

'Because of the dream, it was the same, right down to the cuts—'

He covered his face with his hands. We let him be. The rain came harder against the window. A piece of wood dropped in the fire, sparks flared.

'I must start at the beginning. Only then might you see . . .' He looked up. 'I am captain of a vessel that sails out of Cardiff, *The Severn*. Our orders have kept us nearly two years from home. Corn, cotton, timber, coffee – my ship has moved all that can be bought and sold, to all the great ports of the world. I have seen such wonders, such strange things you would not believe. But never in my life . . .' He cleared his throat and seemed to fight to keep his purpose. 'A month ago, as we were drawing close to Lisbon, I dreamt a man lay dead at the foot of cliffs.'

And then I saw the meaning of his wetness, why to me he was a drowned man, to Anna only dripping rain. He mightn't be drowned himself, but he bore news of it. His body was showing me his tale. That was my looking askance.

'In the dream,' Anna said, 'could you discern the place the man lay? Any sign it was the English coast? Or that of Portugal, or Sp—'

'It was Morwenstow,' the captain said.

'Morwenstow?' Anna glanced at me and I shook my head.

'We're not from these parts,' I said, which was true. My home had been closer to this coast than Anna's, of course, for she was from London, but a few miles made all the difference.

'Morwenstow is north of here,' the captain said. 'Twenty miles or so up the coast.'

'I'm sure I've seen the name before,' Anna said, which made me near fall off my chair. 'In the papers,' she said. 'Was it not mentioned in the enquiry?'

'Sadly, yes,' Captain Ians said. 'The losses there have been great.'
I had no sense what they were talking of.

'It's a big place, then?' I said. 'A harbour ships are making for?'

'The Lord bless you, Mrs Williams! Morwenstow is no more than a few dwellings on the cliff top. And the vicarage, of course. It offers no safe anchorage for vessels. If they are making for anywhere then it's Bude, but even that port is a dangerous one. The whole coast is damned.'

'You appear to know it well,' Anna said.

'I was born in Morwenstow, and spent my youth enduring its storms before putting to sea. Those who visit – and there are precious few, given its isolation – find it a bleak place. But I have always loved it.' Here he managed a thin smile and the shake in his hands eased.

'Given your profession, it must be rare that you return,' Anna said.

'I had not been back for nearly ten years, until the dream. It felt like a summons, given . . .'

His hands began to shake again and he fixed his gaze on his boots. Though he was an old man he put me in mind of a boy who had seen something he was too young to understand.

'The man you dreamt of, him lying beneath the cliff,' I said. 'You knew him, didn't you?'

And then his face was more wet than ever for he was scritching.

'It was Joseph. My brother. I knew it, even though it's been so long since I've seen him. I need you to find who killed him!'

'But Captain Ians,' Anna said, 'you're speaking simply of a dream.'

'I wish I was. Once my ship reached Lisbon, I felt compelled to return home. I found passage to Falmouth and from there took the fastest coaches north. I arrived in Morwenstow yesterday, as he was discovered. It was just as I had seen in the dream. The same clothes, the same arrangement of the limbs, the cuts. They were bringing him up the cliff path as I arrived.'

'Who were?' I said.

'The parson, his men. I . . . I was not myself in that moment, I will own it. I was overcome. To see such a thing. I did not know if I was asleep or awake, and that brought great terror to my mind. When I recovered, I found myself at a loss, for I cannot return to my ship until I know if this poor soul is indeed my brother Joseph and how he met this dreadful end.'

'But you've seen the body now,' I said. 'Surely you can tell if it *is* your brother?'

'In truth, I cannot, for I have yet to see the body at close proximity. The parson has it locked in his deadhouse, where he keeps them.'

'Keeps who?' I said, not liking the sound of a deadhouse.

'The sailors cast on his shores. The parson views it as the Lord's work, but the Devil is in those waters.' The captain leant forward in his chair. 'But Joseph is not a sailor come to grief in a storm. He was killed by human hands.'

'How do you know this?' Anna said.

'Because of the dream. Only my brother lay beneath the cliffs, but it was all around him, a woman's presence. I knew she was there with him, felt it as strongly as I felt the waves' spray on my lips.'

'As if she was the sea herself.' The words were out of my mouth before I knew they were my own. Anna stared at me. The captain too, his mouth fallen open.

'That is a most apt description, Mrs Williams, but how in God's name could you know? Unless you, too, are part of this. That's why I found the paper in the coach. I see it now, all the parts.'

He had grown fretful, seeming to wrap himself in his arms,

and I saw how he would have been after waking from his dream, burdened by knowing what was to come but stuck out at sea, the land before him not his own. So many miles still to go, so many weeks to pass before he could find the truth of what would happen. And when he did, such pain.

He was murmuring to himself. 'I was right to come. It's clear now.'

'Captain?' Anna said. 'What is it that you believe Mrs Williams knows?'

'About the woman. In Morwenstow, they say the man was killed by a mermaid.'

SEVEN

Anna laughed, but soon stopped when she saw he was serious in his claim.

'You surely don't believe these tales, Captain Ians?'

He gripped his hands together in his lap to hide the worsened shake. 'People spoke of such things when I was a boy. Stories to pass the winter evenings, to frighten children. At sea, I have heard men claim they spy the creatures but that is in the doldrums, where their minds are changed by the long calm. They stare so long at the water they fashion the sea cows' long hair and a tail. I have no time for these fancies on board, and would not have given any credence to the talk in Morwenstow, but that was before . . .'

'Before the dream,' I said, 'for that has changed everything.'

He nodded eagerly. 'You see it, Mrs Williams! You see it in me. I am not the same man I was when I put to sea on this last voyage. I am changed, and if that is so, then perhaps all I had thought nonsense before is now real and it *was* a mermaid that killed Joseph.'

Anna shifted her chair so that it shrieked against the floorboards and so spoke her feelings sharp.

'I think it would be best if we kept to matters less watery, Captain.'

'Forgive me, Miss Drake. I have not slept since reaching Falmouth.'

'But that must have been days ago,' I said. 'How are you still on your feet?'

He smiled a sad smile. 'That is another mystery. But I must not give in. I fear what I may see if I allow myself to dream.'

What curse this poor man bore. I wished to free him of it.

'Such things as mermaids are my work,' I said. 'Of the two of us, I am the one for the strange parts of stories, the parts that won't sit easy with Miss Drake's facts.'

The captain seemed more at ease for the first time since his arrival. 'Then I have come to the right place to discover the truth of the dream, and of the poor soul still lying in the parson's deadhouse. There is no constable in Morwenstow and as I rushed there from Falmouth, I had no clue of my next step. I do not believe it was chance that led me to see your advertisement in the newspaper left inside the Bodmin coach. If you will let me know your rates?'

And Anna smiled her truest smile, for here was her truest moment. 'I can assure you, Captain Ians, that they are very reasonable indeed. Fifty pounds to identify the deceased, to discover the manner in which he died and apprehend the perpetrator, if the death be confirmed as unnatural.'

I sucked in my breath. Fifty pounds! What was Anna thinking? We had charged only thirty for our last case, and that was gentry that was paying. I worried she had overplayed her hand, asking so much now. Then I thought of what we had spoken of the day before, Anna's worry of money, and I saw her need to raise our prices. A risky bet, but she was all for risks was Anna Drake.

I needn't have been fearful. Such was Captain Ians' need to

be free of the curse he suspected was upon him, and so be able to sleep again, that he accepted Anna's bargain.

'If you wish to examine the body, then I would urge you not to delay,' the captain said as he stood.

'We will leave as soon as we have made ready,' Anna said. 'This afternoon at the very latest. I must tell you, Captain, not to be concerned if you do not see us there immediately. Mrs Williams and I *will* be in Morwenstow but we may not be as you see us here.'

'You will be disguised?' he said, and my heart fluttered a little, for it was beginning, the case. We would soon be others.

'It might be necessary to adopt different identities, of a *dramatic* kind,' Anna said. 'But rest assured, we will alert you to our presence, and our findings.'

The captain shook hands with us both, for I had no fear now he was drowned. He was dry at last and his skin had found some colour. The water had been a sign of his burden and he had left it behind, pooled across the parlour floor. Our burden now. I led him to the landing while Anna fetched his coat.

'The sooner you can come, the better,' he said. 'I dare not leave Morwenstow too long. The parson is minded to bury the poor wretch with all haste rather than wait for the coroner. He will not hear me when I tell him this is no ordinary sailor washed up on his shore.'

'Rest assured, we will not tarry,' Anna said.

'You will find me at the Bush Inn.'

'Until then.'

Once he was gone Anna set about collecting our things and almost at once the parlour looked bare, as if we hadn't lived there so fully as I had thought. As if we had only ever been waiting to go.

'Shilly?' Anna's arms were full of shawls and blankets. She had stuffed the pages bearing my writing in the grate.

'Hm?'

'I said, will you ask Mrs Yeo about our transport to Morwenstow? She'll know who might take us.'

'All right, but—'

She hurried off in the direction of her room.

'—I must find Mathilda too,' I called after her.

Her answer was the sound of the travelling case thrown open.

The rain was still falling as I crossed the courtyard to the Yeos' cottage. Mrs Yeo welcomed me in warmly, as she always did.

'Mrs Williams! Come in, my dear. Come in. What a day we're having!'

I couldn't see the woman herself for my wet hair was all over my face. I pawed it from my eyes then bumped my head on a milk jug hanging from a beam. Laughter from the back of the cottage – Mrs Yeo's girls playing slaps.

'I can't stay, Mrs Yeo, for we've much to do, but I need to ask—'

'You must tell me,' she said, her voice a-hum with excitement, 'did the captain bring news of a murder?'

'He did, and we've to go as soon as we can, to see about it.'

Mrs Yeo gave my arm a squeeze. 'The Lord has brought you a death! And you'll find the truth of it.' She shook her head in wonder at my cleverness. Well, mine and Anna's.

I asked about a cart to take us to Morwenstow and Mrs Yeo said she knew just the man. Davey was too old to fish but not too old to flick the reins of his mare Clemmie.

'But he won't go today,' Mrs Yeo said, 'the weather like this. Won't be any matter to wait a day, will it, what with the party up Morwenstow already being dead.'

'It might if that party goes in the ground before we get there,' I said, thinking of telling Anna of this delay and not liking that thought at all. 'If Davey won't go, who else would? Any of the fishermen?'

'Not likely. If they're not putting to sea, which they won't with this rain, they'll be keeping close to their hearths. No one will go out until the storm's eased.'

'Can't blame them for that,' I said, though I knew Anna would. 'As soon as Davey can take us, we'll go. Have you seen Mathilda? She went out when the captain arrived and I need to find her.'

At this, Mrs Yeo hesitated. 'You know, Mrs Williams, I did see her. She went dashing off towards the harbour just as I was coming back here, having been in to see you about the captain. Flying, she was! And in all the rain, too. I called out to her. She didn't hear me, probably.'

'I'm sure she didn't. Mathilda's a good girl, Mrs Yeo.'

'Oh, she is! Dear of her. She's not from these parts, is she?'

'No, she's not. But she's with us now, me and Anna. That's where she belongs.'

I took my leave and ran back across the courtyard to the side door we used to reach our rooms above the shop. As I closed the door there was a thump on the other side. I opened it, and there was Mathilda, soaked through and pale. I hauled her inside, cursing her and petting her at the same time. Through all the layers of dress and coat and shawls I could feel she was chilled to the bone.

EIGHT

Mathilda woke me in the night but there were no screams this time. A cough stirred in her chest. By the time the day was fully light she was feverish. I ran for Mrs Yeo.

The good woman came straight from her bed, her hair loose, clad in her nightdress and stout boots. She pulled away the blankets and felt Mathilda's forehead, the back of her neck, while I dithered at the bedside. My poor girl gave no sign she knew we were there. Her eyes were closed and she muttered to herself.

'She's terrible hot,' Mrs Yeo said, 'and yet shaking as if with cold, dear of her. Let's get her wrapped up, Mrs Williams, and then we'll wake up the fire.'

'Anna – we need your blankets,' I called.

'I'm afraid they're packed.' She was in the doorway, and I saw then that she'd dragged her travelling case onto the landing.

'This fever won't break for a little while yet,' Mrs Yeo said. 'Can you wait a day or two before you leave?'

'I fear not, Mrs Yeo. Captain Ians impressed upon us the need for urgency in this case. We must see the body before it's buried.'

'But we can't move Mathilda,' I said. 'Look at the poor state she's in!'

'That's as may be. The fever might not break yet awhile, but the weather has. Can't you hear it, Shilly?'

And I realised it was quiet, for the first time in days. The storm had passed.

'Well then,' Mrs Yeo said, knotting her hair. 'You'll leave Mathilda here with me.'

Anna was speaking, and then it was agreed, and so quick – Mathilda would stay with the Yeos until she was well enough to come to Morwenstow.

'We will reimburse you for any additional expenses incurred, of course,' Anna said.

'Now, don't you worry, Miss Drake. Mathilda's such a kindly soul. She don't eat no meat, do she?'

Anna looked uncertain at these last words.

'She . . . she does not *abstain* from eating meat, Mrs Yeo, but I would assure you Mathilda doesn't eat an excessive—'

'She means that Mathilda's no trouble,' I said.

'Oh!' Anna said, and laughed. Laughed when Mathilda lay so poorly! 'I will have to make a note of that one, Mrs Yeo. Very droll.'

I was made fearful by this arrangement, but there seemed no way to stop it. We had to leave and Mathilda couldn't be moved. I couldn't stay, for Anna would need me for the mermaids and suchlike. There was no other remedy but still my heart was heavy as Anna and I made ready to go.

She fair flew round our few rooms collecting this and that, hurrying me. She told me I must wear a different dress than usual, that I must rid myself of Mrs Williams' mourning colours and that made my breath catch in my throat. Was I to be someone else to go to Morwenstow?

'You're still Mrs Williams,' Anna said. 'And before you ask, yes, you can keep the red curls and the hat. I know how much you like them. It's only the dress that needs changing. Your mourning is over, Shilly!'

And then she was off again and there was no chance to find out any more.

All too soon it was time to leave. I knelt by Mathilda's bed – mine too, but mine no longer. Her eyes were fretful beneath the closed lids, dancing with dreams. Made worse with the fever? I hoped she was spared that.

'Did you tell Mrs Yeo about the bar,' I asked Anna, 'for when Mathilda bites her tongue?'

'I did. You should let the poor girl sleep, Shilly.'

'It'll only be a few days, won't it? Until she comes to Morwenstow?' I stroked Mathilda's cheek. Her skin was clammy.

'We'll have to see,' Anna said. 'There's no point making her travel before she's ready, is there? You wouldn't want to make her worse.'

'Of course not, but—'

'Well, there we are, then.'

'Anyone would think you were glad Mathilda's taken poorly and can't come with us,' I said, and I thought again of their argument, for I was sure it *had* been an argument, whatever Anna might have said after.

There was no reply to this. I turned. Anna had moved to the landing and was putting things in her black bag, the one she always took detecting. And she was wearing trousers.

'Come on, Shilly-Shally,' she called.

My name for being slow, for being late. For being myself. If she was calling me that then it really was time to go.

I pulled up Mathilda's blankets and tucked them so that she was as well wrapped against the cold as she could be, then bent to kiss her.

Her eyes fluttered open and after a moment she seemed to know who I was.

'Shilly! You mustn't let her—'

Mathilda struggled to get out of bed but so feeble it was easy to keep her where she was, and she soon tired of the fight.

'Now, you must stay in bed, Mathilda, and get well as soon as you can so that you can come to Morwenstow and help us with this case, for we'll need you.'

She closed her eyes and muttered something, but I couldn't catch the words. I thought they might have been in her German way of talking.

I hurried down the stairs, made breathless, suddenly, with the certainty that Anna would leave without me. Much as I wanted to stay and look after Mathilda, the thought of losing Anna was too dreadful to bear. She could walk out of my life at any moment, there was the truth of it. I needed to make sure she wouldn't leave me behind.

She was in the street, lifting one end of her travelling case, and a short man, old as the hills, lifting the other. But she wasn't Anna now. The person I knew but did not know, telling me to hurry, was a man.

Another of Anna's selves. He took my hand and pressed hard on my wedding ring, looked me dead in the eye and I knew the game.

'My dear,' he said, 'so pleased you could join us. This is Mr Davey. He has very kindly agreed to take us to Morwenstow. Mr Davey, my wife, Mrs Williams.'

'Good morning to 'ee, missus,' the old man said, then he looked from one of us to the other. 'Betty Yeo did tell me it was to be two women I was taking on the road.'

'It was,' I said. 'But we have had a change. My husband is joining me instead.'

'Right enough,' he said. 'A fine day for it, with the rain gone.'

I might have said yes, isn't it, glad to be with you, Mr Davey, what rain we had, the poor men going out in it, or any such thing. My lips moved but what they said was anyone's business for all I could think was *wife wife wife*.

NINE

Boscastle had been washed proper in the storm. The sea was the colour of polished pewter, the green on the cliff tops bright, as if the Lord had laid fresh turf in the night. Davey's mare was not so fresh herself. Clemmie, Mrs Yeo had said she was called. The creature's back was bowed and I could see the shadows of her ribs. Her grey coat was nicked in places, pink flesh showing.

I climbed into the cart beside Anna, who was my husband now, and she said to Davey seated in front that we were ready, *at last*. Davey flicked the reins. His old mare gave a great sigh I could feel through the seat, and then lurched forward. We were off. How long would it be until we returned?

The hill that led out of the village was steep and winding, and we were slow going, Clemmie a plodder. The freshness of the morning air was soon lost for both Davey and Anna lit their pipes. Now she was a man again it looked more usual a habit. Davey stowed his tobacco beneath his soft cloth hat, such as the fishermen wore. And so we travelled in our own cloud of tobacco smoke. Clemmie coughed, but that was from the effort, I thought, not the smoke. I didn't mind it. The sweet prickle of the pipe was the smell of Anna, the woman beneath all the false selves. Whoever she was being, she was always smoking.

And this new self? Who was he? I wondered. If I was *Mrs* Williams and Anna was my husband, then she must be *Mr* Williams. I had met one Mr Williams before, but this Mr Williams beside me in the cart looked little like the one I had met previous. Where the first Mr Williams was stiff and stern, a newspaper man, this new one was soft and lolling. He wore a stock at his throat but it was only tied loose. His coat was cream-coloured, cut short. His hair was thick about his neck and his whiskers were bushy. I hoped he would take them off before he kissed me.

We came to a bend in the road and Clemmie stopped.

Davey turned around. 'She do need to pace herself.' He had hardly a tooth left in his head and his eyes were all but lost in the crinkles of his face. A thick scar ran up his neck. A dog had had him as a child, I thought. Gave him a good shake too, by the look of it.

'Fortunate we're not paying by the hour for this journey,' Anna muttered.

'Hush!' I said. 'He's a friend of Mrs Yeo.'

'I think our landlady's judgement has been skewed by charity. We might have been better walking but for my case.'

She looked down at the village far below. I did likewise. From this distance, how near the harbour walls seemed to touching.

'So what takes you to Morwenstow?' Davey said.

'A private matter,' Anna said. 'You'll forgive me if I'm unable to be more specific.'

'Oh, I will, sir. I will. It don't surprise me, of course. The things you hear.'

'About Morwenstow?' I said.

'About the parson. Are 'ee ready, Clemmie? Come on then, off we go.' And the cart lurched forward once more.

'You knew of Morwenstow,' I said to Anna. 'When Captain Ians talked of the place you had heard of it before. You said that funny word. Ek . . . Eke . . .'

'Enquiry, Shilly. There was a public enquiry, two years now, in '43. It's an investigation, by the government.'

I didn't know any of these words. They would be hard to work out the spelling for they sounded as if they had many parts.

Anna sighed. 'Like a case.'

'Oh! Was there another murder there?'

She took her coat off for it was warm now. Her black bag was between us. 'Quite probably. But the enquiry wasn't just about Morwenstow. Much of the country's coastline was investigated. Surely you heard about it? It was in all the papers.'

'I didn't have much to do with newspapers until I met you, Anna.'

'Not so loud, my dear *wife*.'

'Or met Mr Williams, rather,' I said. 'The *first* Mr Williams, that is.'

As I said this, Anna's hands folded up and she dropped her pipe. There was all hell-up then, for a stray spark caught the hem of my dress and I was a-smoke. Fearing the cloth would mark, I screamed, as any person with few clothes to their name *would* scream, and Clemmie leapt forward in terror, Davey near tumbling from his seat.

It was all over soon enough. Anna patted out the little flame, Clemmie was allowed another rest, and Davey said his heart had started beating again, after shock had stopped it. We went on our way. But I wondered at Anna. Why me speaking of someone she had once laid claim to being had given her such a start. She was keen to speak of other things.

'Shipwrecks, Shilly.'

'Hmm?'

'The 1843 enquiry. It was looking at why so many ships had been lost.'

'And what was the answer?'

She waved away a fly. 'Poorly fitted ships, poor captains at their helms. The need for lighthouses to guide vessels. Many things, really. But there was another side to the enquiry. A darker side, because there was a belief that in this part of the world, your part, Shilly—'

'And yours now.'

'—ships were *deliberately* wrecked.' She glanced at Davey and when she spoke again her voice was low. 'That people on the coast showed false lights to lure vessels onto the rocks. When the ships inevitably foundered, their cargos were taken. And any survivors, well . . .'

'Well what?' I said.

'They were killed,' she whispered. 'Slaughtered as they tried to come ashore.'

My stomach, which had been jouncing about as the cart jounced, dropped to my feet and slithered away. 'And this was known to happen in Morwenstow, where we're going this very morning to see about a man found dead beneath the cliffs?'

'Well, it was never proved that people in Morwenstow were wreckers,' Anna said. 'But there have been so *many* wrecks there that the place has become known for it. That can't be disputed. My own knowledge of Morwenstow is proof of its notoriety.'

'But do you think that's what killed him,' I said, 'the man Captain Ians thinks is his brother? That he was on board a ship that was wrecked?'

'I wouldn't wish to assume anything at this early stage, Shilly. And neither should you.'

At last we came to the brow of the hill and the road flattened out. Clemmie gave another great sigh, likely of relief this time, and we went on a little quicker.

'The most important thing,' Anna said, 'is for us to study the body. To examine the physical aspects of this case. The elements one can see and touch and smell. The knowable facts. If we get there in time.' She tapped her pipe stem against the side of the cart.

'But you have to own, there's plenty about this case that you can't learn from seeing or touching. It's a kind of knowing. My kind.'

After a pause she gave the briefest of nods, and I was run through with pleasure.

I took her hand in mine. 'I've been thinking of the woman Captain Ians told us about.'

Anna laughed and shook her head. 'Ah yes, the mermaid. Well, I look forward to casting that tall tale back into the sea.'

'We'll have to see about that,' I said.

I thought of the woman swimming off Boscastle. How she'd been safe in the storm's waves. At home there. The way her legs had worked so strong together. Moving as one. As if they were fused. Her voice. I could almost hear it again, there in the cart. Was she calling from the harbour we had left behind? I felt my eyes close in the sun. It was easier to hear her that way. To give in, let go. To listen. The world fell away and I was falling too, sliding into the water. Into her arms.

But there was pain there. A pinch, nails in my arm. Anna clawing me as she pitched forward.

TEN

The cart had tipped and we were in a heap on top of Davey who was crying, 'Clemmie, Clemmie, whatever's the matter with 'ee?'

I clambered out and saw that the matter was the poor horse looked to have died in her traces. She had fallen on to her front knees and then sideways, dragging the cart over. Her wheezing had ended. No breath came from her. The only sound was Davey begging her to get up again.

I went to his side and put my arm around him. He was so little he fit right under, into the crook of me. From what Mrs Yeo had said I guessed the man didn't have much in the world other than the creature now lying dead at our feet, the flies already settling on her unblinking eyes.

The road was under trees, flanked by trees, made green by trees. The mare had fallen on a straight stretch, but there were bends at either end that hid the way beyond. I don't know how long I'd dozed before she'd fallen, couldn't remember when we'd last passed a house. Anna walked a little way in each direction to see what was beyond, came back to say there was only more road, more trees.

'Not a landmark in sight,' she said, wiping the sweat from above her lip. 'We seemed to have been travelling for some time. How far are we from Morwenstow?' she called to Davey.

He was sitting by poor Clemmie, had pulled her head into his lap. 'A few miles, maybe. Not far.' His hat had fallen to the ground beside him, his tobacco pouch nowhere to be seen.

'We could walk,' she said. 'But our case . . .'

Anna eyed her travelling case, which had fallen from the cart and now lay upended in the hedge. The leather bore marks it hadn't had before, and one corner wasn't quite as square as it had been. Together we righted it and pushed it out of the way of the next traveller to come through. I hoped that would be soon, for the day was hot. Clemmie would soon begin to smell.

'The Morwenstow man might be buried and on his way to St Peter by now,' she said.

'If it's no use then we shouldn't trouble ourselves to go on,' I said. 'We don't need the fifty pounds that badly and Mathilda is poorly.'

'This is a setback, that's all. An important one, I'll grant you, but there will be plenty of other lines of enquiry to pursue. No more than a few miles, our friend here says, and it's a fine day for walking.'

'Let's give it up, Anna, and go home. Mathilda will—'

'We're going on!' she snapped. 'We've agreed terms with a client and we will complete the work.' She saw the shock on my face at being spoken to so harsh, and she softened. 'Look, Shilly, we'll never get the agency established unless we have regular work. This case is our chance to make something lasting. Something that's ours. That no one can take away from us. You see that, don't you? You see how much we need this?'

Her thin face was drawn with worry and I was afraid. The fifty pounds Captain Ians had agreed to pay was everything for her.

And there was no sense to be made of that. No good sense. I had a dreadful foreboding that we should go back to Boscastle at once. I tried one last trick.

'But what about the travelling case?' I said. 'We can't carry it to Morwenstow.'

She smiled. 'That's easily remedied.' She took out her purse and counted coins into her hand. 'Strange,' she said, but soft, as if to herself. 'I thought I had more.'

I made sure not to turn away. Not to blink. I hoped I didn't blush. Anna would say it was thieving. I said it was wages.

She saw me watching and went quickly to Davey. She said his name but he didn't seem to hear her, so she put the coins inside his hat, telling him some were for him driving us, some were for the loss of Clemmie, and the last were for him to make sure her case was sent on to Morwenstow, to the inn there – the Bush, where Captain Ians was staying.

Mrs Yeo had given us some provisions and I gathered them up for we'd need them on the walk. As I chased after an apple that rolled away, I saw Anna drop something else into Davey's hat. Her tobacco. She had some kindnesses in her.

She opened the travelling case and took some things from it for her black bag, while I said goodbye to Davey, said how sorry I was about dear old Clemmie. He thanked me and said at least she passed over doing something she loved – a good walk. Given her wheezing up the hills I thought that unlikely but didn't say, of course. He told us the way, said it shouldn't take us more than a few hours. I hoped he was right. The afternoon was well into its stride by then and it was still only April, the days none too long.

Anna locked the case with the key she kept on a chain round her neck. 'On we go then, Shilly.'

* * *

Was it that Davey's directions were poor or that we were bad at following them? Either way we became lost. Lost the light too. We spied one or two bodies far off in the fields, but no one close enough to ask the way. This part of the coast was as lonely as Captain Ians had said. But then I remembered that that was how Anna had seen the moor when she first came there, and that was a place teeming with people, but people going about their lives, birthing, working, dying. They weren't just standing around waiting to be seen by strangers, waiting to be helpful in other people's detective cases.

We were in bad spirits with each other by the time we came across the way-sign. It was painted on a board nailed to a tree. In the last of the daylight I read the black painted letters of 'inn', and Anna read the first words, which were 'The Bush'.

I looked about me. 'We must be in the right place.'

That place was a narrow lane flanked by gorse and thorn trees, fields beyond, all but lost to dusk. I could hear but not see the sea beyond them.

'Well, it's something, at least,' Anna said, peering up at the sign. 'Let's hope this isn't a popular name in these parts. Although anywhere with a bed would be welcome at this point.'

The arrow pointing the way was hard to pick out, but we followed where we thought it pointed for it was the only guide we had. We went on down the lane and there were lights ahead. Windows. My step quickened at the thought of the inn that must be so close now.

'Shilly, wait!'

But I couldn't wait. It had been a wretched day all told, leaving Mathilda, Clemmie dying. I knew what would make it better.

The lighted windows were lower than the lane we were on. How to get down there? I pressed on. The windows vanished and the dusk gave way to something darker, but not night yet, surely? I found I was coughing – the air was bad. Something had rotted. Something large for the smell was enough to bring bile to my mouth.

The sea was louder now, and then there was another sound – sudden and sharp and all through my ears. Birds cawing. The darkness was trees, and the rooks that clamoured from them. The trees were all around me and where was Anna?

I called her name and heard her answer but she was far away, or the birds were too close. I stumbled, and when I put my hands out to save myself my wrist came down hard on a stone slab. There were many of them. I was in a churchyard.

'Shilly?' Her voice was nearly lost in the rooks' noise. 'Stay where you are. I'm nearly—Oh! Do you see it?'

I looked up. A light was weaving through the trees, coming for me, and fast, and there were words in the rooks' caw.

'Get back, you Devil!'

ELEVEN

I dropped to the ground which was wet and all leaves, and hid behind a gravestone. The light was coming closer, dancing over the world as the creature ran towards me. I closed my eyes and tried to think if I knew anything to ward off devils. But then I thought, Shilly, this creature called *you* a devil, and surely devils don't speak so of others? That would be a strange sort of tricksy. I stood up, and the creature gave a shrill gasp of fright, so I was sure then it wasn't a devil, for it would not be so fearful if it was.

The light was a lantern and it was held by a tall, stout man. A man of this earth, dressed in a long coat that glowed reddish in the lantern's light. A handkerchief was tied across his nose and mouth, against the smell, I guessed. When he took it off, I saw he had no beard or whiskers. His eyes widened on seeing me, a shining blue.

'Are you of God's flesh?' he cried.

'I am,' I said. 'Are you?'

And then he hissed, so I thought he couldn't be. Was more likely snake. I cowered behind the gravestone again.

'You ask a man of the Church such a thing!' he shouted. 'You truly are a creature of the night!'

He raised the lantern above his head and was going to bring it down upon me, me who thought him a devil, him who thought me one. I'd be brained and bleeding on someone else's grave before we'd thrashed out our devilishness. But then Anna was there, and I thanked God for that, whether I was of His flesh or no.

'Forgive us!' she said, hurrying through the graves. 'We're looking for Morwenstow. Up you come, Shilly.' And she hauled me to stand.

'What is your business in my parish so late?' said the man, peering at us. He held the light in our faces, as if to blind us. His smooth face now was carved with shadows. He was not so easy to get a purchase on.

'The poor horse died,' I said, 'dear Clemmie, and we—'

'We're here on behalf of Captain Ians,' Anna said.

'Frederick?' the man said. 'This is about the poor sailor in the deadhouse. I have told Frederick – how many times now – that a soul denied rest will walk amongst us. We will be plagued by it, plagued!' He thumped a gravestone with the lantern's stick. 'But Frederick will not listen, even though it is *my* work, given me by God, and I will be the one to face our unquiet brethren amongst these stones. Will I be granted no rest? Will I be forever tortured? Tell me!'

His face was now red as his coat and he leant towards us most powerfully, with spittle on his lips, teeth bared as if to bite us. But at least we knew the dead man hadn't yet been buried. For all our lateness, we weren't too late for him.

'And now Frederick sends strangers to compel me!' the man shouted. 'Who *are* you?'

'Mr and Mrs Williams,' Anna said, her voice lacking conviction in the terror of his rage. 'Forgive us for arriving so late, and without proper introduction. Am I right in presuming you to be the vicar in these parts?'

'You are.' He seemed to find Anna's meekness proper, for he lowered the lantern so it wasn't so blinding. 'Parson Robert Stephen Hawker.'

'Is this Morwenstow, then?' I said.

He pointed the lantern into the dark beyond. 'Though you cannot see it now that night's deep mantle is upon us, we are but a stone's throw from fair Morwenna's walls – the Lord's sanctuary in this benighted place.'

Such a changeable creature he was, blowing from shout to calm in a moment. I didn't know what to make of him. But he was mumbling as if to himself.

'They have reached safety in the dark, and I have found them, which is surely our Saviour's will. I must take them to a place of rest. I must be His vessel in this matter. Yes.' He looked at us, quite fierce, and said, 'You must stay at the vicarage.'

At this he turned on a sixpence and was striding away. Anna set off after him. I caught her arm.

'He doesn't seem a very . . . settled sort.'

'True, but we need somewhere to lay our heads, Shilly. For tonight, at least. And we must keep the parson sweet if we're to see the body. Once that's been accomplished, we can shift ourselves if need be.'

Though I knew she was right I would rather have sought the Bush Inn but I had no light, no knowing where the inn lay, and my love was following this strange man who claimed he was parson of the place. As I followed after, down a slope between the graves, the rooks began their noise again. And from somewhere nearby, the sea turned over, sighed.

The parson led us to the lighted windows I had seen from the road. As we drew close the air grew fresher, the smell of rot easing. I saw the windows belonged to a large house, and were tall, set with many leaded panes, some of them coloured. And so many of them with lights burning, though the hour must have been late.

Anna had noticed this too. 'You have visitors, Parson Hawker. We must not intrude.'

He waved her concern away. 'No visitors to our lonely parish.'

'But the lamps,' I said.

'To ward off the devils, Mrs Williams. To keep this ark in His light.'

The parson opened what I took to be the front door, a huge thing, painted black, studs the size of shillings driven into it. *That* would keep the devils out. He was chuntering on, all gloom now, no raging.

'No company at all, save my flock, and some days I wonder if they're sent to plague me. They will not heed me, though I tell them of their damnation. With the last breath the Lord grants me, I will tell them.'

I was last in the door and there came a noise behind me – feet scurrying, some dreadful snort. I rushed inside and fell into a place of woofs and wet noses. Three dogs, four, all happiness to see their master, and amidst their hairy bustle, cats trod lightly, their tails raised and curled to show friendship. Too many to count.

'Hello, my dears, hello.' He set down his lantern then patted their heads, rubbed their cheeks.

I turned to close the front door but there were eyes in the darkness – a face pushed into the gap from outside. I screamed, and the face screamed, or squealed more like, for it was a pig! Thinking to come into the house!

'Stand aside, Mrs Williams,' the parson said and got between me and the door. 'Now Gyp,' he said to the pig, a fat black creature, 'you know how things stand. 'Tis after ten so you must be away to your lair. Go on, dear boy, go on!' He pulled a scrap of something or other from his coat and hurled it outside. The pig whirled after it with joyful squeals.

The parson closed the door and kicked off his boots. He took off his red coat and beneath it was an old blue jersey. There was red stitching on one side. It looked too fancy to be darning. He caught me looking at it.

'Ah, you have noticed the expression of suffering I choose to wear, Mrs Williams.'

'I—'

'It is of course a representation of the place where the centurion thrust his cruel spear into our Lord's side. I bear this mark in my jersey so that all may be reminded of His sacrifice. You will note, too, the jersey's colour.'

'It is like the fishermen wear,' I said.

'Exactly! For am I not a fisher of men?'

'I think you must be,' I said. And then something fell from him. Some little thing.

The parson set to scrabbling on the floor, as if he was one of the cats. 'Forgive me. The pencil does tend to drop.' He stood tall again and tucked something behind his ear. It was indeed a little pencil.

'For Christ was but a carpenter,' he said, by way of explaining, 'and so I mark his trade. Come now – in we go!'

He bade us follow him into the house, all the cats and dogs with us as if they wished to be our guides. The house was as fine inside as it had looked without. The ceilings were high above us, the passages wide. Doors led off – many of them, and where I could spy the rooms beyond, all of them lit, they were very large, with such finery of furnishings I could but wonder at. The colours of the paper on the walls! The size of the chairs, and so stuffed and shining! This could be no house for a man of the church.

The only sound came from the dogs snuffling along, the cats' shrieks when the dogs fussed at them. And our footsteps too, of course.

'You are alone here, Parson?' Anna asked.

'Ah, what a penance that would be!' He shivered as if just the thought was punishing.

We followed him into a room set out as if a parlour, but the grandest one I had ever seen. There was a deep smokiness in the air, though the fire was unlit, only laid ready for the next day.

'To endure Morwenstow's loneliness without a companion would be more than any of God's creatures could bear. I am blessed to have one of His angels beside me in my work, in the excellent figure of my wife. Now, you must sit yourself down so we can discuss Frederick's nonsense. Not there, Mrs Williams – that is the seat of My Most Righteous Cat and his alone. He will not thank you for disturbing him, I warn you.'

The silver tabby eyed me with satisfaction as I took a chair opposite, then rolled onto his back to show his advantage. His righteousness was all his own. A strange name for a cat but his master was a strange man and no mistake, though he was welcoming, in a way. His rage in the churchyard was forgotten. But we had seen it. We knew it lay within him. And his melancholy.

He eyed us over his not-so-small belly. He dined well, this man of the church, and was in his forties, I guessed, though his hair was yellow-silvery as a child's, the pencil just poking out. His skin was tanned, lined by the sun. Not a parson who kept only to the church, then.

'I'm afraid I can offer you no sustenance,' he said. 'Mrs Seldon who does for us has gone across to the farm. Taken Nancy with her. And my dear wife has gone up to bed. Would that the Lord lets her pass a quiet night,' he muttered.

'Mrs Hawker is not well?' Anna said, then winced as a cat tried to claw its way up her legs.

'In a manner of speaking. She is . . . troubled. I've had a devil of a time trying to keep Mrs Hawker in the house. If I didn't stop her, she might start swimming again, after all my efforts to make her see it's not safe. At her age!'

'Mrs Hawker has a fancy for the sea?' I said, thinking of the creatures who lived in it. Thinking of mermaids.

'She does, Mrs Williams. To hear my wife tell it, she spent most of her youth in the waters off this coast. I would rather she turn her energies to her greatest talent but not a word of a song has passed her lips since the dead man was found.' The parson shook his head sadly. 'She has the most *wondrous* voice. It is a gift from our Saviour. It can be none other. The *purity* of it speaks to His grace.' Then a thought seemed to strike him for he looked sharp at each of us. 'Now that you are here, she might sing again. Visitors might stir her breath back to glory. Yes, yes. Another sign I was right to give you sanctuary. It is for Mrs Hawker's health.'

'Forgive me for prying, but what is it that has so distressed your wife?' Anna said.

The parson slumped back in his chair, slumped back into gloom. 'It is Frederick's doing. He has upset her with his wild theories as to the identity of the poor man lying in the deadhouse. The man denied rest.'

Was that the cause of the stench in the churchyard? This deadhouse, it must have been nearby. And the man rotting inside it.

'It cannot be Joseph,' the parson was saying. 'For all the trials sent us by the Lord, He would not be so cruel as to bring that malcontent back to us.'

'You knew Joseph Ians?' I asked.

He shook his head. 'I have been fortunate never to meet the man, but my wife has spoken often of him, though it pains her so. That is why I have forbidden mention of his name. For her own sake, you see.'

'So Mrs Hawker knew Joseph,' Anna said, 'in her youth?'

The parson frowned. 'I should say so, sir. Mrs Hawker *is* Joseph's sister after all.'

TWELVE

The parson saw our wonderment at this news.

'Frederick did not tell you of the family connection?' he asked.

Anna and I shared a look, for the captain *hadn't* told us that Joseph Ians was brother to the parson's wife. And why was that, I wondered? But there was no time to think for another question rose within me.

'That means Captain Ians, Frederick, he is brother to Mrs Hawker too?'

'He is not very brotherly in his manner at present, upsetting her so.' Parson Hawker's hand tightened over the arm of his chair. Only for a breath, but I saw it.

He shifted the dog who had been trying to wedge itself into the chair with its roly-poly master, and reached into a pocket. He drew out a pouch of some bright cloth, and then said to the dog, which was a little ratting thing, 'Pipe, Timothy! Pipe!'

The dog nipped over to the hearth, its tail a-wag, and bit something that had been left on a stool there. He trotted back to us and in his mouth was a pipe, a long clay one, which the parson took from him with grateful thanks and a ruffle for his ears. The dog curled up on his master's stockinged feet.

'And it is Frederick's interference in my work – in God's work! – that has delayed the burial, for now we face a visit from the coroner when in the normal course of things a note would be sufficient to grant permission to inter. And when will *that* creature scuttle to our shores, I ask you! Or perhaps you know . . .' His eyes narrowed as he stared at each of us in turn. 'That is why you are here, some business of the coroner?'

'Tangentially, yes,' Anna said. 'Captain Ians has asked us to identify the body of the man recently discovered at the base of the cliffs.'

'That will be . . . difficult,' the parson said, and his voice cracked. Was he about to give way to scritching? 'The sea has committed its violence once again and the man's face is—I do not understand why Frederick must torment us with his demands. It is a sailor, washed up on our shores as so many have before. A tragedy, but a common one. I know them all too well. And yet Frederick presumes to interfere. I *must* bury the man, but when will the wretched coroner come? When?' He lifted his eyes to the ceiling and began to mutter a prayer.

'Would it not be better to know who this poor soul is?' Anna said over his muttering. 'To commend him into God's hands as himself? To discover such information, that is the line of work we undertake – private cases, you understand the sort of thing.'

He did not, for the parson only sadly shook his head and bent to fill his pipe from the pouch. Given his talk of devils, I thought there was a part of the case he might understand better.

'We're here about the mermaid too,' I said. 'Her that might have done for the dead man, whoever he might be.'

'Ah yes,' he said, his voice a little stronger now. 'There is much talk here about a woman's involvement.' He lit his pipe and drew deeply on it. The tobacco had a rich smoke – that was the smell

73

that had greeted us in the room. He pointed the pipe stem at me. 'They are the Devil's own, such creatures.'

My blood was cold as sea water then, for he was speaking of me, surely. He had guessed my way of seeing the world that was not like most people, and he would cast me out. But then Anna saved me by asking if he believed in mermaids.

'Of course,' he said, surprised at her surprise. 'They are legion off this coast, drawing unsuspecting souls into their clutches. One of our many troubles, but not so bad as *Wesleyans*.' He slammed his pipe down on the little table at his elbow, and so startled My Most Righteous Cat. 'At least the mermaids keep to the sea. That great fornicator Wesley brings the plague of his band to our fields, to our very doors!' He puffed fiercely on his pipe, but the tobacco's smell was mixed with that of wood burning, for his pipe had marked the table – a new ring in the mess of them that had charred the wood. This man was often angry.

'You've many that are chapel here?' I said.

'Every day there are more, Mrs Williams. They dare not build a chapel in sight of St Morwenna's house, but that doesn't stop them meeting in dark corners, multiplying, like the beetles they are. I will be forced to call on the labour of such devils for the harvest, for what else can I do, lest I lose the crops and there will be such devastations amongst the families?'

He put a hand over his eyes and breathed deeply for a moment.

'The Lord has set me the task to smite them back to the unearthly realms from which they crawled,' he said, as if to comfort himself. I half thought he'd forgotten we were there. Did he think of us as he did the cats so thickly spread about the room? 'That is why I am called to Morwenstow. Why I must suffer such isolation.'

The Lord had given this parson many such tasks. I had never before met one so burdened by his calling, nor one so fiery in it.

But then I had had more to do with chapel than with church. Not that I would be telling him that.

'Have you been parson long in these parts?' I said.

'Ten years.' He looked away. 'Though it feels much longer.'

'To be so removed from life as you are here,' Anna said, 'it must be a difficult place to live.'

'It is easier now than when I took up the living, for the parish was lacking even the most basic amenities. No school to speak of, no safe means to cross the river. No vicarage, even! I gifted the parish all three, and from my own pocket, I might add. This fine dwelling was built to my specifications.' He beamed, worry of Methodists forgotten in his pride, which I was certain was a sin.

I patted the well-stuffed arm of the chair. 'You've a fine place here.'

He clapped his hands and grinned. 'What better way to honour our Saviour than with the finest things in life! Wesley's band would have mankind go barefooted in sackcloth to pay homage, would have us *reduce* ourselves. It is to the glory of the Lord that I keep the larder stocked with cream.'

I liked the sound of that. I liked it very much.

'The vicarage is undoubtedly a great achievement,' Anna said. 'I look forward to seeing it in the light tomorrow, that's if we're not trespassing on your hospitality. If you could direct us to the Bush we would happily install ourselves there.'

'I will not hear of it, sir. Though I cannot condone Frederick's actions in bringing you here, I cannot see you lost in the wilderness either. After all, what was this great house built for if not to harbour those seeking rest?'

To give *yourself* a goodly harbour, I thought, doubting any of the parson's flock lived so lavish.

The clock struck midnight then, which surprised us all. So late it had got in this stormy man's company. The dogs yawned and the cats curled into tighter nests of themselves, and the parson said he would show us to a room. My Most Righteous Cat followed us.

At the bottom of the stairs the cat stopped, as if knowing the parson would do the same, which he did, to tap a kind of clock on the wall there.

'After the storm this week, I hope the weather is set fair,' Anna said.

He did not answer for a moment, only tapped the glass of this weather-clock again, then said quietly, 'For now. But you might hear them tonight.'

'Them?' I said, and a chill passed over me, as if the wind had found a crack to blow through.

'The dead. They are all around us, Mrs Williams. Their calls . . . it is more than I can bear.'

He picked up the cat and led us up the stairs to a landing with more black studded doors, and two passages leading from it. We went no further than the landing, though, for our room was here. He bade us take the candle left burning at the top of the stairs, wished us good night and took himself down one of the passages. I watched him go and wondered at him, so quick to temper and to gloom, but also welcoming to strangers, even those of us with tasks he did not like.

When his candle was gone, I went into the room he said we should use and there was Anna, yellow-haired and in her drawers. Mr Williams was gone – a pile of hair and sticky whiskers on the table. And I was back sleeping in the same bed as Anna. This trip had some good parts, though I felt a stab of guilt then for I hadn't thought of poor Mathilda since we'd arrived. Even now she might be recovered and would join us soon.

The room was as smartly furnished as the rest of the house, with a bedstead of curled iron. I ran my hand over the mattress – soft as a sweetheart's breast.

'The parson must have a private fortune,' I said. 'Or he did until he came to Morwenstow.'

Anna slipped beneath all the many layers of sheets there seemed to be. 'I suspect his pockets aren't bare yet. That tobacco he was smoking, it's Latakia – one of the finest money can buy.'

'You should have asked him for some,' I said, climbing in beside her. The sheets were good. No darns. No stains. The room had been made ready for visitors and kept clean of dust, though the parson said few came to stay. His hopefulness was in these tucked sheets, in the water jug.

'I might see about the parson's tobacco tomorrow,' Anna said. 'That's if we stay on favourable terms. I doubt we will after insisting we see the body. We'll be packed off to the Bush Inn. Enjoy this luxury while it lasts, Shilly.'

'It's not good work for staying friends, is it,' I said, 'this detecting?'

'No, and I doubt we shall stay friends with Captain Ians either, now we know he lied to us. Your feet are too cold, Shilly. Off!'

'He didn't lie, exactly,' I said.

'But he didn't tell us the whole truth either. If the dead man is indeed Joseph Ians, then the person wanting to bury him with all haste is none other than brother-in-law to the deceased, and brother-in-law to the captain likewise.'

'It is strange the captain didn't tell us of his relation to the parson's wife,' I said. 'What might be his reasoning?'

'I'm too tired to guess,' Anna said through a yawn. I caught sight of her false teeth, dull in her own. 'Put out the candle, Shilly. I'm sure much will be clearer in the morning.'

I did as she asked, but as a kiss, blown to her. The last I saw before the darkness was her smile.

* * *

. . . and I felt the sheet beneath me, the coverlet over me. There was the hill of Anna's back. The bed frame. And a sound. A moan. I turned from it, for it was dreadful, but no matter the way I placed my body, it was there. I put the pillow over my head but it came again – the wind, making the sash of the window tremble against the frame, as if the wind sucked at the glass, tried to draw it from the wood. The pull—

. . . and I was rising, pulled by the wind as the glass was pulled. Would be pulled through the glass, out into the night air and—

The sea.

That was where I was meant to go. I had forgotten. I hadn't been listening. But I was ready now.

The stones beneath my feet were sharp. I hadn't put my boots on, but I didn't need them, because I was walking to the water that waited, its dark mouth drawing me to it for it knew me, that water, and needed me and so it called me by my name—

THIRTEEN

'Shilly?'

I thought Anna had hit me with the candlestick to wake me, for my head was sore, so sore it hurt to open my eyes to the light.

She sat beside me on the bed and regarded me dreadful grave.

'Have you ever walked in your sleep before, Shilly? Before we met?'

'Hm? I don't.' I sat up and the room chose that moment to dance. The bed frame was a terrible jouncer.

Anna frowned. 'Are you sure?'

I tried to nod but the room moved again.

'Well, last night might have been the first time. It could be a symptom of withdrawal, I suppose.' Her false teeth tapped against her own. 'But why it's taken this long—'

'What are you talking about, Anna?'

'You don't remember what happened? I woke to see you at the door, scrabbling at it, in fact, as if you'd forgotten how to use a handle.'

'Really? I don't—'

'You were determined to get out. It was all I could do to get you back into bed and you didn't appear to wake at any point.

79

You'd done yourself some damage by the time I caught you, unfortunately. Your poor nails.'

I looked at my hands, and sure enough some of my fingernails had splintered, one quite bad. There was dried blood in the scraps of nail left behind.

'If you were off to find a lover in the cowshed then you seemed rather desperate for them,' she said.

'What?'

'The woman at Trequite, Shilly! The one whose husband thought a devil made her walk in her sleep.' Anna smiled at me, wanting me to share the joke.

'I—'

She patted my leg. 'You needn't look so worried. A bad dream, nothing more. Some breakfast will help. Let's see what delicacies the parson offers.'

I was so slow to get dressed that Anna said she'd go down before me – as Mr Williams, of course. My limbs were heavy, so I sat in the window seat to wait for them to lighten. The view was a fine one for our room looked down a little valley of trees to the sea. The trees were tossed about in the wind this morning, but it had been calm when we went to bed, hadn't it? Something tugged at me, then was away – a wave broken and lost. There were no boats out in the water, and I thought of Mathilda. Was she out of bed herself now, able to watch the Boscastle fishermen, as she so loved to do?

I shook my head and found that the pain I'd woken with had eased, but it had left behind a low buzz, as if a bee was with me. A thrum. That was the noise of the window's sash against the frame in the night. I tried to remember getting up, going to the door. Nothing.

Apart from my name.

It had been a woman's voice that called me. The same voice I'd heard in the wind on Boscastle's cliffs. The parson had said we would hear the calls of the dead, but I had heard something else. Heard the women in the sea who drew people to their drownings. If it wasn't for Anna, would I have got out of our room, gone down to the sea and so to my end? I might even now be washed to shore and put in the parson's deadhouse, my corpse the one making the air bad.

This way of thinking was no good at all. I made myself get up, get on. Tonight I would make Anna tie me to the fancy bed frame, for that must be why it was here – to keep a body from doing as it didn't ought to. With as much haste as I could find within me, I hurried from the room.

And crashed straight into another body. After we had each asked the other for forgiveness, I saw that the body was an older woman, broad-faced, broad-hipped, in a plain dress and apron. Her sleeves were rolled up as if for work. She had a bucket with her, and many clothes tucked into her apron, up her sleeves. Here was the person who kept the lonely guest rooms clean, and here were the rooms before me, the doors on the landing open, the fine linens beyond.

'It's Mrs Williams, isn't it?' the woman said, shaking her rag free of dust. 'I just met your husband downstairs. He tells me you're here about the poor man in the deadhouse.'

'We are, Mrs . . .'

'Seldon. Not much to be done for 'im now, though, is there?' She ran her cloth over the mirror hanging by the stairs without even looking at it. Mrs Seldon must have been working for the parson and his wife as long as there'd been a vicarage. 'No, there's nothing to do but what's right and proper – the parson putting him to rest so the Lord can call him home.'

'Well, I—'

'For we will all be called, Mrs Williams. We will all have our turn, won't we?'

'That we will.'

She closed her eyes and nodded with great feeling. Anna and I were in a place where the spirit was keenly felt, and no mistake. She opened her eyes and I had the feeling she had just said a prayer for me, then she took up her cloths and went into the next room to the one Anna and I had slept in.

'Go careful down the stairs, won't you? The boards are still wet.'

Perhaps I would be called now. If I should fall, break my neck . . .

'My Nancy is seeing to the breakfast,' Mrs Seldon said from inside the room, out of sight now.

I went on my way, but a door caught my eye. I hadn't seen it when we came to bed the night before for it was set back from the stairs. In some ways it was the same sort of door as all the others – black and studded. But in other ways it wasn't, for it was narrower. And it was the only one closed.

When I reached the turn in the stairs, I heard it – singing. I thought it must be Mrs Hawker I was hearing, for hadn't the parson said she was one for that? But then I realised it was coming from above me. Mrs Seldon, singing as she went about her work. And there was no sweetness to it, as the parson had said there was in his wife's song. Mrs Seldon squawked like a rook.

I got down to the hall without breaking my neck and from there followed the smell of meat cooking, and that took me to Anna, who was dressed as Mr Williams, seated at a huge table. There was a white cloth spread upon it and all manner of plates and cups and knives and forks on that. There was a woman seated with Anna, and this I was sure must be Mrs Hawker, the parson's wife.

'Come in, my dear, come in,' this woman said. 'What a delight, waking to visitors!' She was sun-worn as her husband, but much older than him – nearer sixty, I thought. Mrs Hawker had the same nose as Captain Ians, a long one, that looked to be trying to slide into her mouth. And though she smiled her welcome, her eyes were red, as if she'd not long been badly scritching.

'Thank you for having us stay, Mrs Hawker,' I said, and took the chair she pointed me to. On the one beside me, a cat. Of course a cat, in this house. A tatty ginger thing.

'It's no bother, and you must call me Charlotte.'

At hearing this name, I went still as moor stone, for it was my own name. My true name.

And another's, too – the name of my first love, my girl, Charlotte Dymond, who had been taken from me with such violence.

Mrs Hawker was looking at me, a frown now upon her worn, kind face. I resolved to forget this part of her name and only call her Mrs Hawker. She would have to make do with it or I'd be what Anna called *in dis posed* and we'd never get to the bottom of who the dead man was, the captain's dream, the mermaid and all the rest of it.

Anna cleared her throat. 'Charlotte, this is my wife, Shilly.'

I was grateful someone else came into the room then, a woman Anna's age, past forty. She had the same broad face as Mrs Seldon, so I guessed this was Nancy, Mrs Seldon's daughter. She put a plate before me and the sound woke the scrawny ginger cat. On seeing Nancy, he gave an excited chirp and she said, *What you doing in here, mister, waiting for your breakfast? Shall I get you a plate too?* The cat chirped again as if to say, *Yes yes yes* and we all laughed, even Mrs Hawker. Nancy leant over to rub behind the cat's ear and I spied a bit of dirt on her wrist. The parson had said she and her mother lived at the farm across the way. She must have come from milking to see to the breakfast. It was as if I was looking at myself grown older. Myself had Anna not found me.

Nancy went back to the kitchen and Mrs Hawker said I should help myself to the dishes on the sideboard. There I found so many delicious things I decided it was worth a night of strange doings – soft bread and creamy butter, boiled eggs, bacon gleaming with fat. The parson's way to honour the Lord. I was glad to help him with that and piled my plate. It got me a bad look from Anna for doing so, but if we were likely to be asked to leave soon, then I wanted to make the most of our good fortune. It never lasted long.

Anna was asking Mrs Hawker if being the parson's wife kept her from being idle, if she had much to do in these parts.

'Oh, that I do, Mr Williams. The parish is a poor one, I'm sad to tell you. My husband does his best to help but it's more than we . . . Well, we must try. There's no gentry in these parts. No one else who cares.'

'That must make for a lonely time of it,' Anna said.

'We have each other, my husband and I, and each our passions.'

'What are they, then?' I said, sitting down with my full plate.

'Robert is devoted to the poetic arts. He would be delighted to share some of his work with you both. He doesn't have many ready listeners in Morwenstow.'

'And your passion, Mrs Hawker?' Anna said quickly. I didn't think she liked the notion of hearing the parson's poems.

'German. Translations are an absorbing occupation for the winter nights.'

'German!' I dropped my fork. 'Well there's good fortune.'

Mrs Hawker smiled uncertainly. 'Is it?'

'We've left Mathilda – she's our companion. We've left her in Boscastle for she was poorly but she's to come here, and *she's* German!

She would like to talk with you in her own tongue, Mrs Hawker, I know she would. She's—'

'I'm sure our host doesn't need to hear of our domestic arrangements,' Anna said.

There was silence then, for my tongue was stilled by Anna's words. She didn't want Mathilda to come to Morwenstow, but why?

'You'll have a drop more tea?' Mrs Hawker asked Anna, and the talk moved on.

'The parson won't be joining us?' Anna said.

'You'll have to excuse him. It's a leeward wind got up in the night, so he's taken himself off. 'Tis the worry of it, see.'

We didn't, not being people of those parts. I cracked my second egg.

'There's nothing a ship's captain can do in a leeward, 'cept wait, of course. It puts us in an agony of waiting here too, knowing a vessel will likely come to grief on our cliffs.'

'And so bring bodies to your door,' Anna said. She set down her cup. 'Like the man awaiting burial.'

'Yes,' said Mrs Hawker quietly. 'My husband told me why you're here. That Frederick asked you.'

'Do you share Captain Ians' belief, that the deceased is indeed your brother Joseph?'

Mrs Hawker fetched a napkin from the sideboard, to dab her sore, sad eyes. 'It's not Joseph. Of that I am certain.'

'Forgive me,' Anna said, 'but you seem very troubled by the loss. Why mourn a stranger dead, when so many meet their ends here?'

Mrs Hawker took her seat again, and as she did so there was a little moan from under the table and she seemed to ask the floor for forgiveness. I peered beneath the cloth. Two dogs sleeping at her feet.

'It's the talk of him, of Joseph,' she said. 'After so long . . .'

She tried to brighten, dear of her, but it was a struggle. I poured her some fresh tea. When I put the pot down there were marks on the good white cloth. Red marks. Blood. From my splintered nail. I moved the teapot to cover it. But then I saw a burn mark in the tablecloth, same as those on the table the night before, from the parson's pipe, so I didn't feel so dreadful then.

'What Frederick claims,' Mrs Hawker said, 'I don't believe it's true, but it's the strangest thing . . . You'll think me quite mazed.'

'Please, go on,' Anna said.

Mrs Seldon came in then and Mrs Hawker held her tongue, but not to keep her maziness from us, I thought. To keep it from Mrs Seldon, fearful what her servant might think of her.

We sat quiet while Mrs Seldon poured fresh water into the teapot, which meant moving it, of course, and she saw the blood, then looked at me. I felt such a filthy beast then, for she was all proper washed and tidied, her hair put up. I was happier when she'd gone back to the kitchen, and so was Mrs Hawker for she began to speak once more.

FOURTEEN

'All the talk of my younger brother has made him come alive again,' Mrs Hawker said, 'as if Joseph has somehow walked out of the sea. I know that must sound peculiar.'

'Not to me,' I muttered, thinking of Captain Ians dripping wet and pale in our parlour in Boscastle, looking for all the world a drowned man walked from his grave.

'My husband never met Joseph. He came to the parish long after both my brothers had left home, but he has heard the stories from those who knew Joseph in his youth. People remember the badness in others, not the goodness.'

'I would drink to that,' I said, and did so with my teacup.

Anna nodded at the door to the kitchen. 'The Seldons, they knew Joseph?'

'Oh yes. Margaret and her husband were both born here. Peter is sexton at the church now. I've known them all my life, and Nancy too. She and Joseph were thick as thieves at one time. But it's funny what people will forget, for Joseph *wasn't* all badness.' Mrs Hawker looked out of the window, a smile finding its way to her lips, as if she could see Joseph beyond the glass, as if he was with the pig Gyp who was now ambling past.

'What was Joseph like?' I said.

'He was spirited, that I'd grant you, and terrible funny. How he'd make me howl with laughter! Always up to something. It drove our parents to distraction, and no more so than in church. He didn't even try to pretend he was listening to the service. I'd whisper to him, what are you planning, and of course I was his older sister, so he wasn't telling me. He'd just grin and pull these faces.'

The napkin at her eyes again. We let her scritch it out. Warmth against my leg – one of the dogs stirring.

'My brother left Morwenstow before he was eighteen. I have not seen him since.'

'May I ask the cause of him leaving?' Anna said.

'Money,' Mrs Hawker said, and a great sigh left her, almost a groan. She threw the napkin on the table and picked up the cat seated on the chair next to her. 'The root of all evil. Joseph was always needing money for something. Ha'pennies for the fair at Bude. That's when he was a boy, taken with the coconut shy. He made bets with himself.'

'But with others when he got older?' I asked.

She nodded. 'And such schemes he had to make his way in the world. Growing crocuses for London – in Morwenstow, where even trees struggle to stand! He was certain there was copper under Coombe – that's the next village. He convinced the farmers there to dig. They took out a field wall that had stood for hundreds of years. Our father ran out of patience. The rows only made things worse, of course. Then Joseph threatened he would go to sea and our father forbade that too, for that path was Frederick's and he was making his way as befitted his station, with recommendations.'

'I take it there was no such smooth passage for Joseph?' Anna said.

'Our father insisted that one Ians son should be at home. I think he feared the debts Joseph might incur if he left. The tattoo was the final straw.'

'Tattoo?' I said.

Mrs Hawker shivered, as if a draught had crossed her shoulders. 'It was a hideous thing, done with spite. The design . . . Joseph thought if he looked the part of a sailor, our father would relent. The foolishness of youth.'

'What did the tattoo look like?' Anna asked.

'You'll see the likeness in the church,' Mrs Hawker said. 'Joseph's inspiration was a face atop a pillar – a carving. Some hideous old thing from the early church. I cannot bear to look at it.' She stirred her tea with vigour. 'The only saving grace of the tattoo was his thought for me. Not that that helped appease our father.'

'You asked him to get a tattoo?' I said.

'Faith no!' Mrs Hawker said, and near spit out her tea. 'I mean the part of it done for me. We were very close, especially once Frederick had gone to sea and it was just the two of us. Joseph had the tattoo fashioned so he'd always have me with him. Two letters – C and J worked into the design.'

'Forgive me asking this,' Anna said, 'but it might help in identifying the dead man. Where on your brother's body was the tattoo?'

'His arm,' Mrs Hawker said. 'I forget which.'

'Would that be the upper arm or the lower?' Anna said gently, but Mrs Hawker waved the words away. She didn't know. It was all so long ago.

'In some ways it was a relief once Joseph had left,' she said. 'But if I had known he would never return . . .'

'You've heard nothing from him since?' I said.

She shook her head, then set to scratching the cat's cheek. The

89

purr was surely too big for the scrawn of it. 'My husband knows how it upsets me to hear talk of Joseph. He's forbidden anyone to mention Joseph's name. To hear nothing for so long makes for a kind of death, doesn't it? He might well be in the Lord's hands now.' She lifted the cat to her face and kissed its ear. 'He might have been dead all these years.'

A clang then, beyond the room. A pan dropped in the kitchen. Murmured voices. Nancy and her mother, I guessed.

'But not dead on Morwenstow's shores?' Anna said.

'A sad coincidence that would be,' Mrs Hawker said. 'And one I find hard to believe. Frederick's determination that the sailor is Joseph, it's not healthy. Frederick has been at sea too long. This last run has done something to his mind.'

'How so?' Anna said, and I could hear the concern in her voice, for we were talking of our employer. The one who'd brought us here.

'His letters have begun to read like those of a madman,' Mrs Hawker said. 'He distrusts his men, believes the cook to be a poisoner bent on killing him and taking over the ship. And now he has left his post! I doubt the owner of *The Severn* will let my brother resume command after this, and who else will give him such opportunity? He has ruined himself over this business of the dream. He has told you of it, I suppose?'

Anna nodded. 'An unusual aspect of an investigation, I'll grant you.'

'It's madness, my dear Mr Williams, that's what it is! And I must ask you, beg you, not to indulge his delusions. It won't help him recover his mind, and I can't bear any more talk of Joseph. I can't!'

She was upset now, and sounding like Captain Ians himself, him she thought mad – her own brother! The cat wanted to get away from her panic, but she held it down, pinned its back. The purr became a growl.

'I have to make Frederick see he's mistaken. I have to—'

A low cough. It was Mrs Seldon.

'There's a visitor.'

Mrs Hawker's grip eased and the cat leapt free, knocking over the milk jug as it went. 'Heavens. Put them in the drawing room, Margaret. Will you excuse me, my dears? We're rich with visitors today! My husband will be delighted.'

She was bustling off, the dogs awake and with her, but then Mrs Seldon's words brought her up short.

'It's the parson he's wanting,' Mrs Seldon said. 'Says he won't wait. Won't come inside even with the wind got up. He's that teasy.'

'Oh? Who is it, Margaret?'

'The coroner.'

FIFTEEN

He was outside the front door, his back to us. He wore a well-made coat to keep out the wind but it was muddy, and one pocket looked to be hanging off. His collar was grey and only half tucked into his coat. His hat he held, and banged against his leg. So soon arrived and yet ready to be off again.

Mrs Hawker welcomed him, and at this he turned, and when I saw his face I went cold.

His face – I knew it.

This man, the coroner, it was the same man who had laid his rough hands on the body of my first love when she lay cold and gone from me. The same who had decided on the manner of her death, who had told the magistrates of it, then gone to the courthouse to tell the judge and the jury men.

Mr Good. He who spoke the names of death.

He didn't know Anna, for though she had used the name Mr Williams when they had met and talked of cuts and blood and all the rest of it, she had looked very different then. But he knew me, of course, for I had told the magistrates of spirits. He didn't seem a man to forget such a thing.

'*You?*' he said. 'Whatever in the world—'

'Samuel Williams,' my new love said, and grasped the coroner's hand before he'd had chance to offer it, for my new love could see I was in a poor way. 'Here on behalf of Captain Frederick Ians. My wife, Mrs Williams, who I believe you know.'

'I have had the pleasure,' he said, with great sourness. '*Married*, you say?'

Mr Good looked from me to Mr Williams and back again, for he had known me as the Shilly who worked on a farm and owned only the dress she stood up in. Mrs Williams was a different creature, and her husband the kind of man who could buy her many dresses. It pleased me to confound him. It pleased me to be so changed.

'We will need to witness the inspection of the body,' Anna said, in such a voice that meant no countering. 'And I would be keen to hear your thoughts on the manner of death.'

'If you wish to hear about the ravages of the sea, I'd be only too pleased to share them with you,' Mr Good said, sounding anything *but* pleased.

'But you haven't looked at him yet,' I said. 'How can you know what killed him?'

Mr Good shrugged. 'From what the parson has told me, in his *many* letters since the man was discovered, asking me to make haste, there seems little doubt.'

Anna made a noise that was two parts mirth and one part anger.

'I've sent word to Captain Ians at the Bush,' Mr Good said. 'He's the one who has caused this examination to take place, so I think it only right he's present, in the hope of putting his mind at rest.'

'I hope to God it will,' Mrs Hawker said.

'Speaking of which, will the parson be joining us?' Mr Good said. He'd started banging his hat against his leg again. A dull flap, as if he was one of the rooks.

Mrs Hawker's hands fluttered to her throat – no rook she, but a wren. 'I think it best if he doesn't. His health . . .'

'Would you come in the parson's place?' I asked her, to a great *tut* from Mr Good.

Mrs Hawker backed into the porch, stepping on a cat's tail in the doing. 'I'm sure the coroner doesn't need anyone else getting in his way.'

'No he doesn't!' Mr Good said loudly.

'And I . . . I have something I must see to this morning. Forgive me.' She hurried off into the house.

'I hope the parson doesn't expect me to keep her indoors.' It was Mrs Seldon. She must have followed us all to the porch.

'What do you mean?' I said.

But Mrs Seldon only shook her head and held out a handkerchief to Anna. 'I should take this, sir. My husband and I did our best for the poor wretch washed in, but this one was looking for the earth long ago.' Then to Mr Good, 'I should think you'll be in and out quick enough this time, Coroner.'

Anna thanked her and asked if she had another handkerchief for me.

'You surely don't plan to enter the deadhouse with us, Mrs Williams?' Mr Good said.

'Why not?'

'Well . . . It's no place for . . . *ladies*.'

I laughed. I couldn't stop myself. He didn't wish to call me a lady, but he didn't give himself a choice. What he meant was a *woman*. But I was sore, too, even in my laughing, for here was the reason Anna passed as a man, the reason she couldn't be her true yellow-haired self who I loved best. It was men who had the keys and decided who should pass.

'Mrs Hawker has the right idea,' Mr Good said, with such a

poor attempt at a smile that it made his face strain. 'Why don't you wait quietly in the parlour?'

'My wife must attend,' Anna said. 'She is here at Captain Ians' instruction.'

Mr Good sighed. 'Let's get on with it, then,' and he was striding away.

Anna and I went after him. He took the path that cut through the gravestones, climbing all the time. In the daylight the church was there, and beyond that, the sea. The wind was all about us, making the tops of the trees whisper loudly, almost as loud as the rooks who swayed in them. The foulness of the air the night before was worse this morning, and I feared we were making for the cause of it.

'Surely the parson should be here for this?' I said to Anna. 'He's been wanting the coroner to come so badly.'

'And yet now the coroner has come and the parson keeps away.'

To my surprise, Mr Good didn't go to the church. He headed back the way Anna and I must have come the night before, towards the road. On the road's other side, a broad, squat building, whitewashed, with neat windows. Other buildings round it, a tumble of them.

'That must be the Seldons' farm,' I said. 'Is that where the deadhouse is?'

But Mr Good did not go so far as the road and the farm beyond it, for there was a little roof in the churchyard, half hidden by the trees, and as we drew close I saw that it was a small dwelling, with a gate and stile next to it, which marked the proper way into the churchyard. This, then, was the deadhouse, where the parson stowed his dreadful finds.

And this was where the stench was coming from. The rot couldn't be held inside. It was so bad it had pushed through the walls, into our mouths. The taste of the dead was hot bile.

Leaning against the door was Captain Ians. It was only a little time since he had come to Boscastle to see us – two days. But he looked to have grown more fretful since we had spoken. His fingers plucked at his clothes, the same he had worn in Boscastle – the ink stain on his shirt front. He had left the Bush without his coat, though the wind was cold off the sea.

He greeted me like an old friend. Perhaps he didn't have many in that part of the world, his sister thinking him mad, his brother-in-law talking so hard against him.

'This is my husband, Mr Williams,' I said to Captain Ians, 'who you *haven't* met,' but meaning, of course, that he had, for it was Anna beneath the whiskers.

Anna grasped the captain's hand with great firmness, and as she shook it she made sure to look him square in the eye, giving him chance to realise who Mr Williams truly was. 'Captain Ians, a pleasure,' she said loudly, for Mr Good's ears.

The captain's eyes widened in his tired, worn face, but he had the sense not to exclaim his understanding.

'Have you slept at all?' Anna asked him.

'How can I?' the captain said. 'If I should dream of death again, who knows what horror will befall some innocent soul?'

Mr Good gave the captain a dark look at these words, then took a handkerchief from his pocket. Anna and I tied each other's handkerchiefs across our faces.

'If you should faint, Mrs Williams,' Mr Good said, his voice a little muffled by the cloth, 'be so good as to do it in the corner, out of my way. And if there's any talk of spirits—'

'We haven't got all day,' Anna said.

With a *humph*, Mr Good opened the door.

I had smelt the like before, when rats died beneath the floorboards of the cottage where I'd lived as a child, but I'd forgotten how the smell of death could make you wish you were dead too, and I was all regret for my fulsome breakfast. Anna, too, looked to find it bad, but she had seen many bodies in London, for that was a place of murder, so she took my hand and we stepped inside the deadhouse.

Mr Good had been right about the tightness of it. A table took up nearly all the deadhouse. I couldn't look at what it bore, so I looked at everything else. Behind the table, a bench, and shelves above, crammed with jars and pots, heaps of nails. A ball of string. In the corner, a rake. Two pails. The deadhouse was a shed for keeping outdoor things, as well as for bodies on their way to the ground.

I looked at the table, couldn't look away any longer. It was fashioned from planks set over two upturned casks. And on this table was a lumpen shape covered by sheets, with boots poking out one end. Sand on the boots still. Little crumbs of it, and that was terrible to see. It made me think of this man as walking, breathing, thinking. He had been on the sand. He had touched the sand, and now he lay here, dead, but the sand was still on his boots. The sand was still in this world though the spirit of the man who'd touched it was not.

Mr Good stood at the other end of the sheets. There were patches of brown on them that made me think of the damp on our parlour wall back in Boscastle, but these patches were stinking. It was the seeps from the body beneath.

Mr Good took the sheet in his hands and made ready to pull it off but Captain Ians was at his elbow, in his way. With gentleness Anna guided the captain back a pace, to stand with us. He swayed on his feet.

'If everyone is *quite* ready?' Mr Good said, his voice muffled by the handkerchief.

Anna nodded. I told myself, be brave, Shilly.

Mr Good pulled back the sheet.

SIXTEEN

The boots, Shilly, look at the boots. That was what I said to myself. The boots were ordinary things – the leather, the sand. Then I looked a little up his legs. Trousers, of some soft cloth. Dirty, but not torn. And then to his waist – a belt, a buckle, still fastened. But then things became bad. His shirt was torn, and so was his flesh beneath.

This man had been carved to pieces.

I made myself keep looking. Up to his chest, raked open, the gouges inches deep, red and wet. One arm hacked back, the white of bone where a chunk had gone completely, as if some huge creature had bitten him. But there was something there. Some mark on the last bit of the skin before the bite. Green, it was. No bigger than a shilling. I tried to look closer but the light was too poor and then Mr Good bustled me out of his way. The dead man's other arm was only a little slashed about the shoulder. A nothing wound, when seen with the rest.

His neck, which was strangely as it should be, no marks at all. A mole, I saw there. The lump where his Adam's apple had come to lay, the last time he'd swallowed, when he was screaming, surely, in pain at what was done to him? I let my poor eyes rest, looked to the window, to the snip of sky there. Then I made myself set off again in the looking at the body, the last part of the climb.

There was his head, not his face, for that was gone. No eyes. No nose. A deeper gouge where his mouth had once been. A fleck of white there – a tooth? His ears left, but they looked so strange, without the other parts a face should have, I almost wished they'd been taken too. And up to his hair. Some tufts left, matted with blood. That would have been harder for Mrs Seldon and her husband to wash out. How in the Lord's name had they tended this poor soul? Poured buckets of water over him. Sluiced him clean.

What else could you do with such a body that was more outside itself than in? But what had gone with the wiping and the water? What traces of the truth? Anna had taught me the importance of these.

Captain Ians was staring down at the ruin of the man he believed his brother. The man who his sister thought a stranger. The captain seemed unmoved, just stared, swayed, and I wondered if he'd fallen asleep at last, on his feet with his eyes open. But then he sniffed and wiped his eyes with the back of his hand, and I knew he was awake and made mute by grief.

Mr Good was peering at the cuts, poked them with a little stick he'd brought with him.

'The damage is extensive, I will grant the parson that. His letters didn't exaggerate. But this is consistent with a body dragged back and forwards across the rocks. You've seen the rocks offshore here?'

'Not yet,' I said.

'Go down there. This kind of injury, it'll soon make sense.'

'Show me on the body,' Anna said.

He looked at her, she looked at him, then he seemed to decide he'd be quicker away if he gave in to her. He used his stick to push back a flap of skin on the man's chest.

'See the gradations here?'

Anna looked but I didn't dare.

'It's the sawing action of the rocks.' He let go the skin and it landed with a wet flop. 'Quite as expected. Very few of the poor souls the parson collects are drowned.'

'Really?' Anna said.

'The rocks get them before the sea has its chance.'

'What's that?' Anna said. 'There – by the rib. A shine.' She peered this way and that in the ruin of the man's chest.

'Nothing significant, I'm sure,' said Mr Good. He put his hat back on. 'I've seen all I need to—'

'We need more light. Shilly, get that candle lit.'

I did as she asked and then I held it for her, trying not to look at the now gleaming parts of the man beneath it. Anna grabbed Mr Good's stick.

'Now, see here,' he said, but she wasn't listening. Of course she wasn't, because this was her best work – things to see and touch and shine lights on.

She used the stick to pry out the thing she had seen, that now revealed itself in her poking – a thin bit of metal. Two inches long. She got hold of it and held it to the candle.

A key.

'And how would you explain *this*?' Anna said, handing the key to Mr Good.

He shrugged. 'The deceased likely had it on his person when the rocks carved him up, drove it into his chest.'

Captain Ians gave a low moan.

'My apologies, Captain,' Mr Good said hastily.

'Even as the water was swirling round him?' Anna said. '*Through* him, even.'

At this, the captain sank to the floor, but Anna carried on.

'I do not believe this key could have remained inside the corpse as it was washed in to shore. It must have been left with the body after death, either by design or accident. Surely you see—'

'It is of no consequence,' Mr Good said, and tossed the key onto the bench. He snatched the stick back from Anna. 'The rocks did the damage.'

'But there are no signs the body spent time in the water,' Anna said. 'If the rocks were responsible then he would have been in the water for at least *some* time to come into contact with them.'

'Ah, but you see,' Mr Good said, moving to the door, 'the speed a wreck can happen, he might have been washed straight in and discovered before the tide could get hold of him again. I'm sure the captain will support that view. Captain?'

Captain Ians was still slumped on the floor, his back against the wall. He murmured something that sounded like yes.

'There we are, then,' Mr Good said.

'The time death took him?' Anna asked.

Mr Good hmmed and hawed, and was about to speak when Captain Ians lurched to his feet and said, 'He has been dead three days.'

'And how can *you* be certain of that?' Mr Good said.

'Because of the dream!' the captain insisted.

At this Mr Good looked at *me*, thinking this to do with spirits, I guessed. And it might have been, for what were mermaids but a kind of spirit?

'The dream was what brought me back here,' the captain said, 'but the death had yet to happen then. I arrived in Morwenstow as the body was brought up from the shore and I knew from the dream that he'd been killed the night before. The time elapsed was the same in dreaming and in waking life. He was killed, then found almost at once, and has been here ever since. Three days dead.'

'Well,' Mr Good said, and opened the door. 'If we have dreams to guide us in these matters, I should best retire.'

'Before you do so,' Anna said, 'a time?'

A pause and then Mr Good muttered, with great reluctance, 'No more than three days.' Then more loudly, 'I see no reason to doubt my original supposition. This man was likely killed by entering the water and being dragged across the rocks, like so many whose ill-fortune brings them to this coast. May God have mercy on his soul. Let the parson do as he wishes and bury the man forthwith.'

SEVENTEEN

Mr Good left us then, and it was just me and Anna and Captain Ians in the deadhouse, and the stranger-brother before us. We none of us spoke for a moment, then the captain asked us for our thoughts. Mine was lavender – the scent on the handkerchief Mrs Seldon had given me. And sadness.

'Do you share Good's belief that this man was killed by the action of the rocks?' the captain said.

'I wouldn't say I'm convinced,' Anna said.

'I knew it,' Captain Ians said, with some relief. 'Thank heavens you were able to see him before Robert got him in the ground.'

'We'll need to see where the body was found,' she said. 'That will help us make a judgement, but in the meantime, there are several matters that would seem to make the coroner's verdict flawed. First, there is the matter of the key.'

'And look at his trousers,' I said. 'They've escaped the rocks – not a tear in them. His belt still attached. But his belly has been carved to pieces. Only inches between the two parts of him.'

'Quite right, Shilly. Are we to believe the rocks to be so discriminating in their violence?'

'I will own, there's no logic to the sea's rage,' the captain said. 'I've heard tell of limbs washed in, not a mark upon them, save that they've been severed from their owners. And there are the gobbets . . .'

'*Gobbets?*' Anna said.

'Another common horror. The name given to pieces of flesh washed in, separate from the body to which they belong. Those that do not resemble limbs. They are . . . lumps, often.'

I made myself look at the dead man again, at the place in his arm where the meat was missing. 'The rocks do that?' I said. 'Bite such holes in people?'

He nodded.

I could not believe it. Surely it was a living creature did this.

'The mermaids,' I said. 'Do they have claws? They'd need them, for violence like this.'

'Putting mythical creatures to one side for a moment,' Anna said, 'what of identification? Now that you've had a chance to study him, Captain, is there any means to confirm this is indeed your brother Joseph? Beyond the conviction of the dream, I mean.'

Captain Ians looked over the body, what there was of it, and shook his head. 'I wish there was. To be certain, to put his name on his stone . . . But it has been too long. I have not seen Joseph since he was eighteen, when he left Morwenstow.'

'And yet you were certain that the man you dreamt of was your brother,' Anna said. 'How could you tell, after all this time since you've seen him, and the injuries to his face so violent?'

'That was one of the many strange parts of the dream, Miss Drake. In it, he appeared just as he does now, the injuries the same. And yet I knew, as surely as I knew a woman was involved, that the dead man was my brother Joseph. Even after all this time. But such knowledge isn't enough. I would have certainty, beyond any doubt, that this is indeed Joseph.'

'Your sister, Mrs Hawker,' I said, 'she told us Joseph got a tattoo before he went to sea. Said it was wicked to look at. Did you see it, Captain?'

'I did. I was home on shore leave a few days after Joseph went to Bude to have the tattoo done. I knew it at once to be the design in the church. God knows why he chose such an image. Well, I do know. To anger our father. And it worked!'

'Mrs Hawker said the tattoo was on his arm,' I said.

'That's right.'

I set the candle next to the dead man so that we should all better see the part of his upper arm that had a bit missing.

'Could it have been this arm, Captain, that had the tattoo? There is some ink here, I think, just a scrap of it.'

Anna and the captain peered close to the man's skin, then Anna was looking at me, and though her mouth was covered by the handkerchief, I knew she was grinning at me. At her *detective partner*.

'This *could* be part of Joseph's tattoo,' the captain said. 'But it is so small a piece, and to have ink here – it's a common enough site for a sailor to have a tattoo. I'm not sure it's enough to be certain.'

'But it's a start,' Anna said.

We were done with the dead man now. He could go to his earthly rest and the parson would be saved an unquiet soul walking in his churchyard. This one, at least. Anna and I lifted the sheet and covered him again.

Outside, the air was almost sweet after the foulness of the deadhouse.

'I wish you well in your endeavours,' Captain Ians said. 'When more comes to light, you'll find me at the Bush. The light – I forgot to tell you!' He pressed his palms into his eyes with dreadful force. 'The lack of sleep—'

'Please – don't harm yourself, Captain!' I said. 'What light?'

'I've been told that the night before the body was discovered, a light was seen on the cliff, just above where the dead man lay. Someone was up there.'

'A light on the cliff,' Anna said. 'A return to the violence of the past?'

'If you believe tales of wrecking, then you should believe in mermaids too, for nothing has ever been proved.' He seemed to pitch in the wind. 'The waters off Morwenstow's cliffs are treacherous enough without false lights being shown. The enquiry in '43 made that clear, though it did little else for shipping.'

'True,' she said, 'but all stories have their roots in facts, do they not? And I am in the business of facts, Captain Ians. A light on a cliff in this part of the world suggests certain kinds of criminal acts – destruction of property, theft, not to mention murder. Perhaps the deceased was a victim of a false light if he discovered someone setting one.'

'Or he was killed because *he* was setting the light, and someone didn't like it,' I said.

Captain Ians didn't look pleased with my thoughts on this, or Anna's. He said he would leave us to it.

'Can we walk with you back to the Bush?' I said, not liking the way he seemed to teeter, not liking the closeness of the sea. But he shook his head.

'Will you at least allow yourself some rest once you reach the Bush?' Anna said. 'There is nothing to be gained by staying awake.'

He set off in what I supposed was the direction of the inn, though we had yet to see it. 'Until this mystery is solved,' he called over his shoulder, 'I cannot risk it. One dead man is more than enough to feel responsible for.'

'A curious phrase to use, given the circumstances,' Anna said, once he was away.

'I don't think he's confessing proper, even though those are the words for it.'

'Is his goal here simply to excise his own demons, I wonder?' She pulled up her collar against the wind. 'Or something else, something bigger. There seems no love lost between the captain and Parson Hawker.'

'The parson doesn't seem to like either brother,' I said, 'even though he's never met the younger one.'

The captain rounded the bend and winked out of sight.

'And Mrs Hawker,' Anna said, 'though she appeared upset when she spoke of Joseph, it was anger that moved her to speak to us of Frederick this morning. Some family feud?'

'Would this be motive we are speaking of, Anna?'

'It would,' she said, and quite brightly. 'Well done.'

Well done, Shilly, I said to myself. And out loud, to her, I said, 'Shall we find the parson, then? Ask him how the dead man was found?'

'Yes. Let's see if our host has reappeared after missing Mr Good's visit.'

We headed back towards the vicarage.

'We shall have to be beady for locks, Anna.'

'What are you talking about?'

I reached into one of the secret pockets Anna had sewn into Mrs Williams' dress.

'You magpie!' Anna said, and kissed me, quick, on the cheek, for I had taken treasure.

The key that had nearly been lost inside the dead man.

EIGHTEEN

On our way back to the vicarage I asked Anna what would happen to my lessons while we were in Morwenstow for I knew if I went too long without them, I'd forget what I'd worked so hard to learn already. She'd told me that often enough since she'd started teaching me.

'Surely you can see we haven't time for that, Shilly. We have a dead man to identify and a cause of death to discover. You can't possibly mean for us to pause the case so that you can sound your words?'

I tried not to hear the scorn in her voice. I tried not to feel disappointed.

'No . . . I just thought, with me leaving the drink alone. You did promise, Anna!'

She muttered something about *pri or it ties* but I made out I hadn't heard her.

'What about if we made it useful writing?' I said, and pulled my skirt free of a bramble that had crept over a gravestone. 'Something we were going to do anyway, not the names of boats and all of that.'

'Like what?'

'A letter. To Mathilda.'

She tripped then, over what I couldn't see, but by the time I'd helped her up and she'd dusted off her hands, she said she knew how I could have my lessons and make haste with the case at the same time.

'You can read the world around you, Shilly. *That's* useful.'

'What?'

Anna waved at the gravestones. 'We're surrounded by writing every day. Now that you can read some words, you'll start to see it.'

'But the letter—'

'Let's not start too ambitiously, shall we? One thing at a time.'

And then I was certain she started walking faster. Wanting to get away from my plea.

There was no sign of the parson, or his wife, at the vicarage. There were plenty of dogs and cats, though, and some shouting. We found Gyp the pig in the dining room, helping himself to the breakfast leavings as Mrs Seldon tried to shoo him out.

'Geddon with you! Geddon!' she shouted, clapping her hands and stamping her feet as if she was doing some strange dance – the Morwenstow reel.

But Gyp just danced about her, snorting and squealing, as if he knew the Morwenstow reel too, and he liked it. Anna and I took up a corner of the room each to stalk Gyp to the door, and with Mrs Seldon holding high a rolled-up newspaper we got him into the courtyard at the back of the house.

When we'd recovered our breath, I asked Mrs Seldon if the parson was at home.

'You'll find him in the church, getting himself ready.'

'What time is service today?' Anna said.

'Well, it's evensong at four but that's not what he'll be sorting now. It'll be tomorrow's job he's nerving himself for, now the coroner's been.'

'The man in the deadhouse – his burial?' I said.

Mrs Seldon ripped a page from the newspaper and used it to scoop some of Gyp's doings that lay stinking on the carpeting. 'That animal . . . Mrs Hawker's terrible worried for him, of course.'

'Worried for Gyp?' I said.

'The parson!' Mrs Seldon said, and threw Gyp's doings out the window. I hoped there was no one passing. 'Now, I must geddon or we'll have no dinner. You'll be joining us?'

'Please,' Anna said.

'I'll fetch a shawl before we go to the church,' I said, for I had been in enough churches to know the bone-chill of them, even in April, and the wind still with us too, of course.

I was halfway up the stairs when I heard Gyp's squeals and Mrs Seldon's shouting, and guessed the beast had found his way back in. I resolved to shilly-shally and let Anna do the shooing. She could be stern when she needed to be.

I got my shawl, and then as I made to cross the landing I stopped. As before, the narrow door by the stairs was the only door there that was shut. And locked, for I tried the handle. In my secret pocket I felt the key grow heavier, felt it say, try me, Shilly. Try me. So I did. But the key didn't fit the lock.

'You'll never see that one open,' a voice said.

I spun round. It was Nancy. She was a plain creature and no mistake, with her broad face and her too-small eyes. Her hair was a lank cow's lick of brown now greying. Her arms were full of clothes, taking for washing, I guessed.

I quickly put the key back in my pocket. 'I got the wrong door. Thought this one mine.'

She nodded. Did she believe me? I doubted it mattered so I pressed on.

'Why isn't it ever opened?'

She shrugged. 'It's the parson's private place.'

'For writing letters?' I said, thinking of the letters I would like to write to Mathilda, of Anna's secret letters I'd like to read. The parson might help me. Anna didn't seem to want to. Stop that, Shilly, I said to myself. Stop thinking bad of her and fretting about Mathilda. The quicker you find the truth in Morwenstow, the quicker you can get back to Boscastle and sort it all out.

Nancy was frowning at me. 'You all right?'

'I'm fine,' I said quickly.

'Only, you was muttering.'

'I . . . I didn't sleep well. Heard something, on the wind.'

Nancy said nothing. Didn't move away either. She knew what I spoke of.

'You've heard it?' I said.

'We all hear it,' she said, and shifted the washing in her arms. 'Living here, got no choice.'

'What is it? *Who* is it?'

'There's stories. Parson will tell you. He loves all the old tales. Catch him when he's in his study. That's where he does his writing. Downstairs, by the dining room.' A stocking slipped from her grasp and I picked it up for her. 'He's got that many books in there. He'll show you if you ask. He likes talking about his books with visitors. Might help his nerves before tomorrow, and that would help Mother and me.'

'I wouldn't know how to talk to him about books.'

'He won't mind that. Long as you're happy to listen.'

'It's not just listening, though, is it? It's questions too, and if someone puts writing in your hand and thinks you'll know—'

'You don't know your letters?' she said.

A mistake to let her know this, for wasn't I now a better sort of person, married to one such as Mr Williams with his fine coat and his easy way with people like the Hawkers? But Nancy and I were the same kind of person. I'd carried my fair share of other people's washing. And so the words had slipped out.

'I'm learning,' I said, 'slowly . . .'

'It don't matter the time it takes,' Nancy said. 'If it's important, it's worth the wait. We're all waiting for something.'

'But what if it won't come? What if I never learn?'

'Then the Lord will grant it to you in the next world. And sometimes he has to do that, for this world can be cruel. Sometimes waiting isn't enough.'

She was sounding like her mother that morning with her talk of being called by the Lord. And I had some thinking then, of the kind of people the Seldons might be. The kind Parson Hawker didn't like. The kind who met in their own homes to speak of God, and who listened to John Wesley.

There was a crash of glass or china or some such precious stuff downstairs, then shouts of people and squeals of pig.

'There he goes again,' Nancy said.

After she'd gone down the stairs, I waited the time it would take to fetch something from our room, then I went down myself. I didn't go further than the hall, just shouted to Anna from there that I was ready to go to the church and talk to the parson. I wasn't risking Gyp charging again.

Anna came, red-faced and harried. 'The Bush is seeming more and more an attractive proposition.'

'You'd better ask Captain Ians if they have pigs staying before you pay for a room,' I said. 'And speaking of rooms . . .'

I told her of the locked door upstairs, the one Nancy said was never opened.

'A lumber room?' Anna said.

'It would be a small one. Given where it sits next to the stairs, there wouldn't be much that would fit in there. And it would be opened every so often, wouldn't it, if it was a lumber room?'

'That would depend on the things kept there, wouldn't it? How often they were needed. I'm sure it's nothing, Shilly. The main detail to note is that the key found on the dead man doesn't open the lock. Our search for that key's purpose continues.'

'We shouldn't tell the parson of it,' I said.

'I agree. The locked room aside, some of his actions cast doubt on him – him missing the coroner's visit.'

'And if it *is* Joseph Ians lying in the deadhouse, he seems to dislike him.'

'But enough to kill him? Until we know more, we should keep our thoughts about the body to ourselves, Shilly.'

As we made to leave the porch, singing-that-was-squawking rang out from the direction of the kitchen.

Anna winced. 'Dear God, what is *that*?'

'Mrs Seldon.'

'She won't be joining many choirs.'

'But would she lure people to the sea,' I said, 'lure them to their deaths?'

'Mrs Seldon might tempt people to self-destruction if only to spare themselves that dirge. I might be tempted myself.' Anna shut the porch door with great firmness. 'Come on, Shilly. We've got more worldly concerns to deal with. I'm hopeful the parson can help us.'

We climbed through the graves again, back up the path that led to the deadhouse, our noses tucked into our elbows to save us from the smell. But we bore right before reaching the grim place this time, to go to the church. The wind was stronger now, gusting death in our faces, tugging our skirts. Anna said something but I didn't catch the words over the wind, for the wind was like words itself. Words close and whisked away.

The church was an old one, all leaded glass and an uneven roof. The stone around the door was carved in such a way that my eye was caught, hooked and drawn to it. There was a pattern like bad stitching of a hem, and above that were fish, which made the bad stitching like the sea. And we were close to the sea here, for beyond the church was a low wall, and in it a stile that led to fields, and they sloped to the great wide blue – the same view from our bedroom window in the vicarage. The world fell away here, into water, into wind. A body could walk from the church, through the fields, and step out, into death. I turned so that I couldn't see the sea any more. Such melancholy thoughts would have me take myself to my end.

I was going to join Anna when I saw it, and then my step faltered, for amongst the sea beasts carved into the stone at the church's door was a woman. Bare-breasted, bare-bellied, and her lower parts scaled.

Her lower parts – that of a fish's tail.

Anna had lifted the thick ring that served for a door handle, but before she could open the door there came a loud moan, deeper than the wind. I put my hands over my ears, lest the moan should turn into my name.

'Whatever in the world . . .' She shoved the door open and hurried inside with me close behind her, and the moans grew louder still. Became those of a man.

NINETEEN

We had to pick our way through straw to reach him. The floor was laid thick with it, my step uncertain in the poor light, even though it wasn't yet dinner time and we should have had no need for lamps. Though there were plenty of windows, there was plenty of dirt on the glass. There was candle wax everywhere – on the ends of the benches, on the floor. And papers too, drifts of them, all covered in scrawly writing.

The parson was slumped on a bench at the front of the church, the ginger cat beside him. When he saw us he seemed startled, and said, 'You have heard them?'

Anna looked uncertain, but I had a suspicion I knew what he was speaking of.

'I heard the voice last night,' I said as we made our way down to where he sat.

He gripped the back of the bench. 'I knew it. I knew you would hear it, Mrs Williams, though I would not wish to curse you with such a thing.'

There came a moan from outside and the church seemed to shake with it.

'There it is,' he said. 'We cannot escape the sound.'

'The mermaid,' I said. 'That's what you're meaning, isn't it?'

'I speak of the dead, Mrs Williams, not those who might lure us to our ends. *That* is who speaks on the wind in Morwenstow. And they will not let me rest . . .' He looked towards the window as if he feared something would come through it.

'Or it is simply the wind itself,' Anna said gently. 'The sound is unnerving, I would agree, but it is nothing more than nature's sough.'

We were at odds, the three of us. But I was nearer the parson in my wonderings, for the sound *was* powerful bad. It could only be a work of darkness, of the kind I knew most.

The parson turned himself from the window and looked keenly at Anna. 'My wife tells me he has come at last – our deliverer.'

'The coroner?' Anna said. 'He has indeed. Mr Good has given permission for the dead man to be buried.'

At this, the parson put his hands over his eyes and groaned again.

'That's a good thing,' I said. 'Isn't it? You didn't want the dead man troubling you after dark.'

Without showing his face he murmured, 'Were there any effects found on him? Anything that might identify the man?'

'No,' I said. 'We had a good search, too. Him being so—'

'—exposed,' Anna finished for me. 'I'm afraid there was nothing to identify the deceased, Parson Hawker.'

He gave a little sob. 'Like so many whose ships come to grief here. The ground is thick with them, these strangers to Morwenstow. Another leeward wind today. There will be no room left beneath the south trees and then what will I do?'

Anna sat on the bench beside him and gently laid a hand on his shoulder. He was wearing a long brown gown today, made of coarse cloth, and it heaved with his heaviness and his scritching. If he felt her touch, he gave no sign.

'They will have to go in the fields,' he cried, 'and we will have graves all the way to the sea. The wheat will be grown in their blood, the wheat—'

The wind gusted against the window and he tore his hands from his eyes and was on his feet, tripping over his long gown as he rushed to the glass.

'Is it come yet? I cannot see – the waves. May the Lord deliver these poor souls from their pain, and his servant too. Lord, I beseech thee.'

'You fear a wreck, Parson?' Anna said, and the sound of her voice, of Mr Williams' voice, pulled him back from the window and his fear.

'Every day, my good sir. For there is so little I can do once the wind has them. I can but watch and wait for the dead to wash in.'

'Is that what happened with the man you'll bury tomorrow?' I said.

'His ship wasn't sighted here. We have had no sign of it, but he washed in just the same.'

'That would seem to me strange, Parson,' Anna said. 'To have a victim of a wreck in your parish, but not the ship.'

'It is not unknown, Mr Williams. The ship could have come to grief elsewhere and news has not yet reached us. It is the doing of the tide that sent him here, to me, as so often is the case.'

'And how did you hear about the dead man?' I said.

'A man of this parish called at the vicarage to report the grim discovery, for I am known to take them into the Lord's care.' The parson came and sat by Anna again. 'The county pays five shillings for news of any dead sighted, and I pay five more. Though I have but little in this world, I must ensure I receive word of those who need my care.'

I thought of the fine paper on the walls of the vicarage, of the

117

good sheets we had slept upon the night before. Plenty shillings had been spent on those.

'And when the sad news comes, I have the body brought up from the shore. More shillings, and gin, too, for the men I send with the bier are fearful of the sight that awaits them. The smell too . . . Sometimes it will be days, weeks even, before the sea gives up the dead. I do not begrudge the men something to help them. Were it not for the fortitude granted me by the Lord, I would have to have a nip myself.'

He didn't seem rich in fortitude, and I thought a nip might be good for him. I would have been grateful for one myself.

'There was nothing unusual about this body?' Anna said. 'Nothing to make you believe it was anything other than a sailor come to grief?'

'Only Frederick, arriving as the bier reached the fields and spouting his nonsense.'

A movement at my feet and I started back, knocking into the hard angles of the bench end.

'What is it?' Anna said.

'Something's there – in the straw. There – see it?'

The straw was shifting about, and then I spied a scrap of brown, scuttling along. A mouse.

'Never fear, Mrs Williams,' the parson said, when I was only startled. '*He* will see to it.'

I thought the parson must mean the Lord but then there was a growl behind me. We all three turned to see My Most Righteous Cat poking his head out of the pulpit.

'The pulpit is his favourite spot,' the parson said. 'Out of the draughts.'

The grey tabby's gaze was fixed on the straw at my feet and with one great bound he leapt from the pulpit and lunged up the aisle. The straw before him was alive with wriggling. No wonder the cats liked to come to worship.

'With tomorrow's service we will put an end to the poor creature's suffering,' the parson said, and after a moment I saw that he meant the dead man, not the mouse now in the mouth of My Most Righteous Cat. 'And my fervent hope is that Frederick will cease his mad talk and spare my wife further torment.'

He looked at each of us in turn, and gravely, so we could be in no doubt we were to stop our wondering at what had happened here.

'It's good of you and Mrs Hawker to have us stay,' Anna said. 'My wife and I have been struck by your efforts in giving a decent, Christian burial to the strangers lost upon this coast. The cost must be significant.'

He turned to face her and his expression was one of great hopefulness. 'Oh, it is, sir! Such hardships we have faced here as a result.'

'We would like to help,' Anna said, 'in some small way. My wife is part of a committee of ladies who have modest funds to distribute amongst worthy causes.'

At this, the parson leant towards me and I feared he might fall into my lap, such was his excitement.

'What welcome news! I would be so grateful, I cannot—'

'But before my wife writes to her committee, we should like to see the spot the poor man was discovered. To pay our respects.'

He leapt to his feet. 'Of course! I shall take you there myself.'

'There's no need, Parson. You must have much to do before tomorrow's service.'

'It's no hardship. I will find my hat and then—'

'Just show us the way. I *insist*.'

Not wanting to risk losing this lie of money, he was forced to agree. He led the way outside. We were close to the sea, there by the church. I could taste its salty breath on my lips.

'Over the stile here,' the parson said, 'and across the fields. You must bear to the left then and go on a little way. There you shall see the roof of my hut, and the path down to the shore is next to it. That's where our unfortunate sailor was discovered. Right beneath the hut.'

'You've a dwelling on the cliff?' I said.

'Of sorts,' he said, and was able to smile again. The first time that morning. 'It is where poetry dwells.'

'You are a man of many talents, Parson,' Anna said.

'Oh, my talents are but modest – I would not lay claim to any great triumph, though my work is admired in some discerning quarters,' at which he glanced at us from under not so modest eyelashes. 'And how can one *not* be moved to the heavenly arts when surrounded by such beauty?' He swept his arm before him at the fields of thin soil, the stunted trees, the unending emptiness of the sea beyond.

'You do have quite the view,' Anna said, and we three were silent a moment, looking out at the water that was without a ship or boat of any kind. But were there women in it?

'Nothing between us and Labrador,' he murmured, then turned a little to his right. 'But when the Lord wills the sky to clear, the coast of Wales can be seen in this direction, which is only right and proper, given the sanctified ground on which we stand.'

'There is some Welsh connection here?' Anna said.

'Of the most important kind, sir! A connection of *saints*.'

Anna lifted her eyes to heaven, which was the place of saints, for she had had enough of them.

'Our own fair Morwenna, who has given this parish its name, is a daughter of Wales,' the parson said, 'daughter of King Brychan, he who had four and twenty sons and daughters.'

'His poor wife,' murmured Anna, but the parson was lost in the power of his tale, as I was too, truth be told, for I knew the workings of the saints to be wondrous. They could cure all manner of afflictions with their holy water, and cause them, too, if they were treated badly, as Anna would treat them without me to guide her.

'Morwenna's brothers and sisters came unto this land also,' the parson said, 'and their names are likewise hallowed. Perhaps you have heard of them?'

'I doubt it,' Anna muttered.

'St Mabon is one,' the parson said, 'and Menfre, Yse, Cleder. Nectan too, of course. Ah, I see that you are both familiar with this last.'

'It is known to us,' I said. 'The case we had before this one, it was in Trethevy, where Nectan is said to have lived.'

'I know it well. Mrs Hawker and I visited on our honeymoon. Happier times.' He seemed about to slip into melancholy but shook it away. 'The waterfall there is quite remarkable.'

The waterfall – I shuddered, remembering Mathilda in the water, thrashing against the hateful soul who sought to drown her. And what came after – the creature. A chill had throbbed in my bones long after we'd left the woods, and it wasn't from the water's cold. It was fear. Fear at what I'd seen at the waterfall. Was it any wonder poor Mathilda had such troubled sleep?

'I remember a little house at Trethevy,' the parson said. 'There in the woods. A pleasure house, built in the ruins of Nectan's hermitage.'

'So we heard,' Anna said, quite scornful.

'And did you feel Nectan's presence at Trethevy?'

'We certainly felt something,' Anna muttered.

The parson clapped his hands. 'The Lord's glory is amongst us!'

'One can't seem to move without finding it in this part of the world,' Anna said. 'There are more saints in Cornwall than there are coaching inns.'

'And yet the people live in darkness,' the parson said gravely. 'The great fornicator Wesley moves amongst them and turns them from the Lord's light. If they would but return to the one true church they would find salvation. Here in Morwenna's glory is where the Lord dwells, not by their own firesides. Fair Morwenna begged this land from the Saxon king Ethelwolf,' he said, and sat on a bench beside the church, settling in for his tale. 'She wished to bring Christian teachings to the pagans in these parts, and so she sailed across—'

'Would you ask Mrs Hawker to forgive us missing dinner?' Anna said, walking purposeful to the stile. 'We'll likely be out all afternoon.'

And she was away, striding into the wind, with me in her swell – a storm-tossed boat.

TWENTY

We went the way the parson had told us, across the field, and my
thoughts were all of Mathilda. It was the parson and his talk of the
waterfall. The memory of her fighting for her life, nearly losing
her, made my heart beat faster than was good for me. Was she
well, back in Boscastle? Was she happy? Did she fear we'd left her
behind for ever, that we wouldn't return? If she should worry even
for a moment, my sweet girl, I would be ashamed. I had to send
word to her. I had to make Anna help me.

'What a view!' Anna said.

We'd come to the end of the field and there the world fell, for
the field lay on the top of cliffs, the stony shore far below, so far I
thought my insides would purge and I found I was on my knees,
my hands like claws gripping the roots of the grass. The sea was
loud here, even though it was distant, for it was all a-churn, the
blue of it sent white and foamy, and where it smashed itself against
the stones of the beach it hissed and snarled.

'It might be better if you went back to the vicarage,' Anna said.

I made myself stand, kept my eyes from the edge. 'I'll be all
right. Just don't leave me.'

'As if I would! Here's the path, look, that the parson said we should follow. Take my arm. I'll go on the outside, nearest the water, then you've no fear of falling in.'

I nodded, but it wasn't fear of falling that sent me so trembly. It was the fear I might jump. God help me if my name was called.

On we went, our arms together, as if we were on some goodly stroll rather than going to see the place a corpse was found.

I kept my gaze on my boots, but Anna was able to look over the edge.

'I can see why ships fear this coast,' she said. 'There's not a good landing spot for miles. Only the unforgiving cliffs, unbroken. And those rocks on the shore . . . My word. Shilly – you'll have to look at this.'

With her arm locked in mine, I risked a glance, and saw the terror Mr Good had spoken of, that he had been so sure had killed the man who lay in the deadhouse. And now I saw *why* Mr Good was so sure, and the parson, too. Captain Ians' belief that the rocks were not to blame seemed to burn away like sea fog on a warm day.

This coast was set with razors.

They reached out from the cliff face, these black knives, their sharp ends pointed at the sea and at those seeking safety from the waves. So many of them, all different lengths but all of them black and terrible. All of them death.

'This must be the hut,' Anna said.

A thickety bush, some kind of thorn, grew at the edge of the field in which we stood, and in it were wooden planks laid flat – a roof? We went closer and there were steps that led from the path, over the cliff edge.

Before I could stop her, Anna went down the steps, and vanished.

I had to call her twice before she stuck her head out of the thorn.

'The way is perfectly safe,' she said. 'Just don't rush.'

As if *that* was likely. I crawled to the steps, then went down them backwards, not trusting the burden of myself to go upright. Not trusting anything about the dreadful rock knives so far below, the sea waiting beyond them.

'There, you've done it,' Anna said, and took me by the elbow to make me stand again.

We were beside a curious building fashioned from planks – plank roof, plank walls, a door of planks. It was built so that the roof was just below the level of the cliff top, and it hunkered into the thorn around it. But that could give no shelter, surely, for the wind came straight at us, and the air was salty from the sea's breath upon it.

Anna opened the door to the hut and we peered inside. It was a neat little room, all dark wood inside, as without, and a bench running on the three sides that weren't the doorway.

'So this is where the parson pens his poems,' Anna said.

'And waits for the dead.'

'The two go well together.' She turned and looked out to sea. 'And I can think of another purpose for this place.'

'To show a light,' I said.

'Captain Ians says one was shown the night before the dead man was discovered, right above where he lay. That's this very spot.'

'A light to draw a ship onto the cliffs?' I leant against the door of the hut to stop the world from jouncing about. I was feeling as I had done on waking that morning, when the thrum was inside my head. The memory of being called.

Anna peered over the ledge on which the hut was built. 'The path continues down here. We've come this far. Let's see where our victim was found.'

The wind was awful now, so I tied my shawl over my head to keep my hair from my eyes, and to keep my wig from the sea. Anna had only her hands to help her likewise. And so we skittered our way down to the shore, the path all but sheer at times, the small stones loose underfoot. I didn't look at the sea, used the thorn, and the gorse that began to appear, to steady myself. My hands were soon sore but I told myself to pay no heed to the pain for it would be worse to hit the rocks below. To have the sea drag me over them. What was the word Mr Good had used? Sawing. Would that I was spared being sawn.

It seemed to take all afternoon. I felt that I had only ever been slowly putting one foot in front of the other. There had been no Shilly before. There would be none after, for there was no after. Only the path and the hungry sea below. It was like the long wait Nancy Seldon had spoken of. And then I was upright again, when I had been tilted, and my knees went, for we were on the shore.

When I could bear it, I looked up. The hut was surely miles above us, so much cliff between, and the path a snake upon it.

'How on earth do they carry a body up there?' Anna said.

'They must be surefooted as mules in these parts,' I said.

'Quite.' Anna wandered down to where the sea touched the shore, went into the water a little way.

'Be careful!' I said, fearful she might fall and so be one of the sawn.

The beach was mostly stones with only a little sand between them. It wasn't a wide beach for it was hemmed in on both sides by outcrops of cliff. The tide was a little way out, which was why the knife rocks could be seen. There were plenty of them that stabbed from the rest of the cliffs. It was all high, sheer cliffs and the knives, far as I could see.

'Is this where Mrs Hawker goes for her walks, do you think?' I said.

Anna looked up and down the beach. 'If it is, she's not here today. It's too dangerous for her to swim here, surely?'

'Parson thinks so.'

'I wonder if she heeds him.'

We looked about us. The knife rocks weren't tall – only three feet at their highest and tapering to nothing at their ends that reached for the sea. I touched the spine of one. It was rough under my palm. Pitted by the sea but sharpened by it, rather than made blunt. There was blood on my palm. The rock had sliced me open. I thought of the morning in Boscastle, when the bar we used to keep Mathilda from biting her tongue had bloodied my hand similar. The thrum in my head had returned, as if the wind had got inside it and was rattling my skull as it had rattled the window in its frame. I got down low, between two of the knife rocks, to escape it, but there was nowhere to hide on Morwenstow's shores.

Anna's boots in my face, turning about as she looked up and down the beach, the crunch of the small stones beneath them. 'Now that we're here, the suggestion by the parson and Mr Good that our victim is nothing more than an unlucky sailor washed in has been dealt another blow. There's an important detail missing.'

'Sign of his ship?' I said.

'Exactly. Not a splinter of wood here, let alone a mast or a sail. No cargo, either.'

She helped me to my feet.

'And yet we've had some dirty weather,' I said. My words clanged in my teeth.

'True – the storm that hit Boscastle would surely have struck this coast too. We're not that much further north here. Captain Ians came to us just as the storm was easing, and it was that morning he'd seen the body carried up the cliff path. If the storm is meant to have caused a wreck then where's the evidence for that disaster?'

'Parson said the ship could have been wrecked on another part of the coast and it was only the body that came ashore here.'

'He did, but even if that were the case, it's hard to believe that not even a scrap would appear here.' She held out her hands to the shoreline. 'That there would be a sailor but not so much as a splinter from his ship. I suppose they could have cleared the beach for their own ends.'

'Who?'

'The people of the parish. If a vessel is wrecked and any part of it washes onshore, it's fair game for scavengers. There are many who believe there to be a link between the needs of coastal people and the wrecks that land as manna from heaven on their doorsteps.'

'You're thinking of the light again,' I said. 'That someone lured a ship onto the rocks. You think that's how the man died?'

'It's plausible.'

'It's a poor thing to think of people, Anna!'

She shrugged. 'It's a poor thing to do, even if times are hard. To survive shipwreck and then be murdered by those you'd hope would be your saviour – it's a horrific way to die. And all for a cask of wine or a few weeks of firewood.'

'But Captain Ians told us that nothing has ever been proved of purposeful wrecking. You're always telling me how important proof is, Anna. You seem blinded to it here.'

'Our task isn't to hold another enquiry into wrecking, Shilly. That's what governments are for. Our work is to discover who the dead man is, and how and why he died.'

'Well, it doesn't look like he came off a wreck, does it?' I said. 'There's nothing of his ship here, and I *don't* think that's because the people of Morwenstow have cleared every last bit of it. It's because there wasn't a wreck in the first place.'

'There's another possibility we haven't considered – a slight one, but we must address it. What if the dead man *did* wash in from a ship, and he *was* cut by the rocks during his passage to shore, but his ship *didn't* come to grief? He could have been thrown overboard instead, perhaps dead before he even hit the water.'

'And then his ship sailed on without him?' I said.

'It would explain the lack of debris here.'

'But not the key we found inside him.'

'Exactly,' Anna said. 'Given the forceful nature of the water here, it would surely have been separated from the body if he truly was washed in. More likely someone deliberately shoved that key inside him after death.'

'So we're decided he died on land, then,' I said.

'That we can agree on.' Anna tucked a strand of her wilful wig back behind her ear. 'But it seems no coincidence that his injuries are consistent with a wreck victim. Though Mr Good's examination was cursory, the coroner was familiar with the nature of the wounds.'

'So if the dead man was killed on land and looks like dead sailors do in these parts then . . .'

'Then there's a good chance he was made to look like one of those washed ashore to hide his identity.'

Then the wind whipped my scarf from my head. Anna chased it up the beach to the cliff where it snagged on a spindly bit of gorse that clung there. I went to follow, for I had had enough of the knife rocks and the talk of poor people luring others to their deaths.

But I seemed to be looking at the water instead of at the cliff and my shawl snared there. And the wind was in my face, not behind me. And then there was water over my boots. See how it coloured them darker. A snag of weed bright across the toes. And then the water was higher, and my stockings were wet. I stiffened with the shock of the cold, but I was still moving, and the water was higher still, and all the time the words on the wind. Taking shape, taking sound.

I walked into the sea.

TWENTY-ONE

'Shilly.'

A hand on my arm. Another on my chest. Anna in front of me now, not the water.

'What are you doing?' she said, and pressed herself against me, which was a mercy for my body was all for the water. My bones leant towards it.

'I-I don't know.'

I sagged in her arms and we were both wet then, for we were in it up to our knees. All at once I wanted to be away from the sea, far, far away. As far as the moor, even. Anna took hold of me and turned me round, to face the shore again.

'Don't let go,' I whispered.

'I won't, but pick your feet up. It's no good splashing.'

I tried but then I fell, for something had tripped me. A stone, but rolling in the water? That couldn't be right. There wasn't enough weight to it.

Anna bent down to see it better. 'What on earth . . .' She leapt back with a shriek and then she was the one splashing us both.

'What is it?' I said.

She let out a deep sigh. 'The word Captain Ians used when we were in the deadhouse. *Gobbet*. I think we've just found one.'

Neither of us wanted to touch the lump of flesh, but neither did we want to let it float out to sea and be lost. Together we passed my shawl under it, to make a kind of sling, then lifted it clear of the water and carried it into shore. There we laid it down, gentle as if it was a babe. An ugly babe, though. The gobbet was the size of a small ham, grey from having been so long in the water. The skin was torn but the water had taken the blood. Had swelled the whole gobbet too.

'It looks the right size to fit the hole in the dead man's arm,' I said.

'I think you're right.' Anna used the shawl to roll the gobbet over and we gasped, for there on the skin were lines and colours.

The gobbet bore a tattoo.

It was a face, that of a devil, surely, for it had the round red head of a dog but a dog with a beak, a wide green beak, wide as the whole dog head. And in the beak were yellow teeth, a person's full set grinning, and a huge tongue, blue, poking out at us. The eyes were the only part without colour. Just outlines, no beads within them. And somehow that was the worst of it. The empty eyes.

'The green,' I said, 'it's the same as the scrap of ink on the dead man, next to his terrible wound.'

'True. And it's certainly a distinctive design,' Anna said. 'Look there, beneath the tongue. A pair of letters, isn't it? C and J.'

'Just like Mrs Hawker said. C for Charlotte and J for Joseph. This must be Joseph Ians' tattoo, which must mean it's him in the deadhouse.'

'It's certainly looking that way, but we must be sure. Mrs Hawker and the captain said the tattoo was based on a carving in the church. We'll compare them.'

'So we'll have to take the gobbet back up with us.' I wished then we hadn't found the gobbet, for the thought of wrapping it up and carrying it was dreadful. I would tell Anna I was too sore-headed to do it. But she wouldn't likely listen for her teeth were making their tapping sound, her thinking sound.

'The way this piece was parted from the rest of the body, it looks no different from the other violence done to the man. This could also be thought the work of the rocks sawing him into pieces. Mr Good would likely think so, had he stayed long enough to see this missing piece.'

'But you don't believe that,' I said. I covered the gobbet with the shawl for I couldn't bear to see the blind eyes of the devil.

'Surely it's too convenient that the sea should take the *exact* portion of flesh where an unusual tattoo should be. A tattoo that might help identify this man.'

'But the sea gave it up to us.' I turned to look at the water tumbling onto the little stones, onto the black knives. 'It could be that the mermaids want to help, even though it might have been a mermaid that clawed it from him in the first place.'

Anna laughed, as if I had made a joke, which of course I hadn't. These were my thoughts on the case. This was the thrum in my head.

'Captain Ians' dream might have been what brought us here, Shilly, but we don't have to give credence to it in its entirety. I think we can safely rule out the involvement of women of the deep. More useful would be—Well, would you look at that.'

I looked. In the hut far above us, a figure.

'Is it the parson?' I said.

'I'm not sure . . . But whoever it is, they're watching us.'

'I need to get away from here, Anna.'

'I know. You're cold. But if you will go wading into the sea.'

I let her think that was what it was. I couldn't have told her the real reason for I had no words for feeling like I would drown myself if we stayed any longer at the water's edge.

Anna did as I had hoped and wrapped the gobbet in the shawl, then lashed the strange burden to her back. We began the climb up the cliff path. It felt longer than the way down for my weariness was terrible, and my skirt heavy with the sea, which wouldn't leave me. I'd be wet for ever. A drowned woman, walking.

'Last bit,' Anna said, and hauled me over a boulder.

We were back at the hut. Anna opened the door. Empty, but the air was thick with smoke that made my nose prickle.

Anna sniffed. 'Latakia. The parson's tobacco.'

TWENTY-TWO

We crossed the fields and came to the stile. The church was just beyond it. Anna said she would go inside, try to find the carving that Joseph Ians had used as likeness for his tattoo and see if it was the same as the face inked on the gobbet. She didn't want to keep the gobbet any longer than she had to, and I didn't wonder at that.

'You should go back to the vicarage, Shilly. Get out of those wet clothes.'

'You're wet too.'

'You look to be feeling it more than me.' She cupped my cheek in her hand. 'You're very pale. Why not—'

'I would stay with you. It won't take as long, will it, if we look together.' I opened the church door.

It was bright inside, brighter than the grey day beyond and brighter than when we had come last to the church and found the parson gloomy there. I feared there was a service and we had disturbed it, so I stayed close to the door. But then I saw there was no one seated on the benches.

'Did 'ee find 'em?' a man's voice called.

'I . . .' The gobbet? Had this man known what was down there, beneath the parson's hut?

He was at the far end, where the altar stood crowded with lamps. He was much smaller than the parson. Short, thin and with the makings of a stoop. Past sixty and not a hair on his head. He held a cloth. A pail was at his feet.

He came towards us and seemed to see that we were not who he was expecting. 'Forgive me! I thought you were Nancy coming back.'

'It's us who must ask forgiveness for disturbing your work,' Anna said.

We made our way to him, into the light. The straw beneath my feet was thicker than before, and I thought I might lie down in it, to warm myself, for a chill was on me. Had taken root.

'Is it the parson you're wanting? He's back over the vicarage.' The man dropped his cloth into the pail. 'But today mightn't be a good day for callers.'

'I'm afraid we are already troubling the parson as we're guests of the Hawkers,' Anna said.

'Ah – you're the pair!' The man's face brightened. 'My wife told me there was people staying.'

'Then it's Mr Seldon?' I said.

'Quite right, missus. If you'm wanting the church to yourselves I can leave this—'

'Please, don't stop on our account,' Anna said. She gave him our names, Mr and Mrs Williams. 'You're making ready for the funeral tomorrow?'

Mr Seldon took up his cloth again and began brushing dirt and dead flies and all manner of things from the altar. 'Best I can, but I've the farm as well as being sexton, see. Nancy helps me when she can be spared from the vicarage. She's about here somewhere

135

now. I thought you was she when you came in. That's why I asked if you'd found 'em, the flowers. She'd gone out to see if she could find some early ones for the service.'

'Well, we have found *something*,' Anna said. 'That's why we're here.'

She took the shawl, still tied as a sling, from her back and laid it on the floor. The gobbet was resting so the tattoo was hidden.

'Ah that's as well,' Mr Seldon said softly. 'I hoped it might come in, his arm being like it is, with the . . . gap.'

'I gather you aided your wife in preparing the body for burial?' Anna asked.

'I did, sir. Part of sexton's work in the parish, given the numbers that wash in. This was a grim find for you both.'

'But a fortunate one,' Anna said, 'with the burial tomorrow. There's time to put the gobbet back with him. Make him whole as can be to meet his maker.'

'Well, we can but try, though the rest of him is gone soupy since this morning. Almost as if he was holding on for the coroner and now he can let go. Ah, it's a hard thing we must bear in Morwenstow, Mr Williams. The Lord tries us very hard, the parson most of all. Now, you leave that with me, and I'll take it to the deadhouse on my way home.'

'We're not quite done with it yet,' Anna said. At this, Mr Seldon's eyes widened, so she added quickly, 'But rest assured, our actions with the flesh will be most respectful. There is something we would ask you.'

She bent beside the gobbet. With the handkerchief Mrs Seldon had given us that morning, Anna turned the gobbet over so that the tattoo was showing. My heart turned over with it, such was the shock of seeing the inked head again, with the beak and the sightless eyes.

Mr Seldon gasped. 'Why, it's . . . it's the face, from this very church!'

'Can you show us?' I said.

'Certainly, it's just down the aisle here. But I don't understand. How could—Who . . .'

He shook his questions away and grabbed a lamp, gave Anna another, and we set off towards the middle of the church, leaving the gobbet where we had laid it on the floor.

There were pillars down the length of the church, and arches between them. At one of the pillars Mr Seldon stopped. 'It's this one, not that I have much cause to look at it. 'Tisn't a pleasant sight.'

The top of the pillar was lost to us in the gloom. Anna climbed onto the bench beside it and held her lamp up.

I followed the pillar's smooth lines, its ordered squares of stone and mortar, stone and mortar, up up up to where the arch branched either side of it. And at the branching at the top of the pillar was a nasty sight. It took my breath from me, for along with being nasty it was familiar – a known shock.

I was looking up at a stone face. A face with a beak, with grinning teeth and a bold tongue pointed at me. With empty eyes.

Mr Seldon sank onto the bench. 'Of all the things.'

'It is remarkably similar to the tattoo,' Anna said.

'It's the same!' I said. 'Without the colour of the ink, I'll own. But otherwise a perfect likeness.'

There was a noise – a creak of hinges. The church door being opened.

'That'll be Nancy back,' Mr Seldon said, and got slowly to his feet. He seemed to have aged since Anna had lifted her lamp and brought the carved face into sight. It was shocking, I would own, but Mr Seldon had seen it before. What he *hadn't* seen was flesh bearing this likeness as a tattoo, with all the terrible colours.

137

When we were alone again, I whispered, 'This is proof, then. The man in the deadhouse is Joseph Ians.'

'It would seem so, though I think it would be wise to show the gobbet to the captain for final confirmation. Just to be sure.'

'And if the captain says the tattoo is his brother's, then it means the dream was true – the captain did see his brother's death before it happened.'

'Well . . .'

From the far end of the church, towards the altar, came the murmurs of Mr Seldon and his daughter, the clang of pails on slate.

'Which *means*,' I said, feeling my breath run quicker, 'that the part about the mermaid could be true as well.'

'I think we should reserve judgement on that part. But what about *this*?' She held the light close to my face. 'Captain Ians told us about the light, remember, seen from the parson's hut the night before Joseph Ians was found. Do mermaids use lights, Shilly?'

That I didn't know, but I thought it unlikely. Anna did too. Her question was not the kind that sought an answer.

'So we'll take the gobbet to the Bush, then,' I said.

'*I* will, Shilly. I'm not sure it's a good idea for you—'

'Will you be wanting the lamp, sir?' It was Nancy Seldon. She was on the other side of the pillar. How long had she been standing there? 'Only, Father and I are finished here.'

'Thank you, Nancy, but no. My wife and I were just leaving.'

Anna handed her the lamp and we followed her to the door. There was no sign of Mr Seldon, and no flowers in the church, either. Perhaps Nancy hadn't been able to find any. Anna and I went out into the porch and Nancy made to close the door behind us. Then I remembered.

'The gobbet,' I said. 'Where is it?'

'Father has it,' Nancy said, 'to put in the box with the poor wretch. You can have no need for it, surely?'

'Oh, I—' Anna said. 'We did ask him not to, for the moment. Well, no matter. Please thank your father for dealing with it.'

She shrugged. 'That's his job. All of ours who live here.'

Then she pulled the door to with some force, for she was strongly made, like her mother but with thicker arms. She bade us goodbye and went down the path through the churchyard, towards the vicarage. The air after her was warm with beeswax, cut sharp with vinegar.

'Please say we don't have to fetch the gobbet back from the deadhouse to show Captain Ians the tattoo. Because I'm telling you now, Anna, it won't be me that goes inside to get it.'

The look on her face at the notion was enough to ease me. 'That would be a foul business. What was the word Mr Seldon used about the corpse? *Soupy*.'

'We've seen the tattoo, and we've found the carving that matches it. That's enough proof to put to the captain, isn't it?'

'It's enough for me, Shilly, but the captain is the one paying us.'

TWENTY-THREE

We were in sight of the Bush. I had been all for going straight in, but Anna caught me to see if I was back-sliding on the matter of drink.

'Is this wise, Shilly?'

'You don't have to worry. Not a drop has passed my lips in months.'

'All the more reason to avoid such places. What was it you used to call them — dens of iniquity? Why give yourself such temptations?'

'I can't skirt it for ever. The world is full of inns.'

'This part of the world seems to be.'

I took her hands in mine and she flinched at the chill.

'I'll not be much use to you if I never more step foot in inns or kiddlywinks or beer shops. That's where the rogues are!'

'True.' Her gaze went to the Bush behind me, the glow from the windows. 'And it might help warm you up. If you're sure you can resist . . .'

I hurried towards the inn before she could change her mind.

The floor was slate, and dirty with mud. It was quiet inside, the fire louder than the few men who were there. And they were *all* men. We got stares for we were dressed much finer than their working clothes. I took the bench nearest the hearth and told Anna I would have a small beer.

'But we're not staying,' Anna said. 'We just need to tell the captain about the tattoo.'

'He'll likely need a drink after hearing about that, won't he? Because if the tattoo is the same as Joseph's then this means the dead man truly is his brother. Even though he had the dream, the truth will be sad for him, and we can't let him drink alone. I'll just have a drop. Like you said, Anna, it'll take off the chill.' I said it like I didn't even want it. But I did want it, of course I did. Such wanting doesn't leave a body.

She gave in at last and went to fetch the drinks and I did my best to breathe, to fight the swell inside me. This was a test I'd given myself, like the tests we set those we were suspicious of in our detecting, because what I'd told Anna outside *was* the truth – I couldn't keep from such places for ever. And I wanted to prove I was changed from the weak creature I was when she first met me. For if I did that then she would have to help me with my writing. And some writing in particular, for I'd decided I'd write to Mathilda. So I said to myself, Shilly, you will drink this drop of small beer and this alone, and you'll leave the Bush soon as you've talked with Captain Ians. And you won't take anything with you, neither. No sliding half-bottles into your coat pocket for Anna will find them, she always does. And then all this goodness will be undone.

She was back with the glasses. 'The barman has sent up to the captain's room. He'll be down shortly.'

I took a deep breath and reached for mine. But Anna pulled it back so I couldn't get it.

'You're certain about this?' she said. Her face, her own

beneath the whiskers and the eyebrows, the powder and the paint, was all fear.

'Certain,' I said, making sure to look her in the eye.

She pushed the glass back to me. I lifted it.

'What shall we drink to?' I said.

'To tattoos?' she said, and found a smile.

'To tattoos.'

Our glasses met with a clink I'd missed hearing. I put my glass to my lips and took the littlest sip. It was sharp and sour and good. But I wouldn't be undone. I was Mrs Shilly Williams now, and Mrs Shilly Williams had hold of herself. I put the glass down and stood.

'What are you doing?' Anna said.

'Going to the bar.'

Her eyes widened.

'To beg paper and ink,' I said. 'We're going to write to Mathilda.'

She opened her mouth to speak but I made out I hadn't seen. She was going to tell me no, we wouldn't write, but I couldn't fathom why. All I knew was the pitching that worry gave me. Why didn't Anna want Mathilda to join us? There would be room for her at the vicarage – half the bedrooms were ready for visitors. Mrs Hawker and she could talk about German things. The parson's wife was sure to love Mathilda's sweet nature. All who met her did, Anna too. But there had been that row between them before we left Boscastle. What had caused that bad feeling?

The man behind the bar found me paper but ink gave him more trouble. He was built like the barrels that sat on the floor – broad-chested, sturdy. He was bearded and none too clean about the mouth. Looking for the ink he cast about and blew air through his nose like a horse. He smelt so bad, it would have been no surprise to see flies round him, like he *was* a horse truly. The smell was of spirits. Once that smell would have made me trembly, made me thieve and lie, but today it did nothing but make me want to purge. I was truly a new soul. Them that was chapel would have known me born again.

While he was rootling, I had a notion I would speak to him. There was something we had yet to discover. Something important, even though Anna didn't think so. Better to rootle for this when she was out of hearing.

'I'd have one thing more from you,' I said, 'aside from the ink. About the sea.'

He stopped his search and frowned at me. 'The sea?'

'About what's in it. *Who* is in it.' Now he truly was uncertain of me, but I pressed on. What had I to lose from this stranger? 'The man in the parson's deadhouse. I've heard tell it was a mermaid killed him.'

He went back to rummaging. 'There's many here that say so.'

'Will you tell me about her?' I said.

'It's a nasty story.'

'Please. I . . . I need to know.'

Something in my voice must have told him just how *much* I needed it, for he ceased his rummage, put his hands on the bar, palms flat in the little puddles of spilt beer, and he spoke.

'She must have had a name, but no one here remembers it now. It all happened so long ago. A Morwenstow girl, she was, and beautiful – that people *do* remember, because it wasn't right, see, her looks.' He leant forward. 'Unnatural. People said it was because her mother bathed her in a pool of water used by mermaids when they were visiting these parts, and the girl took on their beauty – her skin so pale you could all but see through it, see the seawater that had begun to run in her blood.' He laughed. 'My own mother told me this to stop me going in the sea. Thought that would frighten me more than any talk of currents.'

'And did it?' I said. 'Frighten you, I mean.'

'It did, but that was because of what happened next. The squire's nephew came calling, and this girl had no sense in her beautiful head for she lay with him. He'd never marry her, her parents being working people, and when she told him she was with child he left the parish.'

This part I had heard before, in many stories.

'What happened to her?' I said, already guessing the answer.

'Oh, when the child came, she and the babe both died. The squire's nephew came back to Morwenstow then. They say that's when it started. The calls.'

I felt my own blood run cold as seawater at mention of this. I couldn't stop my shivers.

'For though the girl had been buried in the churchyard,' the barman said, 'some part of her had swum down, down through the earth and into the sea beneath. She was free now, wasn't she, and she could take her vengeance. She called him, the squire's nephew, and he had no choice but to go to her. His body wasn't his own when she called, oh and it was the most *awful* sound, they say. Ungodly.'

'What did she do to him?' I whispered.

'Well, she killed him, didn't she?'

'How?'

The barman shrugged. 'Some say drowning. Others say she tore him to pieces with her teeth, or with her claws. It don't matter, really. The end is still the same, however the story's told.'

'But what was it that made people think it was the mermaid that killed the man in the deadhouse?'

'The noise. She's always calling. When the wind gets up we hear her, and she's good for business. People need a draught after that. People like yourself. I see it on you. That's why I'm telling you.'

I mumbled my thanks, ashamed, somehow, that my wretchedness was so clear to strangers. I wasn't so good at hiding myself yet as Anna. I still went into the world naked.

'But that night,' the barman said, 'the night before that man was found beneath the parson's hut . . . Well.' The barman shook his head. 'It was much worse than usual. Them that came in here was took bad with fright. Did very well out of her that night.'

'Why?'

He looked me dead in the eye. 'That night she was screaming.'

'It could have been the storm,' I found myself saying, and it was as if Anna was with me, speaking with my tongue.

The barman smiled. 'It could have been. No way to know, is there? Unless she calls you too. But you'd never have the chance to tell anyone the truth.'

I shivered, for he was right, and that was terrible.

'The people she calls,' I said, 'what is it marks them out?'

'Love,' he said, and shrugged, as if it was the simplest thing in the world rather than the most difficult and wondrous and all the time sleepless longing. 'Aye, it can be the love of a wife for her husband that the mermaid knows,' he said, and I realised I had turned to look at Anna still seated with our drinks. 'All kinds of love that's lost,' the barman said, 'for the mermaid lost twice over, didn't she? First the squire's nephew, then her child. Our screaming mermaid calls them that hurt the most.' He laughed. 'If you believe such tales.'

'Women loving other women?'

'All the kinds of love you can think of. Mothers for daughters, fathers for sons. Friendship. It's the strength of it – they say that's what she's drawn to. If you've a passion and you're hurting, she'll call you. Now, you'll be wanting another?'

'Hm? No, I'm not—'

'For the captain.' The barman nodded across the room. 'He's come down, look.'

I took the glass the barman gave me and went back to the fire. The cold was deep inside my bones now. My wet clothes had been chilled by the wind on the way back from the hut and I couldn't feel my feet. But it was more than that. It was the story of the woman made a mermaid by her rage. A woman screaming into the wind.

The captain was looking rough as ever but he made an effort to greet me, and seemed excited. It was soon clear why.

'I have just been telling the captain about the tattooed gobbet and its likeness to the carving,' Anna said.

'It can only be Joseph's tattoo,' Captain Ians said. 'Your description is as I remember, and it matches the carving too.'

'There's the bit of the tattoo left on the body,' I said. 'The same green ink, of the beak, I think.'

'It is him lying in the deadhouse. There can be no doubt now.' The captain banged the table with his fist and our glasses jittered. 'I *knew* the dream was true. And Robert so keen to tell me I was wrong. Charlotte too.'

He was tugged two ways, between relief and despair. To be right, but about such an awful thing. A deep sigh escaped him. He had been proved right about the dream, but that meant the loss of a brother. Frederick and Joseph Ians had not met in this world for many years. Our discovery of the gobbet meant they never would

146

again. There was only the hope of the next world, as the Seldons kept on about.

For myself, I felt relief. We wouldn't have to go back inside the deadhouse to get the gobbet. Joseph Ians would be buried the next day and the foul air would begin to clear from the churchyard. And we were closer to finishing our business in Morwenstow and getting back to Mathilda.

'I will tell my sister,' the captain said. 'As I'm sure you'll have gathered, staying at the vicarage, she and I have not shared the same belief about Joseph dying. We've been at odds, and Robert hasn't helped matters. But it's all over now. We have the truth, or some of it, at least.'

'Mrs Hawker will be saddened by the news,' I said.

'She will, but she can't be kept from it. Not with the funeral tomorrow. She should know she's saying goodbye to her kin rather than a stranger.'

'Well,' Anna said, 'that's one part of our work done. What remains is to discover who killed him, for we are in no doubt that he *was* killed, and on land. There is the matter of the key which can only have been thrust inside Joseph after death, and now the tattoo, which was distinct enough to identify the body and conveniently removed from it.'

'You believe that the murderer *cut out* the tattoo?' the captain said.

'Quite so, to prevent identification. If it wasn't for the effort of my wife here,' and at this Anna flashed me the briefest of smiles, 'the gobbet might have been washed out to sea on the next tide and the identity of Joseph Ians never discovered.'

'I am grateful to you both,' the captain said, 'and I pray to God that the truth of my brother's death will soon come to light.'

Anna stood and shook his hand. I stood likewise but the slates seemed to have grown soft since I had sat down, and I could not stand so well. It was the cold of the sea. I needed my bed.

It was only after we were on our way back to the vicarage that I remembered I'd left most of my small beer untouched. And my note to Mathilda unwritten.

TWENTY-FOUR

My shivering worsened with every step closer to the vicarage. Anna helped me up the stairs to our room then sat me on the bed.

'Here, lift your skirt,' Anna said.

I couldn't take off my wet clothes myself for my hands were ashake. My legs and feet felt as if the sea pressed against them still. That push and sway of the waves. With the nimble fingers of someone who has often changed her clothes with great haste, Anna got my dress unbuttoned and whipped it over my head. I was thankful the chill hadn't taken her so bad as me, though we'd both been in the water that afternoon. She was strong, even though she was so thin and older than me too.

'I wasn't being undue in my praise for you finding the gobbet, Shilly. It really was fortunate that you saw it.'

'I didn't.'

'But that's why you walked into the shallows. Wasn't it?'

'I didn't *see* anything,' I stuttered through my chattery teeth.

Anna's hand stilled on my stocking. 'You felt it, whatever it was? Your . . . way of feeling?'

'It was a voice. She called me—'

'She?'

'I couldn't fight her, Anna. She knows my name! The barman at the Bush told me all about her, how she was cast aside by—'

Anna sat back on her heels. 'Who knows your name?'

'The mermaid.' I said it in a whisper but she heard me, that creature, for the wind blew hard at that moment and made the window *hmmmm* in its frame. We both jumped.

'That's her,' I said, 'making ready to call me. To call me to my death!'

'It does sound something like a voice, I'll grant you,' Anna said. 'But it's surely just the wind, Shilly.'

I pressed my face into her breast and sobbed. She let me cry, and the warmth of her body eased the shakes. She helped me back to sitting and joined me on the bed. Her arm around me, but the best of it was she didn't tell me no, Shilly, you're a liar, you're mad, you're a drunk, or all three crimes together. She didn't try to stop me talking. Instead she asked me to tell her what I had heard on the beach.

'Will you take off Mr Williams?' I said. 'I would rather tell you than him.'

'If it would help.' She peeled off her whiskers, with some wincing for the glue made the whiskers cling. I helped her unpin her wig and she fluffed her yellow hair beneath so it stood at all angles, like a cornfield roughly shorn to stubble.

'There now,' she said, and put her arm around me again. 'Tell me what happened.'

'It's as if she speaks in the wind,' I said. 'That's how her voice reaches me.'

'And what does she say?'

'That I should come down to the sea. That I should join her. And my name, Anna. My *true* name! The way she says it – it gets inside my head and thrums there. It dulls me. Takes away all my thoughts so all there is, is her.'

Anna put her hand to my forehead and I leant into her touch. 'Does it hurt?' she said. 'A headache?'

'Bad, it is, but it's worse what she does to my legs. Her voice is like a charm that sets me walking and I don't even know I'm doing it until I've moved. If you hadn't got hold of me today . . .'

'And last night, when I woke to find you trying to open the door, it was the same – this voice, calling you?'

I nodded. 'And before that, too, in Boscastle, just before Captain Ians came. I saw one of them, Anna, from the cliff.'

She leant away from me a little, as if to see me better. 'You saw a mermaid at Boscastle?'

'I think so, though I didn't know it then. I couldn't see her tail parts all that clear. But the rest of her looked the same as the carving at the church door. I'll show that to you. It's above—'

'I saw it. I wondered if you had too.'

'Why would there be a carving of a mermaid here if they didn't have them in these waters? The parson says he's seen them.'

'Our host is somewhat highly strung. Here, wipe your face.'

I took the handkerchief she offered but I smelt the deadhouse again for it was the handkerchief Mrs Seldon had given her, and that she had used to turn over the gobbet.

'Wouldn't your nerves be bad too if you had to live here,' I said, 'with mermaids calling all night and dead men carried to your shore in pieces?'

'They might,' Anna said. 'But bad enough to murder someone? That's the question we should put our minds to.'

'You mean, did the parson murder his brother-in-law? What would be his reason, Anna? He's never met Joseph Ians. His dislike might truly be because the memory of the man upsets his wife.

That's not enough to kill Joseph if he did return to Morwenstow.'

'So who does that leave as a suspect – a mermaid?'

There was no scorn in her voice, and that left me tongue-tied. I wasn't used to this – what was the word? *Faith*.

'I suppose it does,' I said.

As if to confirm our thinking, the wind came at the window again. All at once the shivers were upon me anew and I wanted to crawl into quiet and safety. To find a place no one would know my name.

Anna seemed to understand this for she said, 'I think it best you get into bed, Shilly.' We truly were thinking the same way at last. 'There's nothing to be gained by you falling ill. The funeral is tomorrow and I need you with me. We need to keep an eye on those who attend, including our hosts.'

I had time to think it was a shame I was too poorly to enjoy Anna taking off my clothes before she had swept me under the bedclothes and was putting Mr Williams' whiskers back on. She was leaving me.

'Where are you going?' I said. The bedclothes felt heavier than they had previous. Mrs Seldon must have come and put more on.

Anna opened the door. 'To find something to help you rest.'

My heart leapt at this for I thought she must mean drink but then I thought no, Shilly, don't be a fool. You've promised you won't touch it in return for Anna teaching you your reading and your writing. But then I thought, it's been a day or two since Anna got the paper out and made me follow the words with my slow finger, so a little drop wouldn't upset the bargain. It might only be fair. We would write to Mathilda and tell her of our doings in Morwenstow. Of the mermaid, of love. No, that might frighten the poor girl and I didn't want that. Never that for her. I would write of the sea which was not the same sea here as at Boscastle for there are no boats here, Mathilda, are there boats where you are, is the *Merry Maiden* at rest, are you at rest now, after your fears for Anna, what were they, Mathilda, tell me, please—

And then the door was opening and Anna was back with a bottle! But it was only a small one, green, and as she uncorked it the smell was dreadful bitter.

She sat on the bed and poured a spoonful. 'Fortunately, Mrs Hawker had a tincture. Here – open up. It'll help your headache if nothing else.'

Her voice worked as powerful on me as the woman who spoke in the wind for my mouth was opening and the bitter water was on its hateful way down my throat. I coughed but none left me.

Anna looked at me, sadly, I thought, and sighed.

'You mustn't worry,' I said, and patted her hand. 'I'm only a little poorly from the cold. The rest of me is well.'

She looked down at my hand on hers. 'Yes,' she said faintly. 'But try to rest all the same.'

'You'll stay with me? If she calls, I might try—'

'I wouldn't worry about that, Shilly. The tincture will keep you abed.'

My eyes were closing and I couldn't open them. 'What . . . What is it?'

'Laudanum, Shilly. It'll help you sleep. I hope that's all you need. Heaven knows I'm not the one to . . .'

Her voice quietened away in the darkness of the room. Perhaps it *was* time to sleep. A silent sleep.

'You do believe me, Anna, don't you?'

The sound of the door opening, then closing. Between those sounds I thought I heard her speak but it might have been the voice in the wind. It might have been my own.

* * *

153

I was cold. So cold I ached. The sea had got inside me. I had to get my blood moving or I'd turn into moor stone and never move again. And I had to do it at once for I had need to be somewhere, that was certain. I had already waited too long. Quick, Shilly, you must come home quick. I tried to run but my feet wouldn't work. They were all pins and needles, for there was nothing beneath them. No floor. No ground. I was hanging in the air, and I was turning. Slowly. But turning still. A shriek of metal above me, and somewhere close by, someone sobbed.

I could not move my neck. Where my neck should be was a burning place, but burning with cold. How could this be? My hands were still mine, for when I touched my neck I felt the deep cold of metal. I felt the metal of the hook that had pierced me.

And when I screamed my voice was not my own and I knew where I was. Hanging on a meat hook in the butcher's shop back in Boscastle.

And the sobbing – it was Mathilda. Mathilda crying for me.

TWENTY-FIVE

When I woke I knew I hadn't been called to the sea but I was wet all the same, and from salt water likewise. I had been scritching pools of it.

'Anna?'

I reached for her in the bed, in the darkness of the room. She wasn't there. I dried my face on the pillow and sat up. There was no wind at the window, no thrum in my head. My shivers had gone. But the coldness was with me still, for the dream had been bad. Was it a sign of some bad thing to come? I had felt the need to hurry somewhere – back to Boscastle? But I had felt, too, that I was already too late.

Voices outside the door. Anna's voice in Mr Williams' mouth, and the deep swell of the parson. They drew closer, then the door was opening and Mr Williams was wishing the parson goodnight. I tasted smoke, smelt drink, too. Anna was granted more fineries as a man than a woman.

She closed the door and I said her name again, startled her – I felt a tremble in the bed frame as she knocked into it.

'You're awake,' she said.

'Will you light a candle? I've had enough of the dark.'

More stumbling and then a flare and the room was furniture once more, the fireplace, the curtains. And Anna ridding herself of Mr Williams again.

'What time is it?' I asked.

'A little after midnight. You've been asleep some time.' She sat in the window to take off her boots but she was all a-sway. 'How do you feel?'

'Better than before. No shivers.'

'And the woman – she didn't call?'

'No, but—'

'Thank heavens for that.' Anna dropped her boots by the door and fell into bed beside me. 'You can't be having laudanum every night. No good replacing one vice with another. But if it helped ease your head that's something.'

'It did. Though . . .'

She was on her back, Mr Williams' hair still on her head. I lifted it off then squeezed myself close to her.

'I haven't done any writing for a day or two, Anna.'

Her eyes were closed. 'Hm?'

'I want to practise tomorrow.'

'If we have time.' Her words were slurred. Tiredness, or something else, something the parson kept in a cabinet in his study?

I pinched her cheek to keep her awake and she slapped my hand away, but no other part of her moved. *She* was turned to moor stone.

'I want to write to Mathilda,' I said. 'Or to Mrs Yeo, at least, to see how Mathilda is. If she's ready to join us.'

'But we might not be here too much longer,' Anna said. 'Better to save Mathilda the journey.'

'You mean we might be closer to the truth? Did you learn something tonight?'

'I learnt the parson's port is as fine as his tobacco.' She laughed, her eyes still closed. 'He is a strange creature. His wife too. They were sorry to hear you were indisposed.'

'Because you made me so, Anna! I don't want any more from that green bottle.'

'It was for your own good.' She put her hand on my thigh, and though my heart was glad I couldn't keep from thinking of Mathilda. Of myself on the meat hook. I didn't want to tell Anna of my dream. I couldn't bring myself to put it into words, so I sought something else to say instead.

'Does Mrs Hawker know of our discovery yet? Has the captain told her that the dead man is her brother?'

'Not yet. He must be planning to tell her in the morning. Mrs Hawker might as well have one more peaceful night. Heaven knows, tomorrow will come soon enough for sadness. It gave me a chance to ask some further questions.'

'Oh! And what did you find out?'

She yawned. 'That the Ians childhood was a happy one, until Joseph's schemes with the copper and the crocuses got out of hand. Apparently, Mrs Hawker and Joseph used to go down to the beach where we were today, to swim. They weren't supposed to – their mother had forbidden it on account of the current. They never invited Frederick. Mrs Seldon's daughter – what's her name?'

'Nancy.'

'Nancy, yes. Well, Nancy was invited to these secret swims, for she was very thick with the younger Ianses. Is that a word? Anyway, this carried on right up to the point Joseph left Morwenstow, and now Nancy is their servant.'

'Did you make Mrs Hawker cry,' I said, 'asking her about her brother?'

Anna let out a belch and I moved to be free of the smell.

'I did, but I told her my asking was to learn more about Joseph, which would help stop Frederick's delusions, as she believes them to be, and that seemed to give her courage. It stopped the parson roaring at me too. He was most genial once Mrs Hawker had left us to the port. Such fine port . . .'

'And what did *he* tell you? Anna – are you listening?'

She wasn't. Her breath had stuttered to soft snores. I kissed her, to taste the port and her beneath it, then opened our door and darted for the landing, for more candles. Across from our room was the one that was always locked, the one Nancy said was the parson's special room. Had Anna asked the parson about it tonight? I thought it unlikely. She didn't think the locked room mattered. It was another key she was interested in, the one tucked beneath a dead man's ribs.

From the landing I took all the candles I could see back to our room and set them in the window. All this talk of fine port and tobacco, the parson could afford to keep the darkness from me. I searched for my shawl, then remembered it was likely with the gobbet in the deadhouse. Not that I wanted it back after it had been used for *that* purpose. Mr Williams' short, cream coat would have to do to save me from the draughts tonight. Would that the travelling case would reach us soon. I made myself think very hard on it, thought of it atop a cart that was even now on its way to Morwenstow, bringing us fresh clothes.

So settled in the window, I waited for morning. If the wind should blow tonight, and in its breath the woman who called me by my name, Anna would be no help keeping me from my own end. I thought of Captain Ians, likewise afraid to go to sleep. Was he even now sitting up in the Bush Inn, longing for dawn? I resolved to ask him for his wakefulness remedies when next we saw him. And I resolved two more things also.

One, I would have no more of the tincture from Mrs Hawker's green bottle. It had given me the same muddle as drink but with none of the warm forgetfulness that was pleasant.

Two, I would make Anna write to Mathilda tomorrow. I would know that she was well. I could not rest easy until then.

TWENTY-SIX

But there was no time for letters in the morning, for Anna and I were both of us shilly-shallying, both of us sore – Anna sore-headed from the port, me sore-necked from sleeping crooked in the window seat. It was Nancy who woke me, knocking to see if we wanted breakfast. There was candle wax all over the window seat, and some on the floor below – what would she think of us! And Anna, abed still, as herself, Mr Williams' hair on the end of the bed frame. I opened the door a crack to say to Nancy thank you, yes, we'd be down quick as you like.

'Well then,' she said, 'I'll leave the dishes. I was all for cleaning up, thinking you'd already gone to church, but Mother said she hadn't seen you go.'

Anna murmured from the bed.

'Is your husband taken poorly?' Nancy said.

I put myself more in the way, so Nancy shouldn't see there was a woman in my bed when she thought there should be a man there – the man she'd met, with whiskers and a cream coat.

'He's no good first thing,' I said.

''Tis hardly early,' she said, turning towards the stairs, 'being gone nine. But if you don't keep as regular hours as *some* folk . . .

I'll leave the eggs and freshen the tea, given you're not attending.'

I leant out onto the landing to call after her. 'Attending what?'

'Why, the funeral. Parson said your husband was keen to pay his respects but if you're not—'

I shut the door at once and shook Anna awake.

The noise of the rooks followed us into church and were only a little quietened by the door being shut. The parson was speaking of tongues, the pain of silence. He gave no sign he'd heard us come in late, so lost was he in his words, but some heads did turn. I recognised Mrs Seldon as one of those looking at us, her husband beside her, his bald head bent in prayer.

The cats lolled by the font, with My Most Righteous Cat at the heart of them. He'd have to share the pulpit with the parson today, and I thought he wouldn't like that. He pressed his holy cheek against my knee, and I scratched him behind the ear. A blessing for us both.

'Shilly!' Anna hissed, and I saw I was to follow her to a bench on the left side of the church.

'For man walketh in a vain shadow,' said the parson, 'and disquieteth himself in vain. He heapeth up riches, and cannot tell who shall gather them.'

We were gathering our riches that morning at the funeral, going about our paying work. Though how it would help us, I didn't know.

I was glad of the straw to silence our boots. But not glad of the new smell that rose from it, a terrible sweetness. We took our seats then I fished from the straw a weed. Wormwood. If I hadn't felt so sick from the smell I might have laughed at such efforts to keep the air fresh. I asked Anna what we should be doing at this funeral for someone we didn't know.

'Watch, and keenly so,' she whispered. 'Make a note of who is here, and who isn't – is there anyone we might have expected to attend but who is absent?'

Mrs Seldon was looking at us again, and looking stern at our whispering while the parson spoke. I picked up a hymnal and held it open before our faces. I couldn't have read it, of course, but it would hide us from those we watched.

But Anna snatched the book from me.

'What are you doing?' I said. 'It's so our mouths shall be hidden, and our detective plans likewise.'

'That only works if the book is the right way up, Shilly.' She turned it, and the letters on the front looked more like I knew them to be. 'Now, what was I saying?'

'We're looking for those who haven't come,' I said.

'Yes. And those who *did* come, how do they behave?'

'So seeing who is scritching, then?'

'And who isn't. The signs of relief can be loud as those of pain. The same is true of guilt, Shilly.'

'What does guilt look like?'

'It can take many forms.'

'Well we'll have a job of it, then!'

'Keep your voice down. It's a delicate science. You must look for changes in sweating, in the colour of a face. See where gazes are directed.'

That sounded a hard business to me, for weren't people always blushing and sweating and looking about them? That was what bodies did, the guilty and the good. We were doing some of it now, looking at the parson. Where would it end? With everyone a detective?

I shook my head and pushed the hymnal out of the way, into Anna's face. I'd do my best. I could do no more.

The church wasn't even half full. Mrs Hawker was seated at the front, with her brother Captain Ians beside her. They had made friends again. He must have told her about the body. The Seldons, all three, were a few rows behind Mrs Hawker and the captain. And the rest of them in church? Working people. Farmers. Some labourers. No fishermen, there being no harbour nearer than Bude.

Parson Hawker loomed over us all from the pulpit and his voice was loud enough for a full church, a bigger church, for the entire Kingdom of Heaven, where he said the poor wretch was bound. Beneath the parson was the coffin. A plain box, set on a trestle. No finery spent on the man inside, for until the day before he'd been thought a sailor washed in from far away. Anna and I had found the truth too late for anything better to be given him. Joseph Ians needed to go into the ground before the bad air of his body gave sickness to everyone in Morwenstow. The smell of the deadhouse was with us in the church, the wormwood no use against it. I pinched my nose and hoped the service would be swift.

It wasn't. The parson spoke lengthy of redeeming and rising and suchlike, and spoke of Joseph by name. Spoke of the prodigal son and the need for forgiveness. It looked to me that the captain and Mrs Hawker bent their heads lower at this, but perhaps that was what everyone did when such things were said at funerals in churches. Perhaps I should have done it too, were I not detecting.

Then the parson said we would stand to sing and I was glad for the change, for I liked a song. Who didn't? Those with moor stone for hearts. But church hymns were not so sweet as chapel ones. I'd sung both in my time. Church songs were gloomy as the buildings that housed the singers. I liked the cheerfulness of chapel tunes, the jounce of them. Tunes I was sure Mrs Seldon and her daughter liked. But that suspicion I was keeping in my pocket, for I didn't think the parson could know of the Seldons' ways or he wouldn't have them in his house.

But a song was a song and it would do us good to lift our voices to the Lord and stop the rooks' noise outside being so loud. Guilt might be carried in singing as well as sweating, and I should find it there. I resolved to listen very hard.

The hymn we were to sing was called 'Ride On, Ride On, In Majesty', the parson said. I didn't know it but most in the church did as from the first it was sung quite hearty, with Mrs Seldon's dreadful voice drowning out the others. Then another voice rose clear over the rest, over even Mrs Seldon's squawk. It soared high above them all. A woman's voice. One I knew.

It was the voice that called. I pressed my head to the coolness of the wood to ease the thrum there once more. Would that it didn't shape into my name. Would that no one called for that poor wretch—

'Shilly?'

There it was – she had called me by name and I would walk into the water. I put my fingers in my ears to stave off drowning long as I could.

And then I was rising. The waves bore me up, into Mr Williams' face, and Anna's, there, beneath it. She who had hold of my elbow.

'You've never heard a soprano before?' she said, and her words were things to cling to in the thrum of my head.

'What?'

'The high notes – that's a soprano, and a fine one at that. The parson was right.'

'But that's the voice I've heard, Anna – the one that calls me to the sea. That wants to drown me!'

'Really? But . . .' She looked to the front of the church, and I looked likewise.

The singing was pouring from Mrs Hawker's mouth.

Was it truly her voice I'd heard in the wind? Was *she* the creature who waited in the swell, who carved bodies with her claws? When Captain Ians had dreamt it was a woman who'd lured his brother to his death, was it his *sister* he was thinking of?

Anna's face was all concern and I feared she might give me more of the laudanum, so I did my best to slow my breath, to think. Mrs Hawker stood, on two legs, so how could she be a creature of the sea? But if such creatures could change their shape when they had need, like the cunning women who ran themselves into hares to better outrun their chasers . . . The barman at the Bush had told me that the woman betrayed by the squire's nephew had done the same. After her death she'd sunk through the earth of the churchyard and into the sea beneath. Who was to say that Mrs Hawker couldn't do the same to change herself, and others like her in these parts?

At last the singing stopped and everyone sat down again. The parson was in his pulpit, My Most Righteous Cat seated on the floor beneath him. The cat looked up at his master, as the parson looked up to his and called upon him, the Lord, to spare Morwenstow from the ravages of the sea.

'For your servant is bowed by the task, for he is . . . he . . .' The parson wiped his mouth and I peered at him in the gloom of the church. Was that sweat above his lip, around his nose? The sweat of guilt? A moan from him, cut short as he cleared his throat. 'In the darkest of hours, we beseech thee, merciful Father, to look . . . look upon . . .'

And then he was desperate to escape the pulpit, fumbling himself from its high wooden clutches, which sent My Most

Righteous Cat racing to the back of the church, his tail high in alarm. The parson crashed onto his hands and knees, then laid himself flat on the cold slates. His face was pressed against them, his brown gown a puddle of cloth around him. He moaned again.

I looked to Anna who was watching, her mouth wide open.

'Is that what guilt looks like?' I said.

'It might be,' she muttered. 'But why does no one help him?'

We were the only ones shocked by the parson lying on the floor, by his noise. The rest of those in the church looked on idly, if they looked at all. Most were talking to their neighbours, in quiet tones of everyday talk, not surprise. The woman in front of us said something about the beer gone bad at the Bush, and the woman with her cursed this news.

'Should we help?' I said. 'It seems a cruelty to leave him there. He's wretched.'

'That he is,' Anna said. 'But it's not our place to—Oh, there we are, look. Mrs Hawker is assisting him.'

She was indeed. Mrs Hawker placed a hand on her husband's back and leant in to his ear. I couldn't hear her words over the rest of the talk in the church and they seemed to do no good anyway for the parson didn't get up, only moaned louder.

'Do you think his heart has given out?' I said.

'No – his jaw is working just as always.'

'He's confessing? Maybe we should get closer—'

Anna pulled me back. 'Let's wait. Something tells me this display is a regular occurrence.'

Mrs Hawker said something to Captain Ians and he got up to help her, with some reluctance, I thought. The captain was very grey about the face. Together they heaved the parson to his feet. Mrs Hawker patted his cheek, which cheered the parson and he was on his way again as if nothing had happened.

'You were right,' I said to Anna. 'He does do such things regular.'

She shook her head in wonderment. 'How long will he run on now?'

'We might be here all day.'

Now it was Anna's turn to lift her eyes to the heavens. 'Spare us that.'

The service did indeed run on, and on, and on. There was no more of what Anna called *thee at ricks*, but not much to keep me watchful either. A man at the back took a newspaper from his coat. The cats had fallen asleep by the font. My eye was drawn to the slate slabs of the floor, for there were letters there. Now that I had some learning of them, I found that my eye often caught on letters, even when I wasn't trying to see them. It was like they were stones in a path that tripped me. But this was a good kind of tripping for it was practice, and Anna said I needed that more than anything.

The letters I saw on the slates were put together to make words, and some of them I knew. There was LORD – that was carved many times, and likewise 'rest' and 'wife'. Beside them were other shapes I knew were numbers, but I hadn't got to learning them properly, and I didn't think they were so important as words for knowing things. I wouldn't trouble myself with them. There was only so much a body could do in a day, and one who was meant to be detecting too.

Reading the words on the slate left me glum for they made me think of Mathilda still in Boscastle, and my letter to her still unwritten. I would make Anna write it later. As soon as Parson Hawker had freed us from the church. He'd been in such a hurry to get the dead man buried, rushing Mr Good to come and look at him, and now he was taking all the time in the world to commend the corpse to the Lord. The air was more fouled by the minute from the corpse's seeping, and I was more tired, for detecting was hard.

Sometimes it was more than I could bear.

TWENTY-SEVEN

The funeral had at last ended and all in church had followed Parson Hawker and the coffin to the churchyard. We were the last to leave and found the captain not far from the church door. He leant on an old slate gravestone that was itself leaning. He still hadn't slept – I saw that in his eyes, on his skin. Somehow smelt it on him too. Could he not bear to be at the graveside as his brother was lowered into the earth? Looking at the state of him, it might have been he just wasn't able to walk that far.

'It must be some comfort to know your brother has been laid to rest in the soil of his home.' I looked over to where the parson stood beside fresh-turned earth, Mrs Hawker with him. 'He's not being buried under the trees on the south side, where the sailors go, those whose names aren't known. There's many denied such mercy in this world.'

'Mercy, Mrs Williams? I suppose so,' the captain said. 'To think that if you hadn't discovered the gobbet and proved my belief about Joseph being the dead man, my brother would have been buried in sight of the family plots but not with them – that would have grieved me. You have done both he and I a good service, but you must forgive my low spirits. It is difficult to find relief in my brother's final resting place when it was coming home that killed him.' And the captain, too, looked across at his sister and his brother-in-law by the graveside. 'Joseph came back to Morwenstow and he was murdered.'

'Tell me, Captain,' Anna said, in a voice made to sound reasonable but which was anything but. 'When you engaged our services, why did you not tell us that Parson Hawker was brother-in-law to you and Joseph?'

He was confused by this. 'I didn't think it important. It made no odds. Joseph was dead. *That* I knew.'

'But it is a significant detail to omit, Captain, that the deceased may be related to a suspect in the case.'

'A suspect? To whom do you refer?'

Anna didn't answer straight away. A useful breath to take. Then she said, 'Why, the parson, of course.'

He straightened and made some effort to brush down his quite filthy coat. 'Perhaps it was wishful thinking on my part not to mention the connection between myself and Robert.'

'What do you mean?' I said.

'In a perfect world I wouldn't find myself brother-in-law to Robert. He is not a relation one would wish.'

'He is an eccentric, I'll grant you,' Anna said. 'His behaviour in church today . . .'

The captain shook his head. 'Such things I could bear, if he behaved with decency towards my sister.'

'He hasn't?' I said.

'Not since the day they met.' The captain turned his face from the churchyard, and from the couple now making their slow way home. 'He has used her poorly, squandering her inheritance on lavishness he can ill afford.'

'You mean the things he has built here – the school, the vicarage,' I said.

'And the lives they live. You are staying with them. You cannot fail to have noticed.'

He looked to each of us in turn, and I wondered if Anna regretted the fine port and finer tobacco she'd enjoyed the night before.

'And as if that wasn't enough, I find it unconscionable that he should live in such a manner when his parishioners, the very people he is here to minister to, suffer such hardships as they do. Look around you. This is a poor parish. And yet the *parson*,' and here the captain allowed himself a brief but hate-filled glance towards the vicarage, 'smokes the finest tobacco and demands his own unique supply of writing paper from the most expensive firms in London! He'll be in the poorhouse himself before long. That I could countenance, but the fact he will take my sister with him . . .'

This speech was too much for the captain in his weakened state, and he clutched the gravestone. How long until he was in his own grave?

'I take it you've shared these fears with Mrs Hawker?' Anna asked.

'I've tried. My letters receive only defensiveness in return. All I've achieved is to drive a wedge between us and so deepen my sister's love for this devil of a man.'

'And this has worsened since you returned,' I said, 'with the claim the dead man was Joseph?'

'It has, Mrs Williams. And so I fear to say more, which leaves me spouting bitterness to strangers. Forgive me. I must learn to guard my tongue, or it will be my fault the shares are lost.'

'Shares?' Anna said.

'That's all my sister has left of her inheritance. And not for long, if Robert has his way. But perhaps . . .' His gaze darted between us.

'Perhaps you could help me in my petition, make my sister see.'

'If you would tell us a little more about the share arrangement,' Anna said, 'then I'm sure we could find our way to—'

'I am grateful to you, truly,' he said, and he looked so pitiful, this old sea captain, clinging to a gravestone, looking quite dead himself with tiredness.

'We'll sit over here, shall we?' I led the way to the bench beside the church where we would be sheltered from the wind, and from unwanted gazes.

When we were seated, the captain began.

'There is a ship that trades from Bude, *The Eliza*.' Captain Ians rested his head against the wall of the church but did not close his eyes, despite the tiredness that lay so heavy on him. 'She's a small concern, moving slate, sand for the fields, but she's a reliable old girl and has served our family well for many years.'

'You own her?' I said.

'In part. She's divided into shares, which are owned equally by four parties – myself, my sister Charlotte, and Joseph. Our father left them to us.'

'And the fourth in the partnership?' Anna said.

'Sally Grey, a widow. She was a dear friend of both my parents and tended my mother in her last illness. Such kindness my father didn't forget, and he left provision for her in his will – a quarter of the shares in *The Eliza*.' The captain looked across the fields, to the sea beyond. 'I've not been a good friend to Mrs Grey since leaving. My father would be ashamed at my neglect. But after so long away . . . Well. I must call on her soon, once all is settled here.'

'Mrs Grey is nearby?' I asked.

'At Coombe,' he said. 'She has been unwell lately, so Charlotte tells me. A bad case of the pox.'

'Best you do stay away, then,' I said. 'You've got enough to concern you without that.'

'And what is the parson's position in this business of the shares?' Anna said.

The captain gripped the side of the bench. 'He pesters Charlotte to make her shares over to him, but that would not be . . . wise.'

'Why not?' I said.

'Because Robert would be forced to sell them before too long. Though *The Eliza*'s trade is small, she brings in a healthy annual sum. My mind is made easier knowing that Charlotte has that income to defray Robert's expenses. Without it . . .' He shook his head. 'The wisest course would be for my sister to make her shares over to me for safe keeping.'

'Which would give you the controlling share,' Anna said.

'True, but there's safety in that.'

Safety for you, Captain Ians, I thought but didn't say. What I did say was, 'And what of Joseph's earnings from *The Eliza*? You've not seen hide nor hair of him for years. Where's his money gone?'

'It's been saved for him,' the captain said. 'Charlotte and I have been very careful in that regard. We did so in the hope he would return, or at least send word of his whereabouts.' The captain quickly wiped his eyes. 'And now we know exactly where he is.'

'What will happen to Joseph's savings now?' Anna said.

'In the terms of the agreement, as laid down by my father, the money saved for Joseph will come to me.'

'And do you know the sum of this legacy?' Anna said.

After a pause, the captain answered, and quietly at that. 'It is somewhere in the region of two thousand pounds.'

The wind had dropped, and the rooks, for once, had left us. Even the sea was quiet, as if waiting, for a truth was coming clear. All three of us on the bench felt it.

'Sad as it is, your loss, you have gained from your brother's death,' I said.

'I have, Mrs Williams. I would not dispute that. But it is nothing to the loss of a brother.'

'A brother you haven't seen in more than forty years,' Anna said. 'A good trade, some might say.'

He got to his feet and stumbled back from the bench. 'You cannot think this money motivated me to . . . to *kill* my own brother?'

We said nothing. We would lend him the rope to hang himself.

'It is preposterous! I charged you to investigate Joseph's death. Why would I do that if it was my own neck I risked in doing so?'

'True,' Anna said, and I marvelled at her calm in the face of such anger from the captain, who was, after all, the one paying us. 'But it wouldn't be beyond the bounds of possibility to employ an investigator to ensure someone else hang. But come, sit. We are speaking of generalities here. We make no charge against you.'

Oh, but we might! And the captain wasn't eased by her words. He stayed standing, his eyes wild.

'Captain Ians, please. Mrs Williams and I meant no offence. We were speaking simply of the facts in this case.'

'I—Quite so. But still, I would not have you think such things, even just to entertain them. Now, if you will excuse me—'

'I have one last question for you,' I said. 'If you get Joseph's money, what happens to his shares?'

'They pass to Charlotte.'

'And if Mrs Hawker should give Joseph's shares to her husband,' Anna said, 'as well as her own—'

'God forbid she would be that foolish,' the captain muttered.

'—then Parson Hawker would have the controlling stake in *The Eliza*,' Anna said. 'And I'd imagine that means he could force a sale if he wishes.'

The captain nodded, his gaze on his boots. 'He could. Which is why Charlotte must be persuaded to resist Robert's demands. Any help you may give in that quarter, I would be indebted to you.'

You're already indebted, I thought.

'For Charlotte's sake, you understand. Not my own.'

'Of course,' Anna said.

He took his leave of us then, and hurried away, back to the Bush Inn, and to his guilt? He had told us much, and not come out of it well.

TWENTY-EIGHT

'The funeral service might not have run quite as expected,' Anna said, 'but the parson did strike one right note. *He heapeth up riches, and cannot tell who shall gather them.* Joseph Ians had *quite* a heap of riches waiting for him.'

'He wasn't here by chance, then,' I said. 'He had a strong reason to come home to Morwenstow. But now he's dead, his brother will do the gathering.'

'A motive for murder if ever I heard one.'

'But Mrs Hawker and the parson,' I said, 'they're the same. Each stood to gain if Joseph should die.'

'Which means we have three suspects to consider. And it's a curious state of affairs.' Her false teeth began to clack. 'None would seem to be in competition for the gain. They *each* benefit from Joseph's death without compromising the others. The captain gets Joseph's earnings that have been saved for him, Mrs Hawker gets Joseph's shares, and if the parson has his way, those shares will be made over to him in time. Could they be working together to see Joseph dead?'

'I'm not sure,' I said. 'The bad feeling between the captain and the parson seems truthful. They wouldn't put their heads together. Mrs Hawker is likewise at odds with the captain and her husband has forbid her to talk of the other brother. There's no peace between the parties.'

'So each has their own motive,' Anna said, 'and we must assume they would act without the knowledge of the others.'

'And now that we have found their motives,' I said.

'Yes?' Anna looked at me with some eagerness.

'We must discover what they were doing when Joseph Ians was likely killed. There is a word for it, I forget—'

'Alibi, Shilly.'

'That's it. It means knowing the time and a person's business and such.'

'It does, indeed. The captain has already provided us with details of his whereabouts when Joseph's body was discovered – on his way back to Morwenstow, and from the open sea off Portugal, no less. Though he stood to gain from his brother's death, his alibi would seem to rule him out. We must ask Mrs Hawker and the parson for their movements.'

'And there's another soul we must think on, Anna.'

'Hm?' She had stood and was using the edge of a grave to scrape mud from Mr Williams' boots.

'That Mrs Grey, the widow who owns the other quarter of the ship shares. Her with the pox.'

'True, she might have an interest in Joseph's fate,' Anna said, 'though it's not clear to me yet what that could be.'

'I'll put her in my pocket for now, then.'

Anna stopped her blasphemous boot scraping and frowned at me. 'Your *what*?'

'My pocket. For things that might be important but we haven't the truth of yet, so we can't know. If they're important, I mean.'

'I see. And what else is in your . . . pocket?'

'Well, the captain's dream is in there, and the mermaid, of course.'

'It's a big pocket, then,' Anna muttered.

I made out I hadn't heard her. It was best to just press on when she went teasey about my way of looking at things. Forcing her to hear me was the only way. It was one reason I knew myself to be a louder person these days. I was sure I never had need of so much shouting before I met Anna Drake.

'And the Seldons,' I said, folding my arms. 'They're in my pocket too.'

Now she was keen, now she was without scorn. 'Really? Why?'

And I told her of my suspicion that the mother and daughter working for the parson were Methodists, who were the parson's most hated kind of person, and that though they hid it from him, I had spied it out.

'It's because they think me like them,' I said. 'For the way my voice sounds, for I'm only just learning to read and write. So they are less . . . less . . . Oh, what is the word!'

'Guarded? They let their guard down?'

I didn't understand her. She tried again.

'They are honest with you?'

'Yes.'

'What they make of the two of us together then, I can't think. This incarnation of Mr Williams might need to come down in the world. Or was he forced to marry his scullery maid? It seems unlikely. Or he could—'

She could never stop her making of other selves. Anna herself had told me the word for such habits – *com pul shun*. It was like a lady I had seen in Blisland, where I was born. She would not take off her gloves, not even for eating, they said. My mother knew a woman who knew another woman whose sister worked in the lady's house, and *she* told my mother that if this lady was made to take off her gloves then she would scrub her hands with a hard brush until the skin came away in folds and there was blood all down her arms. The lady had a *compulsion* to wear her gloves. Anna had a *compulsion* to be someone other than herself. And me? My *compulsion* was Anna Drake.

'Well, well,' Anna said, and took her pipe from her coat. 'It's not just the mysteries of life that you contribute to Williams and Williams Investigations. It's religious learning too.'

'Religion *is* a mystery, Anna.'

'And philosophy too!' she crowed. 'Oh, Shilly, what a wonder you are.'

And she leant down and kissed me, with her whiskers and her breath all the parson's fine tobacco, but a kiss! As she went to pull away, I kissed *her*, hard and long, and she gave in to it, to me, as she wished to, I knew she did. I drew her onto my lap. What a pair we would have looked to anyone passing – a woman with a man on her knee, her hand at his waist, her hand at his breast.

'Anna,' I murmured into her cheek. 'You love me, I know it. Why can't we be as we were once before? What harm does it do? We are all the time together anyway. To be as married people are truly, not just these names we use, these rings.'

She leant into me and I felt her boniness beneath her man's coat and shirt.

'Because . . . because I—'

'What is it? I have kept from the drink, truly I have.'

'I know, and I know how hard that's been. But there is something I must tell you. Shilly—'

'Whatever is the matter? It can't be so bad to cry over.'

She stood to wipe her eyes. When she was done, she had wiped away her willingness to tell me her secrets too.

'It's nothing,' she said, just the same as when that letter had come, back in Boscastle. Just as she'd said when she argued with Mathilda. Whatever it was she was keeping from me, it was keeping us apart too.

She ducked inside the doorway and I knew her to be repairing the powder that had washed from her face with her tears. The powder that helped shape her face to that of Mr Williams. My husband, the stranger. Would that I could have her as a wife and so know her truly.

When she stepped back into the weak sun she was all business again. There would be no more sitting on laps and kissing. Not for a while, at any rate.

'Alibis, Shilly.'

Was she speaking of her own?

We returned to the vicarage. Where there might be easier answers.

TWENTY-NINE

The vicarage seemed inhabited only by creatures. The cats slept on the fine chairs in the room where we had sat with the parson on our first night and which Anna said was a drawing room. The dogs slept under the dining-room table. Gyp the pig had stuffed himself beneath the stairs, wedged between an old trunk and what I took to be a tin bath full of shells and pebbles. His snores made the tin bath rattle.

Anna went upstairs to see who was about, and I went to the back of the house, where at last I found a person, and that was Mrs Seldon, napping before the fire, her knitting in her lap. I let my foot clang one of the fire irons and she woke. I asked where the parson and his wife were to.

'They're having a rest, the pair of them,' Mrs Seldon said. 'Service this morning has taken it out of the parson. He do get quite upset with the burials.'

'So I saw. Him falling to the floor!'

'Today was a quiet one.' Mrs Seldon picked up her knitting. The wool was red and lumpen. It made me think of the clotted blood on the body of Joseph Ians. 'I can't bear to see the parson like it any more,' she said. 'Some would say we're cursed in Morwenstow, the number of souls who end up on the beaches. Parson says it's the lack of faith.' *Click click click* went her needles.

'Would you say that?'

She looked up from her needles. 'Morwenstow is strong in believers.'

'And what do you say of the dead man being Joseph Ians?'

'I say it's terrible sad. If it's true, that is.'

'You doubt it?'

Click click click. The red wool twitching. 'All I know is the way his body was torn to pieces. How you could tell anything of the poor wretch, let alone a name, is beyond me. But there we are. What do I know? I'm only the one that sees to *all* the bodies that wash in here.'

'We found something that makes it certain the dead man is Joseph. A tattoo he was known to have. It was on the gobbet that washed in.'

Her knitting slipped from her hands to the floor. 'My husband told me about the flesh. I didn't know nothing about it being Joseph's tattoo. But he'd have no reason to come back to Morwenstow after all this time. What was there here for him?'

Mrs Seldon didn't seem to know anything about Joseph's earnings from *The Eliza*. I wasn't about to tell her either.

'His sister, for one thing,' I said. I picked up her knitting from the floor, and as I did so I saw there was something in the grate. A yellow flower, bright amongst the new wood waiting to be lit. I put it in my pocket inside my head.

Mrs Seldon took the knitting from me. 'The rows there were on him leaving, I wouldn't have thought *that* would be enough. No, it can't be him.'

'But what about the tattoo?' I said. 'It was of a carving in the church!'

She shrugged. 'I daresay there's plenty got them. Why, them

carvings could be in all the churches between here and Australia.'

I opened my mouth to tell her what I thought of that notion, but then I closed it, for could she have been right? The carving looked strange to my eyes, but perhaps it wasn't. How was I to know?

Mrs Seldon was murmuring to herself. 'No, no. It can't be him. It makes no sense. No sense at all.'

She wouldn't be convinced, but that didn't matter. Convincing Mrs Seldon that the dead man was Joseph Ians wasn't my work. I thought I would try a different track. I took the seat next to her.

'You knew Joseph as a boy, Mrs Seldon, didn't you?'

'It was such a long time ago,' she said.

'Mrs Hawker said he used to be great friends with Nancy.'

'Did she now? Well, that'll be *her* way of remembering.'

'It's not yours?'

Mrs Seldon looked at me. 'Different sorts of people see the world different, don't they? See a person's standing only when they want to. One thing I do know, all this talk it's Joseph means we'll have no peace in this house. You might want to shift yourself to the Bush, Mrs Williams. It'll be quieter there, even with those who've given in to drink parading their wickedness.' She got to her feet. 'Something came for you. I would have told you at breakfast, but you were so late rising.'

'Something for me?'

'A letter. I left it on the table in the hall.'

Another letter. And it had found us here, at Morwenstow. Whoever was writing to Anna, she had given them this address.

Before I could say anything more, Anna herself appeared in the kitchen. From the pallor of her face I thought she must have heard Mrs Seldon tell me of the letter, but Anna didn't speak of it. Instead she asked the old woman who it was that had found the body on the beach and brought the news to the vicarage.

'Inchin Ben,' Mrs Seldon said, with some dislike for the words, I thought. If she had been a church person, of Parson Hawker's kind, she would have crossed herself. 'And no surprise that was!'

'Is he one of the watchers?' I said. 'The parson told us he pays men to look out after a storm, to see the bodies come in.'

'No he is not!' Mrs Seldon said, and scooped her knitting onto the table with force. 'Inchin Ben is nothing to do with anyone, and that's how it should be.'

'Why is that?' Anna said.

'Well, he draws the luck from others,' Mrs Seldon said. 'He's been saved from that many ships going down. It ain't natural.'

'You would rather he'd been drowned?' Anna said, barely able to hold fast to her scorn.

'It'd be more proper than him living when so many with him didn't. You ask anyone round here, they'll tell you. Inchin Ben is bad luck for he'll *take* the good luck from you. I'd keep away from him, if I were you.' And here she looked at me for she liked me best, I thought, for she thought me poor.

'And if we *were* to risk our luck,' Anna said, 'where would we find this man?'

'Coombe,' Mrs Seldon said. 'But don't expect to come back again if you do go and see him. You'll be over the cliff edge, and it'll be him to blame.'

'Mrs Seldon, wait,' I said.

She turned in the doorway.

'His name – why's he called Inchin Ben?'

'It's obvious, isn't it?'

Anna and I looked at one another.

'He's taking a liberty,' Mrs Seldon said, as if we were soft, 'taking people's luck. Creeping, he is. Creeping for all that's good.

Inchin for it.' And her shoulders shook as if someone had just walked over her grave.

Once we were alone, Anna said, 'I definitely want to meet this man now.'

'You think there's more to learn from him of the body?'

'We can't rule it out. But there's something else in your pocket that we must now take out and examine, Shilly, with the help of this Inchin Ben.'

'Oh?'

'The light that was seen on the cliff, the night before Joseph Ians was discovered on the beach beneath. We need to know who lit it, and to what purpose. I'm hopeful this curious man can help with that.'

'But what if Mrs Seldon's right and he does take our luck?'

'He'll be lucky to *find* any between you and I. Come on. We'll need to be back before the daylight goes if we're to avoid the fate Mrs Seldon has foretold for us.'

'Anna, you mustn't joke about such things! You might not mind falling onto them knife rocks but it's not the way I'm going, I'm telling you.'

We were back in the hall, heading for the door.

'Oh yes? And how will you go, Shilly?'

'In bed with you, my heart giving out with pure joy.'

She blushed, just as I'd hoped.

'Go and get your boots on,' she said. 'I just need to . . .'

And she was away to the table. To collect her letter. Into the pocket of her cream coat it went. If she couldn't find the words to tell me the truth of what was going on, I would have to find it out myself. I would have to read that letter.

THIRTY

Anna must have thought to read the letter herself before we left, for she was some time coming to the front door. I had my boots on and thought I'd wait for her outside. The porch smelt too much of dog, and maybe pig too. I had to move the parson's lantern out of the way to open the door and when I did I saw a cart coming down the narrow lane from the road. And on the back of it, a sight I knew well. Anna's travelling case. My thinking had brought it. Anna had no sense of the good things I could do for her.

The cart pulled up outside the vicarage. The driver was sore for he'd taken the case to the Bush first, where Anna had told Davey to send it, of course, and then he'd had to come on further, hearing that the owner was at the vicarage.

He fair threw the case to the ground. It was more battered than the last time I'd seen it, as if it had been thrown from many other carts since it had been thrown from poor Davey's. But it was locked still, so that was something. All Anna's other selves stowed safe within it.

As we didn't know the way to Coombe, where we were to find Inchin Ben, I asked the driver. He had a young face but few teeth left in his head.

'Two ways you can go,' he said. 'Along the cliff there, past the parson's hut and only turn inland when you reach Duckpool. Or take the road here and go past Tonacombe and Stanbury. 'Tis the same distance.'

'How long to walk there?'

He licked one of his few teeth left. 'An hour, I should say.'

Anna came out then, and together we carried the case up to our room.

'The driver said the way to Coombe is inland,' I said. 'The road.' I wasn't going back to the cliff edge if I could help it. If I should hear the woman's voice again, then I wanted no chance to throw myself onto the knife rocks or cast myself into the sea. A field would suit me better if my body should act wilful against me. Turnips were not so bad to fall on.

We set down the case and then my hand was on the door of our room ready to leave, for I was thinking we would be off now, as we had planned. But Anna stayed me.

'I've an idea we should take others to see this Inchin Ben of Coombe, Shilly.' She took the little key from the chain at her neck and opened the case. I remembered then the key I carried, the one found inside Joseph Ians, and felt for it in my pocket – a real pocket this time, not the one in my head. The key was still there, but we hadn't yet found the lock.

Anna threw back the lid of the case and clapped her hands. It was like she was greeting old friends, and in a way, she was. All these other parts of herself.

And parts of *me*, too, for she said we should both go to Coombe as men!

'You think Inchin Ben will like men better than women to talk to?' I said.

'It seems a safe guess. Mrs Seldon has led us to believe he's a

187

grizzled sailor made an outcast by his community.' Anna knelt by the case and began to sort through the layers of cloth. 'He mightn't have had much to do with women. Better to assume his stance and go as men than risk going all the way to Coombe as ourselves and then be turned away.'

I sat on the bed. I hadn't ever passed as a man before. Anna had only lent me women, one woman, Mrs Williams, who was my great favourite. Anna enjoyed her men, I knew that. To put them on wasn't just for detecting, for speaking to those who would spill their secrets more easily to men than to women. Men's clothes gave her something else. Something I wished I could give her. If only she'd let me.

'Ah – here we are!' She pulled out a pair of short coats made of a dark-blue wool and laid them gently on the bed. Then she was back to rootling.

I was handed two pairs of trousers, not breeches, for these were long. One pair was grey and the other cream. Then there were shirts and waistcoats, and a heap of white linen strips. I feared they would be tied around my neck.

She eyed me poking the strips. 'It's not just the clothes, Shilly.'

'I know, I know. It's who wears them. You're always telling me. So, who will we say we are to get Inchin Ben to speak to us?'

She took one of the coats into her lap and sat back on her heels. 'Well, the belief hereabouts has been that the man found on the beach was a sailor washed in from a wreck. I doubt Inchin Ben will have heard the truth yet. Mrs Seldon made him out to be quite the pariah, so it seems unlikely he was at the funeral.' Anna smoothed the coat's cloth along her thigh. 'If there *was* a wreck, then the owners of the vessel would make enquiries. They would send their agents.'

'Why? What good would it do once the ship had been lost?'

'I don't suppose you're familiar with the concept of insurance, Shilly, but it's a significant matter. If a ship is lost, the owners can make a claim for her value. Can get their money back. Or some of it, at least. But they need information about the circumstances of the loss to make that claim.'

'You seem to know a lot about lost ships,' I said, thinking this might be part of her past. This might be her way of telling me who she was, what had been her life after her foundling start with the butcher and his wife. For all I knew she might have been a sea captain herself. I wouldn't have been surprised.

But she just shrugged. 'Such matters are often in the papers. It's a common enough occurrence, sadly. But that will help us today. Inchin Ben will find no strangeness in such visitors as shipping agents.' She stood and held out her hand to me. 'Time to get dressed.'

My trousers were too long so she pinned them. Likewise the shirt, which bagged about my shoulders and looked foolish with the waistcoat on top, the shirt all puffed out. I wasn't made for Anna's men, and I told her so, hoping she wouldn't make me do it, for I had no wish to be rid of Mrs Williams' long red curls, her fetching mole painted by her mouth.

'Don't be ridiculous, Shilly. These clothes weren't cut for you, that's all.'

'Who were they cut for?'

'Why, for me, of course!'

But the stitches in them told another story, one I saw by detecting – the very thing she'd taught me. I saw the tucks and the darts. Anna had *made* the clothes in her travelling case fit her, using her gift with needle and thread. Because they hadn't fitted her so well before that. Because they had belonged to someone else, and who were those souls that now went without their coats of good wool, their silken petticoats? Perhaps she was a thief as well as a seamstress and a sea captain. My list of Anna Drake's talents was getting longer by the day.

The waistcoat had some curious ties on the inside of the cloth, and the trousers were made likewise too, for all down the seams of the legs were little buttons and loops. I had come across such things before with Anna's clothes. They were made to turn to purposes most other clothes didn't, and I was sure those purposes would come clear soon enough.

She bade me put the coat on then tied one of the linen strips around my neck, just as I had feared. A stock. And it was as if someone's fingers were at my throat and they were trying to crush my breath.

'It's too tight,' I said, scrabbling at it. 'Can't my shipping agent have lost his stock?'

'No, he can't. And you'll get used to it.' She stepped back and eyed me. 'I wasn't sure this would work, but you know, you make a convincing man, Shilly.'

I didn't take that as a kindness.

'It's fortunate you don't have much fat on you,' she said, and resettled the coat on my shoulders. 'Your shape is very . . .'

'Very what?' I felt I could barely get enough air to make my words come.

'Flat,' she mumbled.

'Well thank you *very* much!' I put my hands to my chest. She was right, of course. Barely anything to cup. 'It would be harder for Mathilda, I suppose.'

She was rootling in the case again and didn't answer.

'Her figure is more fulsome than mine,' I said. 'You'd have to bind her breasts.'

She took two small bags from the case. Bags of hair, I knew.

'Here we are,' she said.

'Anna?'

'Hm?'

'We must write to Mathilda today. Promise me we will.'

'Of course.' But she wouldn't meet my eye.

'I can't do it by myself yet. You know I can't. You must help me.'

'Lean forward. I must take these hairpins out.'

I did as she said, for the pins held Mrs Williams' hair in place and I couldn't very well wear that as a shipping agent. Leaning thusly meant I could no longer see Anna's face.

'Please, Anna. I need to know she's well.'

'Mathilda is in safe hands with the Yeos. You mustn't worry, Shilly.'

'But I saw her, in a dream. She was—'

'It would be harder with the three of us here, wouldn't it? And needlessly so. We're better as a pair, you and I.'

'You mean for detecting? Only for detecting we should be without her?'

A pause. My heart began to race.

She yanked a pin free. 'Got it. Of course I mean for detecting. You mustn't worry. Now, lift your head.'

Mrs Williams' hair was taken from me. In return, I was gifted a wig of black hair that hung long and ticklish to my ears. Anna put on one of yellow.

'The colours are to work with our own features,' she said, 'rather than against them. Now, the final touches.'

She got her paintbox and greased me. No redness on my cheeks and lips now, as Mrs Williams enjoyed. Instead, my eyebrows grew thicker, darker, and my lips paled. My cheeks grew whiskers, as did Anna's. I looked at my hands. Though she hadn't touched them, they looked different somehow. They didn't seem my own. And my stockinged feet likewise. A flutter came into my belly. A flutter that was good and bad, sad and keen.

'Take a turn about the room,' Anna said, and she sat on the bed to watch me walk up and down beside it. The trousers gave a strange feeling to my legs, for there was cloth sliding between them, but, I had to own, they were kind to moving. I had no bunching like I did with my skirt.

'I should think it would be easy to run in such clothes,' I said. 'Easier than skirts.'

Anna nodded, and lay back on the pillows. There was a look on her face I hadn't seen for some time. For too long. A look that made me slow my walking. Made me run my hands up and down my coated chest.

'And better to climb things too,' I said. 'Trees and such.'

I lifted one leg onto the bed and leant into the stretch. Leant towards Anna. I ran my fingers up and down my thigh. And then her hand joined mine and she reached for my trouser buttons.

'Come here,' she said, and caught me.

I let her pull me from the clothes she had dressed me in. She took my breast in her mouth, put her fingers to the part of me she knew better than any other. I closed my eyes. In that darkness, I was made a shining thing.

THIRTY-ONE

We were later starting for Coombe than we'd meant, but neither of us minded. If darkness should fall before we were back at the vicarage and we stumbled to our ruin, I found I didn't care. I didn't fear it. For Anna and I had lain together. If today was the day my life ended, so be it. I would die in happiness.

The vicarage was still quiet as the pair of shipping agents crept down the stairs. They were light on their stockinged feet as they made their way to the porch and found their boots. One of them whispered to the other, what of that letter left on the hall table for you? Who is writing to you, Anna? Is it one of your other loves, some stranger before me? But the yellow-haired man kissed his companion's words away before the front door and all was silence again.

And then the door was opened, and they were two men on their way to see about a ship. If their hands should touch as they walked, their fingers brushing as if seeking the heat and scent of each other still on their skin, well – who was to know? Only those two – a secret shared.

As I closed the door behind us, I heard a woman, sobbing, deep within the house. Mrs Hawker mourning her brother. Time for us to find Inchin Ben of Coombe, the taker of other people's luck and the finder of Joseph Ians.

We walked close to one another. Closer than we had in many months. I carried with me the feeling of her lips on my breasts. And she – did she feel, still, the flick of my tongue between her legs? She wouldn't speak of it, and that was no surprise, for she couldn't, didn't have the words. Never had done, for as long as I had known her. But that didn't matter. What was between us wasn't silence. It was speaking without words. It was breathing without breath.

It was us. It was we. And on we went, together, to Coombe.

The road took us past some large, grand houses on the way. Anna told me that the signs at their gates bore the names the driver had given me as landmarks. Stanbury and Tonacombe. Manor houses. And we passed some low houses, too, poor things of moor stone with windows no bigger than my two hands placed together. The kind I had lived in. Before Anna. I walked closer to her still. Thankful.

She took out her pipe and filled it. The air around us was soon rich with a smell I recognised.

'The parson had some of his fancy tobacco to spare, then?' I said.

Anna blew a plume of smoke into the air with great joy. 'He did! And for that I'm so thankful, I might just offer up a prayer.'

There were not many people about. Few passed us on the road, and none of them on a horse or in any sort of carriage. They were all working people, their corduroy and their worsted muddied and patched. And I one of them, hid twice over – a working woman passing as a better man.

It was a pleasant enough walk through fields and along lanes. Much better than the drop of the cliff, the wind seeking to whisk us into the sea. Much better to have the trees lining our way. But the trees were bent over, stunted things, like old men broken by work. As I imagined my father to be, if he were still living. I didn't often think of him. It laid me low. So I sent the thought away by telling Anna I knew nothing of shipping agents and would likely be no use at all in making Inchin Ben believe I was one.

'For you're always telling me, Anna, the clothes aren't enough. The wearer has to speak the right words, have the right learning for such a person.'

'True,' she said, and drew on her pipe. 'But your young man could be rather shy.'

'Oh, could he?' I said.

'I think he might have to be, Shilly. Or aloof.'

'What's that?'

'He thinks himself better than others. Takes on an air of coolness. Not friendly. Can you manage that?'

'It'd be easier than knowing about *en sur ance*.'

'I dare say it would, and a person can be crafted from silence as much as they can from their noise.'

'So they can. You yourself, Anna.'

'Take this for a stretch, would you?' She handed me her black bag that she took everywhere detecting. It wasn't heavy, but it was bulky and made difficult to hold with all that was stuffed in it.

'What have you got in here?'

'Essentials, Shilly. You'll see why later.'

'Letters?'

She wouldn't meet my eye.

'There's something in them you don't want to share,' I said. 'Why?'

She walked a little faster. 'You're right. I don't want you to read my correspondence, but that's simply because it concerns a private matter. A trifling, dull, tedious matter, but one that is mine alone. If you had letters, I wouldn't try to read those.'

'I don't get any letters.'

'But you will one day! Just because words exist, it doesn't mean you have a right to all of them, Shilly. Not all the letters in the world are for you.'

I supposed she was right. Wasn't she allowed her secrets? She had let me know her again today, in a different way, a better way, and that was all that mattered in the end.

The road sloped down and then there were more cottages, and these were poor indeed, with holes in the thatch and foul-smelling water pooled at the walls. As we walked on, there came coughing. It came from a dwelling ahead of us. We heard the burden of the lungs of the people living there before we had even passed their door. There sounded many. A whole family, perhaps. The door itself had fallen open. It looked to be missing hinges. Anna's steps slowed as we came level with it.

'What are you doing?' I said.

'Surely we should see if they need help.' She peered in the doorway. 'Hello?'

The air was bad within. It made my nose burn. I grabbed Anna's arm and pulled her back onto the road, put myself between her and the door.

'There's poor people everywhere, Anna. If we stop to help them, we'll never get to the end of this case.'

Anna shook me off. 'That's a hard line to take. What if there's someone in there who just needs a drink of water, something to help their throat?'

'And what if there is and they give you that cough?'

That stopped her going in, but she didn't start walking again.

'I'm disappointed at your lack of charity, Shilly. It behoves us to—'

A noise within the cottage made us both start.

A figure shuffled into the doorway. A man, dreadful thin, with long hair and a long beard, both these bits of him straggly.

'Forgive me, sir. I was up with the children. You've come from the parson?'

There was a light of hope in his crusted-up eyes. He had a blanket wrapped round his shoulders, and as he came closer, he leant into a corner of it to cover his cough. The blanket's colour, its weave – I knew it. It was the same as was on our bed at the vicarage.

'I'm afraid not,' Anna said. 'We were simply passing and heard signs someone was unwell.'

As this pitiful creature stood before us, these words seemed foolish. Unwell – the man was surely dying! And more of them inside, too, for the coughs above rattled down to us below like terrible rain.

'Ah, there we are.' The man shuffled back. 'He'll be along later himself, no doubt.'

'Parson Hawker? He visits you often?' I said.

'When he can, though he's none too well himself, dear of him.'

He began to cough and doubled over, and once again I saw Morwenstow's bowed trees made man before me. Anna moved to steady him, but he waved her off and propped himself against the ruined door.

'He's a good man, the parson. When he heard we was wisht again, and my youngest taken, he came on his little pony with all he could carry.'

'How kind of him,' Anna murmured. 'And what kindness may we do you?'

He looked from one of us to the other. Had Anna forgot herself for once? Forgot the kind of men we were? She had, because before I could remind her, she agreed to bring in some firewood, and so, of course, I helped. If she was taken ill, then I would be too, so I thought it the best course to get the business done quicker and so be away.

There was payment for our pains, though. Anna asked where we might find Inchin Ben.

The man was beset then by another coughing fit, which was only partly caused by his body. Part of it was shock.

'You don't want to see him,' the man spluttered, once he could speak again. 'He'll take—'

'We know,' I said. 'And we're going to see him.'

The man shook his head, as if we were the ones in need of pity. 'Along a little way. The fine door. You can't miss it. But sirs, if you do see Inchin.'

'Yes?' Anna said.

'Don't 'ee be coming back to my cottage again. We haven't any luck to spare.'

And with the little strength left to him, this poor, dying man shoved his broken door closed in our faces.

'Well,' I said, 'Captain Ians is wrong about his brother-in-law.'

We started on our way again.

'The parson might be short of money,' I said, 'but it's not just from liking that tobacco and other fine things.'

'Agreed. He clearly gives much to the poor of his parish. And they're in need of it. Ah – but not all of them, I see.'

Before us was another cottage, this one not so badly kept. Its door was closed proper but it was a strange door. The wood was dark brown and shining with oil, like it was made from the same wood as the fine furniture in the vicarage. And it was in two parts, like a stable door, but set with shiny metal and there was a curious round window, set high. I had never seen nothing like it. But Anna had.

'That wood has seen other uses,' she said.

'Where?'

'A ship. It would seem Inchin Ben takes more than just luck, Shilly. He takes wreck spoil too.'

She knocked on the stolen door. It opened at once. As if the creature inside had been waiting for us.

THIRTY-TWO

Inchin Ben wasn't as Anna had thought he would be.

He wasn't grizzled. He wasn't old at all. The youngest man we had met so far in Morwenstow, saving the driver who'd brought Anna's travelling case. I thought Inchin to be no more than twenty-five. His hair was brown and curly, his eyes were greenish. The colour of the sea in Boscastle's harbour. A quieter sea than the one that surged about Morwenstow's cliffs. And he was a quiet person, too. His voice was soft when he said yes, of course we could come in. I felt sure he would have talked to women as keenly as he would men. But luck could be taken from men and women the same, so I made sure not to touch any part of him, not his clothes even, as I passed him in the doorway. I would keep my own luck close.

He said we should go through to the room at the back of the cottage. It was made of the same fine, polished wood as the front door. The walls, the floor, the ceiling – all was made of wood. Not all of it the same shade, though, or the same lengths. It made me think of the parson's hut.

I caught my shoulder on something sharp – the corner of a cupboard, set high on the wall. They were scattered about the room. Too many for such a small space. Each of them bore hooks and hinges and handles. But no locks. The key in my pocket would be no use here. And it was easy enough to know why. No one would dare creep into Inchin Ben's house to steal, so he would have no need to lock anything away. *He* was the thief in these parts. A thief of luck.

The metal of the cupboards gleamed gold in the lamplight, for though it was only afternoon and not yet dark outside, there were many lamps lit. And all of them fine-looking ones. There wasn't a candle without a glass shade. The room was warm. My skin beneath my whiskers was damp with sweat, and I feared the sticky paste Anna used to keep them on my face would slide off, take my whiskers with it.

'Please, sit,' Inchin said, and we did so, on good chairs – narrow, they were, as if made to fit a tight space, but plenty of stuffing in the seats and fine curly bits on their backs.

I looked at how Anna was sitting, with her legs a little apart and her hands clasped between them. That was how I must sit while wearing trousers. While I was a man. I thought I should put gravel in my voice too, so I shouldn't be thought girlish. But then I said to myself, Shilly, no one has called you girlish in all the days of your life. There's no danger of that now as you sit here in trousers and whiskers.

'We're here on behalf of Goodwin Grant,' Anna said, 'a company trading out of Wapping. You have heard of them?'

Inchin hadn't, and I wasn't surprised for Anna had no doubt made them up. She was good at quick lies. Too quick, I often worried.

'We believe one of our ships was lost in these waters recently. Our task is to find if any of her cargo survived. Or parts of the ship herself.' She looked about the room. She smiled.

'And why do you think I can help you?' Inchin said, but still soft, still gentle.

'It was you that found the dead man on the beach near the vicarage,' I said, feeling this an easy thing to say. There was no difficult ship business yet. I would turn shy when that came. And what was the word Anna had said? *Aloof.* That too, if needed.

Inchin blinked several times, but didn't look away. 'I did find him, yes.'

Silence then. He was in no hurry to tell us what had happened.

'We believe,' Anna said, 'that this man may have been crew of our vessel. If you could share the circumstances of discovery, I would be grateful.'

'You could have spoken to the parson,' Inchin said. 'He'd have told you. Why come here, to my door?'

'We take our instruction from Goodwin and Grant, and that instruction is to go to the horse's mouth, so to speak. To pursue a thorough investigation.'

Silence. Those green eyes blinked.

'Forgive us for disturbing you,' Anna said.

'Nothing to forgive,' he said. 'There's not many that come calling.'

'So we've heard,' I said, and Anna shot me a look. I supposed that might be thought rude, though it was the truth. 'I only mean that, there's talk about you in these parts. About your—'

'Luck?' he said. He shook his head. 'My luck being the luck of others that I've taken to preserve myself?'

'Something like that,' I muttered.

'Would you think it luck to have no company in life, sir? To be shunned?'

'To be living at all, after being wrecked,' I said. '*That* is luck. I should think I'd be grateful for having that.'

He studied his hands. 'Ah, you would, would you, sir? I don't blame you for saying so, if you've never faced it.'

'Drowning?' Anna said.

'No, sir. The land. Seeing it, I mean, so close. So close you could all but reach out and touch it.'

And he did reach out, as if there was something before him, and as he did so the lamps flickered. All of them. Anna grabbed my arm.

'There's agony in it, to see the land, lights, houses. People too, on the cliff, watching. And none of them able to help for you're trapped, see, once the lee wind blows.' His voice had dropped to a whisper. 'There's nothing will stop a ship being driven onto the rocks once a lee has her.'

The lamps were a flicker, a flicker, and I could feel a draught blow in. A storm must have got up and the wind was coming down the chimney. But there was no chimney in this room. There was no hearth. Only the wood. The wood of wrecks.

Inchin was whispering. 'You think, I'll get up the mast. I'll tie myself on. The others there with you. And when she leans, I'll lean with her, and we'll jump clear.'

And the wooden room was no longer a room in a cottage safe on land. It was the belly of a ship. I saw how it would be, pitching in the swell, the world shaking. Thinking, this, this is how I go.

'You tell yourself, come on now. 'Tis only a few feet. You've jumped further to cross a stream.'

Shadows and light, shadows and the wind across our faces. I could taste salt. Anna was hunched into me. I held her tight. I wouldn't let her fall.

'And you want her to lean so bad, like you've never wanted anything more. And then you hear her start to go. You hear it before you feel it. The crack, like bones breaking but slow. Then she's shifting, leaning, and down you go, the land coming nearer. Your mates screaming. You can see the grass on the cliff. The little yellow flowers. And you jump.'

As if his last word was a charm, the lamps steadied. Every one of them. The room came back to itself. I blinked in the light. I expected it to be all topsy-turvy after the storm, the wood splintered, the chairs floating. And us? Torn to pieces.

But we were seated as we were before. The wood of the walls and all the cupboards was the same. Not a nick in it.

Anna wasn't holding on to me. I was holding on to her. She pushed me quickly away, for what men from shipping companies did such things?

This man that I was. A fearful man. A man who had seen a glimpse of Inchin's life, and his near death.

'And when you've lost the maziness of it,' he said, 'when you can move again, you find there's grass between your fingers. You look about you and see that you alone are saved. And that, my good sirs, is a burden like no other.'

'How many times have you escaped shipwreck?' Anna said.

'Seven.'

'And each time the sole survivor?'

He nodded. 'The others were all got by the rocks. They was as close to living as I was, as close to getting that grass between their fingers. And yet the sea chose to drag them over the rocks, back and forth, until they weren't whole men no more.'

'Like our friend on the beach,' I said quietly.

'Like our friend.'

He hadn't wept, he hadn't wailed. But in his voice was pain.

'We appreciate your candidness, Mr . . . Ben,' Anna said. 'You've clearly seen much of the ravages of the sea.'

'That I have. But the man I found didn't come in off a ship.'

'Really?' Anna said, and did a good job of finding some surprise, for of course we shared this way of thinking with Inchin Ben. We, too, believed Joseph Ians had been killed on land.

'No trace of any ship out there,' Inchin said.

'And you would be looking?' I said.

He said nothing, but then he didn't need to. The signs were all around us. We were sitting on them. And I didn't blame him.

'If you don't believe the man was killed by the passage of coming into shore,' Anna said, 'what *would* you say did for him?'

Inchin shrugged.

'Could it have been a mermaid killed him?' I said. 'That's what people are saying round these parts.'

'They are indeed, sir.'

'And?'

'And there's reason for it,' he said. 'The voice people hear when they're near the cliffs, a woman calling. It's enough to make you believe the stories.'

'What does she call?' I whispered.

'Ah, now, there's many answers to that question. Some say she calls the squire's nephew, him that left her. Some say they hear their own names called, because the mermaid knows they've lost someone close to them and she's looking to trick them. Others, they'll tell you it's just the wind.'

'Which do you think it?' I said.

The lamp nearest him had begun to smoke. He blew it out. 'There's a great many things about this world I wouldn't claim to understand. Why was I saved seven times, and all those with me drowned?'

We none of us had an answer to that.

THIRTY-THREE

But there were other things we could ask. Easy questions, about known parts of life. Safe parts. Those of clocks.

'Tell me,' Anna said, 'what time did you discover the body?'

'Early,' he said.

His face was dry when mine felt awash with sweat. It was running down the back of my shirt and I cursed my waistcoat and coat over it. I started to take the coat off, but the flappy sleeves of the shirt got caught and I was like a fish tangled in a net. Anna pinched my leg and I knew I'd best give it up. It seemed it didn't do for shipping agents to take off coats indoors.

'Could you elaborate?' Anna said.

Inchin scratched his cheek. 'Well, let me see. It would have been . . . not long after daybreak. And the poor wretch can't have been there too long before that.'

'Oh? Why?'

'Because I'd been the same way the evening before. About seven I walked that path, along the cliff, coming home from Morwenstow. He weren't there in the evening, but the next morning, first thing, coming to Morwenstow again, I saw him. Right below the parson's hut. I went straight to the vicarage to tell the parson, for he collects them, for burial. He's a good man, Parson Hawker.'

'And what were you doing on these walks?' I said.

He said nothing for a moment, then looked away, at the cupboard door nearest him. 'I was going to church.'

'Morwenstow church?' I said.

He nodded.

'But the times you say you were walking,' Anna said, 'there are no services held at Morwenstow then.'

'That's why I go.'

'Forgive me, I don't—'

He got up so quick he made his chair start back, and then went to the window. 'I go when I know the church will be empty. I must give thanks for my salvation.'

'Not chapel, then?' I said, sure there would be a meeting house closer to him than Morwenstow's church.

He bowed his head. 'They don't let me in. Fearful, they are. But the church is always open, and the parson, he's—'

'—a good man,' Anna said. 'So you've told us.'

Inchin spun round. 'Because it's true! He's shown me kindness when few would. And not just me.'

'The family a few doors away,' I said, 'them coughing. Parson has tended them?'

'More times than I can count. He'd give the Sanders the shirt off his own back.'

That might be all he has left before too long, I thought.

'Round here,' Inchin said, with anger in his voice now, 'people have little enough as it is. If the harvest is poor, if they'm taken ill, they can be dead sooner than folk like you can imagine.'

'Such suffering is a blight on this land,' Anna said. 'But some have found ways to survive in these coastal parts. To thrive, even.'

'What the Lord chooses to bring to shore is the Lord's business,' I said. My shipping agent was taken with religion, I decided.

'But it's another matter if a light is struck to lure a vessel in,' Anna said.

The lamps flickered. I wished she hadn't spoken of such a thing. It was like saying someone was a murderer, and that was taking a chance when you didn't know the person you were calling such. When you didn't know if they was really a raging person behind those cool green eyes. A man too full of luck might try anything. But Anna wasn't afraid.

'I understand a light was seen the night before the body was discovered,' she said. 'At the hut.'

Inchin didn't move from the window. 'It was still daylight when I passed that way late afternoon, and daylight again by the time I saw the dead man the next morning. Daylight alone was the only light I saw. But there was something . . .'

'Yes?' I said.

'In the evening, when I was leaving the church. There was someone there.'

'Inside?' Anna asked.

'No – the church was empty save for me. But when I opened the door, there was someone there. They hared off, soon as they saw me. I didn't think anything of it at the time, but then he turned up, the man on the beach, so badly cut, when I knew no ship had gone down. And now you're here.' He narrowed his eyes. 'Asking me questions.'

'Did you see who they were,' I said, 'the person at the door?'

'No chance to. He was all cloaked, the weather being so dirty.'

'Did you see which way the cloaked figure went once they'd left the church?' Anna said.

'Opposite way to me. I went over the stile and started on my way back here, past the parson's hut. The man went left from the church.'

'Towards the vicarage, then,' Anna said.

Inchin shrugged. 'I didn't stop to find out.'

'Why?' I asked.

'I wanted to be home before the daylight went. It don't do to be on the cliffs in the dark.'

'It is a treacherous path in places,' Anna said.

'It's not the path you need worry about,' Inchin said. 'It's what's on them. There's a good reason the parson carries his lantern everywhere with him.'

'I see,' Anna said flatly. 'And on the subject of lights, we're no clearer on that which was seen on the cliff.'

'Well that's your lookout,' Inchin said.

Anna smiled. 'Or is it yours?'

He shook his head. 'You've asked me plenty questions today, sir, and I've helped you best I can. Now I got a question for you in return.'

'Have you indeed?' She looked at her nails.

'I have. Was this light moving?'

Anna and I shared a look.

'No one has said so,' I said. 'Far as we know it was fixed.'

'Well, then,' Inchin said, 'it wasn't used to lure a ship onto the rocks. No ship's captain worth his salt would plot a course by a still light in a storm.'

'Why not?' I said.

'Because he don't want to come into shore. That's where the most danger lies. He's safer in deeper water, isn't he? Wait it out. And if he should lose his bearings, he'll make for a *moving* light, because a moving light means—'

'Another ship,' I said. 'Because a ship is always moving, even if

209

it's stopped in the water. The water around it never stops jouncing about, so the ship jounces likewise.'

'It does,' Inchin says. 'A still light is no light for a wrecker.' He leant against the wall and folded his arms. 'But I would have thought agents like yourselves would have known that.'

It was time to take our leave.

THIRTY-FOUR

'For someone who claims not to do any wrecking,' Anna said, once we were away from the cottage, 'Inchin Ben seems to know quite a bit about how one might go about it.'

The sky was all dark clouds. The wind a damp breath on the back of my neck, chilling my sweat.

'I don't think Inchin claimed *not* to be a wrecker,' I said.

'No, you're right, Shilly. He didn't say one way or the other. But he did say a great many other useful things. If we take Inchin at his word—'

'Have we any reason not to?'

'Not that I can see. So, if we believe him, we now know that Joseph Ians was killed between dusk and daybreak.'

'That's a goodly length of time, Anna.'

'True, but it's something. And the light – if it *was* moving, if someone here planned to draw a ship onto the rocks and wreck it, then perhaps Joseph saw something he shouldn't, and that's why he was killed.'

'I let you down with the light business,' I said, feeling very low. 'Me showing Inchin that I didn't know ships would only follow a moving light in a storm, it ruined the disguise.'

She clasped me round the shoulders. 'You'll get better at not showing your hand.'

'I'm sorry all the same.'

'It takes time, that's all. Look at me, having to get used to . . . well, you. The things you see.'

'You're getting better. You don't tell me I'm foolish so often. Or blame the drink.'

'Can't blame drink when you've given it up, Shilly.'

'Which I *have*!'

'I know. So that means that now you're just you. No . . . *diluting*.'

That one was new.

'By which I mean watering you down,' she said. 'Like poor beer.'

'Oh. That's good then, is it?'

She laughed. 'I'd say so.'

'And you believe me about the woman I hear calling? The woman who might be a mermaid.'

'I do, though I wouldn't claim to understand it, and I can't believe Mrs Hawker is a mermaid, Shilly. I know you think her voice is the one you've heard calling, after hearing her sing at the funeral, but it can't be true. She's as flesh and blood as you or I.'

'I don't know what to think any more.'

Anna held me close as the wind sought to take me from her. As the air grew wetter.

'But it's not just me,' I said. 'Others have heard the voice. The barman at the Bush, he told me people hear it all the time on the cliffs.'

'Perhaps someone *is* out here,' Anna said. 'Someone with

something to shout about. And speaking of the Bush – we need to find out if the light seen from the hut was moving. It was Captain Ians who told us of it in the first place. Let's see if he has any further insights.' She glanced at me. 'You will be all right, going back there?'

'I had no trouble yesterday, did I?'

'That you didn't.' She squeezed my arm. 'But if the temptation should become too much, just wait for me outside. It shouldn't take long. Better a little wet from the rain than risk undoing all your hard work.'

'It is hard,' I muttered.

'I know.'

By the time we passed the manor houses again, dusk was closing in and the rain was hard upon us. My cheeks felt the heaviness of wet whiskers, and my hair, too, was heavy. Wigs were not so good in the rain as real hair. I was glad when the Bush came in sight, and not for the reasons I had felt in the past when making for inns. Today I wanted only to be dry. I had no longing for the inn's waters.

Anna went in first and I was following when I caught sight of a familiar face on the path that ran between the inn and the cliff, and coming this way. Nancy Seldon.

She was a little way off and hadn't seen me. She was walking into the rain, her head held high, as if she was enjoying the cold. No shawl or hat. She was twenty paces from me and bearing towards the inn. I didn't think she would go inside.

Anna had not come out to find me, so I guessed she was talking to the captain, likely thinking me fearful to join her because of temptation. I would put her right when she was done, but for now it was hard to look away from Nancy, though the rain had me wetter by the moment. Her every muscle seemed to strain into the wind, her mouth open, her jaw working, as if she was eating the weather.

I shrank back into the doorway of the inn, which hid me, and then I remembered I was not myself that afternoon – I was a shipping agent. A man. So I could watch Nancy if I wished, for men watched women all the time without fear. It seemed to be their right to do so, when they chose to see us at all, and so I watched her, and I wondered.

Her hair looked to be soaked, wetter, surely, than the rain could have made it. Her dress too – the cloth dark with water in patches. She must have been in the sea. Was Nancy afflicted as I had been since coming to Morwenstow? Did she hear a voice on the wind and find she had risen from her bed, her chair, left the hunting of flowers on the cliffs? If she did, then she was able to resist the thing I feared most – that I would get into the water and be drowned, or torn apart by a clawed creature, for here was Nancy walking by the cliff alone, daylight nearly gone. Here was Nancy, coming home.

She passed me. She neither turned to see me in the doorway nor gave the sense she was purposefully ignoring me. I did not think she knew I was there. Should I call her?

Then the door banged and Anna was at my side.

'The captain was just back from a walk, fortunately, though he couldn't—Shilly, are you quite well? You look like you've seen a ghost.'

'A ghost? Not that.'

Anna frowned.

'It's nothing,' I said. 'What did the captain tell you?'

'He couldn't say if the light seen at the hut was moving.'

'That's a pity,' I said.

'He didn't see it himself, of course. But he did advise me of who we should ask about the matter. The name of the person who told him of the light in the first place.'

'And who was that?'

'Mr Seldon.'

THIRTY-FIVE

It was late by then. Too late to call at the farm to ask Mr Seldon about the light he had told the captain of. That would have to wait until tomorrow, so we started back towards the vicarage and as the cloth slipped between my legs I remembered how I was dressed. As a man.

'I can't go back like this,' I said. 'The Hawkers will think a stranger has come into the house!'

'They will. Which is why you won't be going very far as you are. And neither will I.' Anna tapped the black bag we'd carried all the way to and from Coombe with no need, until now, to open it. 'The church will do.'

I half wondered if we would find Inchin Ben in the church, but he wasn't there. No one was, but still we chose a dark corner to change ourselves. That time of day, the church had more darkness than light. And it was cold. I didn't want to take my trousers off, but Anna said I must.

'It won't work otherwise,' she said.

'What won't?'

'This.' And she ripped my trousers in half.

'Anna! That's so wasteful! We'll never have money for the agency if you do such things.' I still had on the shirt and waistcoat and coat on top, but my lower half was quite free. I stood in just my drawers and shivered.

'Oh, ye of little faith. They're not ruined, Shilly. Quite the opposite, in fact.'

And I saw that the cloth hadn't been torn. She had just pulled apart the hooks that ran down the seam of each leg. The trousers had become a single piece of cloth.

She knelt behind me and wrapped the cloth around my waist. It fell to the ground.

'Stand still while I do you up.'

Her fingers moved nimbly from my waist down my legs as she did the hooks up again, but this time only one set, so the cloth became a skirt.

She took off my coat. 'Now, tuck your shirt and waistcoat into the skirt.'

I did as she said. She walked a circle of me, hitching the skirt higher on my waist. From the black bag she took pins and pinned the skirt tighter, so that my waist was small and what was left showing of the waistcoat looked like a bodice, for of course it matched the print of the trousers that were now a skirt. Then she took a shawl from the bag and tied it over my shoulders, which hid all the shirt save for the collar and the cuffs. My hair was in the black bag too, or Mrs Williams' hair, rather, and her red lips and the mole that sat by them. Anna put me back together and changed her hair to that of Mr Williams.

'You won't put his clothes on?' I said. 'The things he has been wearing most days?'

I was thinking of Mr Williams' cream coat, where she had stowed the letter that had come to the vicarage.

'I didn't bring them. Mr Williams can get away with this more fashionable ensemble, just for getting up the vicarage stairs.'

The agents' wigs went back in the bag with my coat, which she folded carefully to fit. And we were ready.

As we left the church, I told her she was very clever to make clothes work so many ways. For men's things to become women's.

'Would that I could make more than men's clothes work for us, Shilly,' she said sadly.

I kissed her. But it wasn't enough.

The vicarage was quiet on our return. It was dark, too. I fell over something in the porch. As I picked myself up, my fingers found glass – a little pane. And round it, something hard and smooth. Bone, was it? I lifted it back to where it had been, propped up against the wall – the parson's lantern. But no light it gave us tonight. There was only one lamp left burning in the hall, and that turned low. Anna carried it as we sought something to eat, and the light made the house a sea of shadows that we swam through.

The long table in the dining room was empty, the cloth unmarked. If the parson and his wife had eaten supper, all was put away. Mrs Seldon had gone home to the farm on the other side of the churchyard, I guessed. We were free to wander as we wished. I found some bread in the kitchen and we warmed it over the fire's embers. Mrs Seldon had forgot her knitting. The wool was a puddle of lumpy blood on her chair.

As we crossed the hall and started up the stairs to bed, Anna said, 'Under other circumstances I would fear our hosts thought us rude not returning for supper.'

'And for going off all the time. For having private business.'

'That too. But with Joseph Ians identified, the Hawkers have much to occupy them.'

'Have we done them a service, us coming here, or given them a curse?'

'I suppose that depends on your point of view, Shilly. If the truth brings opportunity or merely pain.'

'Or both,' I said, thinking of the ship shares, thinking of the earnings of the ship.

'The least we can do tonight is ensure we don't disturb the Hawkers' slumber.'

We had reached the landing. There were no lights left burning upstairs. The passages that led away were dark mouths. Anna lifted the lamp brought from downstairs and our door loomed before us. All at once I had a strong need to get on the other side of it and shut out the rest of the house, the rest of Morwenstow, the sea beyond. To be in a very small place where I could see all the walls at once.

'Shilly!' Anna hissed. 'You're catching at my heels.'

I kept as close to her as I could without jumping into her arms. My hand was on our door.

A sound. On the landing behind us.

I was all for rushing into our room but Anna had the light and she turned away. Towards the sound.

A rustle, of paper? Drawers opened and shut. And a man's mutter.

It was coming from the corner of the landing. The parson's locked room.

'Shilly, look – a light under the door.'

As I looked at the strip of light it grew larger, for the door was opening! The sea was all around us then, as if someone had taken a great gulp of spray and blown its salt on us. And then there was a pair of stockinged feet in the light, and a hefty set of legs, and the long brown gown of Parson Hawker.

It was he who screamed, thinking us devils, of course.

When he saw we weren't, just his house guests who spent more time out the house than in it, he began to breathe again. And shut the door of his secret room behind him.

'Forgive me,' he said. 'I was . . .' He shook his head and the candle he carried shook likewise, sending waves of shadows across his jowly face and the pencil tucked behind his ear.

'It is we who must beg forgiveness,' Anna said. 'Startling you so when you have urgent business to attend to.'

'Business?'

'That which keeps you from your bed so late,' she said, and nodded at the door to his secret room, now closed on us.

As if her words had reminded him, he quickly locked the door, then put his hand to the wood and gave a great sigh. With relief, that whatever was inside was safe from us?

'My dear?'

We all three jumped at that, but it was only Mrs Hawker, coming to see what the upset was about. I caught a glimpse of her face before the parson swept her back down the passage, wishing us a night of good rest. She was pale as the moon, apart from her eyes. They were red as Mrs Seldon's knitting wool.

Anna and I went to our room then, at last, and I made to lock it, but there was no lock to do so!

'You were closer to him than me,' I said to Anna in a whisper. 'Did you see anything in there, before he shut the door?'

'Only a piece of furniture. Or a dark shape that *could* be furniture. A bureau?'

'Wreck goods?' I said.

'Ah, you smelt it too, then.'

'You mean the sea water?'

'I thought it fishier than that,' she said. 'The parson loves his cats, doesn't he?'

'So?'

She set the candle in the window and I thought of false lights. False lights that needed to move to do their dark deeds.

'*So*,' Anna said, 'the parson might keep the cats' food in that room.'

'But why be so creeping about that? Fish for cats is no crime.'

'Not for most people, I'll grant you, Shilly. But the parson is a peculiar individual.'

'He is, but . . . I think there's more to the parson's room than that, Anna.'

She climbed into bed and the creak was dreadful loud. 'Something connected to the death of Joseph Ians?'

'It could be,' I said. 'Even Nancy said she never sees in that room and she's here all the time.'

'Why aren't you getting into bed, Shilly?'

'There's no lock on this door.'

'And do you think we need one?'

'If she should call me, if she should say my name . . .' My words turned to water with my sobs.

Anna sprang from the bed. 'You're not getting out of this room, Shilly. Not if I have anything to do with it.' And with no care for the shriek it made, she dragged the chair from the corner and wedged it under the door handle. 'There. If you try to move that in your sleep, I'll know about it.'

'And you'll stop me?'

She put her arms around me and led me to the bed, as I had dreamt for so long that she would. All those cold and lonely nights in Boscastle, fearful she would never love me again.

'Of course I will. No harm will come to you while I'm here, Shilly.'

My sleep was warmed, and quiet, knowing she believed me.

* * *

I woke in the night, but not from a woman calling me to my end. It was my needing to piss. That call I didn't mind. When I tucked the bowl back under the bed, I caught sight of Mr Williams' cream coat hanging on the end of the bedstead. Anna was still asleep, her head mostly hidden under the coverlet. I reached into the pocket of her coat.

The letter she had stowed there was gone.

Had she known I would try to read it and so hidden it, burnt it? What was it she didn't want me to find out?

Anna's letter might be gone but I would have another – a letter for myself. I would write to Mathilda. But I had no paper, no ink. No matter. I would choose the words tonight and then in the morning I would write them down. Somehow, I would find a way, even if Anna gave me no help.

I got back into bed and thought to begin. But what was the way to start a letter? What came first? My name. Mathilda would want to know who the letter was from so I would first write *Shilly. Shilly is writing*. And then Mathilda's name, so she would know it was for her. *Shilly is writing to Mathilda.* My eyes had closed. I quickly opened them. What to put next? *I am not asleep. I am thinking of you. Are you better now? Can you come to Morwenstow?* I yawned. *I am not yawning. I am awake. Mrs Hawker is kind and will speak German with you. I am awake. I am awake.*

THIRTY-SIX

The sun woke us, for in the surprise of Parson Hawker coming out of his secret room the night before, we'd forgot to draw our curtains. But it was good to rise early, Anna told me, as she slid from my arms.

'We can catch Mr Seldon at the farm before he starts for the day.'

My head was heavy as Anna's travelling case, and felt as tightly packed too. I buried my face in the pillow and spoke into its soft crush. 'Why do we need to go to the farm? I've forgotten . . .'

'*Because* Captain Ians said it was Mr Seldon who told him of the light on the cliff. Someone was out there the night Joseph was killed. It might be the *same* someone Inchin Ben saw fleeing the church. If we can find that person, we might have our murderer. The light is where we must start.' She laughed. 'I sound almost biblical. The parson must be having an effect on me.' She put her hand gently, almost fearfully, on my back. 'You didn't try to get out of the room last night. She didn't call you, the woman you hear?'

'No. I got up, but it was only to piss. Then I wrote to Mathilda.'

Anna sat up sharply. 'You have ink and paper? Who gave them to you?'

'No one. I don't have them, Anna.'

She slumped back against her pillow and though she tried to hide it, I could see she was relieved at this.

'But what would it matter if I did?' I said. 'You've taught me writing. Well, some of it. You could be teaching me more.'

'We have been rather occupied, Shilly.'

Had we? I did feel weary. Perhaps we had been working hard. Perhaps she was right and it was because there was no time, that was why there hadn't been any lessons since Boscastle. Not another reason. Not because she didn't want me to learn, to write my own letters. To stop me reading hers.

'I wrote my letter in my head,' I said, 'to Mathilda. I have the words.' What had I chosen? *I am awake. I am awake.* And then I had fallen asleep, and my dreams . . .

I pressed my face deeper into the pillow. My dreams had been me turning on a hook in Mr Yeo's cold room again, back in the butcher's in Boscastle. Mathilda had been weeping somewhere nearby, but I couldn't go to her.

That morning in Morwenstow I couldn't speak such things to Anna. They were too bad. If I spoke them, they might be made true. Let the dream be one of them *hal oo sin a chuns* Anna said I would have from giving up the drink. The sip I'd had in the Bush had set it loose. Let it not be the other thing. The thing that was me seeing the truth askance. The truth hidden. The truth to come. Dear God, let it not be that.

Anna patted my shoulder. 'It's looking to be a beautiful day.'

She wasn't wrong. The sun streamed through the big window at the turn in the stairs and I stopped to look at the world through it. The world made green and gold and flashing with light. Morwenstow was a beautiful place sometimes.

That was when the parson caught us.

'A fair morning, at last.' He was at the bottom of the stairs, tapping the weather-clock again. He was dressed once more in his blue jersey with the red stitched mark of the spear that had pierced Jesus's side, but today he'd added a bright-green hat woven with specks of silver, like all the stars had fallen from the heavens onto his head. His little pencil, worn to praise Jesus who had been a carpenter, was half tucked inside the hat, the writing end grazing his ear.

Anna and I carried on down to meet him. He was a different man to the one we had seen the day before, the one who had lain on the floor of the church, overcome by the task of burial. His colour was up and he fair danced with some unspoken business.

'With the demands of the funeral, I've not had the chance to thank you, both, for your efforts in identifying my wife's brother.'

'It is Captain Ians you must thank,' Anna said. 'He was the one who invited us to your parish.'

At mention of the captain's name, the parson fell to looking at his nails, like a boy who'd been told off and knew such a telling was the right one.

'I have been unduly harsh with Frederick, I see that now. It was him making poor Mrs Hawker so upset that caused it, and I couldn't think that Frederick's claims could be true – that he should have dreamt his brother's fate.'

'It is somewhat fanciful,' Anna said, but she could say no more, for the captain *had* been right.

'And Frederick's belief that it could be Joseph at all,' the parson said, 'that Joseph should be returned to his home, after so long away!'

'What do you make of that, Parson?' Anna said.

'Why, that the Lord has a plan for each of us.' He smiled. 'After the follies of his youth, Joseph Ians was brought back to the home he spurned.'

'And died doing so,' I said.

The parson nodded as if this was great wisdom I had spoken. 'The Almighty's punishment is just, Mrs Williams. My wife has yet to come to this point of view, but she will, in time. And you will help her, I'm certain.'

'It would be our pleasure,' Anna said. 'If we may trespass on your hospitality a few days more? Now that we have discovered the truth about poor Joseph, my wife and I would like to explore the parish.'

For we couldn't leave yet. We had only half the truth so far. Half of our money still to earn.

'Of course!' the parson said. 'This is excellent news.' He stepped towards the dining room. 'Come – Nancy is just putting out the breakfast.'

'We must forgo breakfast, I'm afraid,' Anna said.

'Nothing wrong, I hope?' He sounded true in his concern.

'Just a small matter my wife and I must attend to in Bude.'

This the stirrings of a lie, of course. I hoped the parson wouldn't ask us too many questions. He looked as if he would, but then Nancy was at the door to the dining room and he wished us a pleasant day. We were out the door, at last. But we weren't going far. Just across the churchyard to the Seldons' farm.

The farmhouse faced the church, the rest of its buildings clustered behind it, as if the farmhouse was a mother hen, the sheds and the barn her brood. As we drew close, I heard the cows. A sound I had lived my days by on the moor, where I'd met Anna. These cows were louder than the rooks. It was good to have some change from the birds.

Anna knocked. And knocked again when there was no answer. I was thinking we would have no luck learning of the light Mr Seldon had seen, but then a dog barked somewhere, and Mr Seldon himself came round the side of the house. He didn't look near so pleased to see us as he had when he was cleaning the church. This morning he smelt of cows, their dirt and sour milk. The dog had followed him. A dusty-coloured thing with long ears. It looked old as its master.

''Tis early for callers,' he said, and stepped between us and the door.

'Forgive the intrusion,' Anna said. She seemed always to be asking for forgiveness. That was a weary word for detecting. 'Could we come in?'

'My wife tells me you been to see Inchin,' he said. The dog growled. Mr Seldon rested his hand on its head.

'That's not why we're here,' I said. 'We need to ask—'

'Can't let you in if you been to Inchin. We're calving, see. Can't risk it.'

But that wasn't why he wanted to keep us out. There was something else. Something in the house. I knew it, sure as I knew my own name and how to spell it.

Anna looked to swallow a few different replies to Mr Seldon's fear for his cows, before settling on, 'Of course,' said tight and unwilling.

He wanted us gone. That would be how we'd get answers from him. We had nothing to bargain but that.

'We don't want to keep you,' I said, 'and we won't have to if you can help us.'

'We're trying to discover the last moments of Joseph Ians,' Anna said.

He would not ask us why, for that would make us stay longer. A noise from within the house. A chair, scraped on the slates. He looked quickly at the door. Anna took a step closer to it. The dog growled again, Mr Seldon shuffled backwards, but Anna stood firm.

'I gather you told Captain Ians that you saw a light that night, at the parson's hut.'

'I did.'

'When was that?'

'Close to ten, I should think. Now, I must be getting off.'

'And the light,' I said, 'was it moving?'

He eyed us both, quickly, slyly, for he knew what that question meant. He knew we were asking, did someone set that light on the cliff to draw a ship onto the rocks in bad weather?

'You know how bad the weather was that night?' he said. 'The storm. I couldn't tell what was sky, what was water out there. All I know, I told the captain, and now I'm telling you. I seen a light on the cliff.'

A flash of blue in the window nearest the door. Someone had walked past it, inside. Mr Seldon saw me looking.

'If that's all,' he said, 'I've got to ring the bells for service.'

'It isn't all,' I said.

'Earlier that evening,' Anna said, 'towards dusk, did you see anyone near the church?'

'I saw the parson leave,' Mr Seldon said. 'Then Inchin come. I've told the parson he shouldn't let that man in the church.'

'Are you regular at church yourself?' I asked. 'Beside the cleaning and the bells. For worship?'

Another pause. 'Of course I am.'

'I'd think you'd have to be, really,' I said, 'being sexton, your wife and daughter working for the parson. You'd have to be *church*, rather than anything else, for you all to keep your work.'

He coughed. 'There was another there that night. As Inchin

was leaving there was someone by the door, and Inchin scared 'em away, as he does.'

'Did you see which way the other figure went?' Anna said.

'I thought he must be going to the vicarage, but then when Inchin had left, the other man went round the side of the church, going back on himself, to the stile.'

'Did they climb the stile and go across the fields?' I said, thinking of the parson's hut just a little way further.

'I didn't see,' Mr Seldon said. 'I had to keep my eye on Inchin going across the fields and it was the last of the daylight. I had to make sure he didn't come anywhere near here, didn't I?'

'That would have been unlikely,' Anna muttered. 'The poor man seems to understand very well the animosity towards him.'

'But you never know with him,' Mr Seldon said. 'He would creep and then—'

'The person who went to the stile after Inchin,' I said, 'what did they look like?'

Mr Seldon shrugged. 'I couldn't say.'

The dog gave a yawn, which turned into a whine, then dropped to the floor, as if its old legs had been pulled from under it. With its head on his front paws and eyes closed, it looked quite dead.

'Could you at least tell us what the person wore?' Anna asked.

'Something heavy, for the wind was up, wasn't it? Been terrible dirty, the weather. A big old coat, with a hood.'

Which was the same as Inchin had said, but I didn't think Mr Seldon would like to be told he was in agreement with the man who stole others' luck.

'What about the person's features,' Anna said. 'Did you see if they were old, young?'

'I couldn't say nothing on that, what with his face being covered.'

'Covered?' I said.

'With a scarf or summat. What with that and the hood, a wonder the man could see anything. Now, I'll thank you to let me get on—'

The front door opened, and there was singing.

THIRTY-SEVEN

Mrs Seldon stood in the doorway, her clothes changed from those she wore while working in the vicarage. Her apron was gone. She wasn't the one singing and thank the Lord for that. The singing was from the others in the house. The others still hidden.

She looked aghast to see us on her doorstep and quickly shut the door behind her. The singing softened, but left a scrap on the wind, almost a taste, it was, if sound could have a taste. Warm, and thick. Like good bread. It wasn't the call of the sea. It wasn't a call to drown a person.

Mrs Seldon took her husband's arm. 'We—I, *I* was wondering where you'd got to. And now I see we got visitors!' She kicked the door with her heel and at once the singing stopped.

Should we try to go in? I wondered. Press Mrs Seldon's manners, for we were guests of the vicarage, after all. But seeing her standing there, gripping her poor husband's thin arm fit to snap it, I couldn't be so cruel. Let us get what we needed and so away.

'We were just asking your husband about the light he saw on

231

the cliff,' I said, 'the night before Joseph Ians was discovered. Your husband's been very helpful.'

She glanced at him.

'Did you see it too, Mrs Seldon?' Anna asked.

'I didn't see nothing. The weather, it was—'

'Yes, I know,' Anna said. 'What is it you say in these parts? It was *dirty*.'

'Well it was! I wasn't going out in that, and I had no need to.'

The dog scrabbled to standing and began wagging his tail, and then there came a footfall behind us. Anna and I turned.

Nancy was in the road. She must have been coming home from the vicarage, and on seeing us stopped. She carried a basket propped on her hip.

I hailed her, said how fortunate it was we should be speaking with all three of them together.

'Isn't it?' Mrs Seldon said, and licked her lips.

'Parson can spare you, then?' Anna said.

Nancy shrugged. 'I got the dinner done, ready to be put on, and the mistress . . .'

'Is she down at the water?' I said. 'Parson told us she likes to swim still.'

'I couldn't say. What she does is no business of mine, is it?'

And no business of ours either, that was the unspoken part.

'It's understandable Mrs Hawker would want some time by herself,' Anna said. 'Given the news of her brother.'

Anna and I stood between Nancy and her parents, Nancy and the house – and what was going on in there. I could guess.

'You knew Joseph Ians,' I said.

Nancy nodded, shifted the burden of the basket at her hip.

'You must be grieving too, then,' I said.

'For Joseph? It's been a long time since I seen him. More than

232

half my life gone since then. I'm sorry for the mistress, though, and for the captain. They've took it bad.'

'But they will all be reunited in the next world,' Mrs Seldon said, and seemed to stand taller with the words, her husband too. Even the dog knew the call of the Spirit for he raised his head and stared at me.

We asked Nancy about the light too, for why not make a set?

'Your father says it was close to ten when he saw it,' Anna said.

'I was in the vicarage until nearly midnight,' she said. 'I saw no light on my way home.'

'That's late,' I said. 'What kept you so long from your bed?'

'The parson,' she said. 'He'd got it into his head to take some things to a family in Coombe. They been very poorly.'

'The Sanders?' I said, thinking of Inchin Ben's coughing neighbours.

'That's them. Parson had me turning out the cupboards for blankets and potted meat. All the socks the mistress had knitted. The ones Mother done too. It was all to be taken to the Sanders the next morning, but then Inchin come early to say there was a dead man on the beach, and . . . Well, then you came.'

'And here we are!' Anna said, and smiled.

Silence then, and in it, loud the creak of a floorboard behind the door.

'We should be on our way, my dear,' I said, and took Anna's arm.

The relief on the Seldons' faces was so great, I nearly laughed. It was like we'd told them they wouldn't be hanged.

Mr Seldon hurried past us in the direction of the church. Once Anna and I had reached the road, there was the sound of the Seldons' door opened then shut, quick as you like, then I heard the bolt slide home.

'They're a fearful lot,' Anna said.

'You would be too if you'd lose your work because of your praying.'

'You're certain of it, then, Shilly, that the Seldons are Methodists?'

I nodded.

'Well, let them have their meeting and sing their hymns,' Anna said. 'They're not doing any harm, though the parson would have us think otherwise.'

'They're doing harm to Inchin Ben,' I said. 'There's cruelty from them that's chapel, and kindness from the parson in the church.'

And as if the parson had heard us talk of him, the church bells rang.

'Well, we know where the parson is for the time being. Once the service has finished, we'll ask if he, too, saw the figure fleeing the church.'

'Both Inchin and Mr Seldon believe that person to be a man.'

'They do indeed,' Anna said.

'I don't see why they should. Neither of them saw anything of the person's face or their body to know such a thing. They've just decided it to be so.'

'That's because *they* are men. They see the world through men's eyes.'

'And what of the man we're going to see now? The one we told not long ago that we were going to Bude, which must be some way from here.'

'I'm sure the parson will accept our change of plans, Shilly. We'll tell him our trip concerned the matter of the charitable ladies who might look favourably on his cause.'

'With Joseph Ians dead and Mrs Hawker getting his shares

in the ship, the parson might not need our ladies now.'

'Something tells me Parson Hawker will always be in need of charitable ladies,' Anna said.

And so we had ready our lie.

THIRTY-EIGHT

But a lie wasn't needed, for when we went into the church, the parson was most pleased to see us.

'The Lord welcomes you, my friends!' he called from the pulpit.

I could see at once why he was so pleased – there was no one else in the church to hear him preach, save the cats. They were scattered about the front two benches, sleeping or licking themselves, or having a good scratch of the benches' wood. My Most Righteous Cat shared the pulpit with the parson, as if *he* was preaching, and the parson *his* pet! Then I spied Mr Seldon towards the back. There because he had to be, I guessed, as sexton, to keep his job. His heart would be back in the farmhouse with his wife and daughter, and those singers.

I sat in the row behind the cats, for they were there first so it was only right, and Anna joined me. The parson started talking and kept on for a good while. His words swum in and out of my head, and they were all long and unknown to me. Anna and I said our Amens when bid, and stood and sat likewise, and all the while I was thinking of the Seldons' farm so close by, and others there with Nancy and her mother – a house full, praying, while the parson's church was empty. I glanced to the back of the church. Mr Seldon was asleep.

At last the service was over. The parson stepped down from the pulpit and came to sit with us. The cats climbed about him, putting their tails in his face, their cheeks on his hands. Here was love. Did he need more than that in his church? It seemed he did, for he was low in spirit at the empty benches.

'You see how it is,' he said. 'I offer the chance to know the one true God and it is spurned.'

'There was plenty at the funeral,' I said.

He nodded, but with sadness. 'There was indeed, Mrs Williams. The end of a life draws the penitent souls, especially burials of those washed in to shore. It is the nature of living so close to the sea, I think. It is always on our minds here. But the daily word of our Saviour . . . Well. You see how it is.'

The door opened then softly closed. Mr Seldon on his way back to his cows, his duty done.

'Mrs Seldon and Nancy don't join you?' I said.

'When they can. But the demands of the vicarage and the farm weigh heavy on them.'

Do they indeed, I thought, but what I said was, 'I should think you could have a rest instead of doing a service. If no one's coming, you could be napping here with the cats and no one would mind.'

He gave a sad laugh at this. 'I could, Mrs Williams, I could. But my sacred duty is to redeem the souls of this parish. The services are said for them, though they may not be in church to hear the words. I spent much of last night working on that sermon too.'

'My wife and I enjoyed it very much,' Anna said. 'A stimulating set of ideas.'

The parson beamed. 'Well – that *is* gratifying to hear. If a humble man of the cloth might beg your indulgence.' He looked at her from beneath his long, girlish eyelashes, shyly. 'May I ask which area *particularly* spoke to you?'

Anna's face drained of colour and her mouth hung open. She hadn't thought to be so pounced, had been lost as me listening to the long strange words of the service.

'There is so *much* to commend, Parson. How to begin . . .' She looked to me, but of course I was no help. She had started down this path. She would have to get herself away from it. 'That is to say, the tenor of your words, the *gravitas* . . .'

'Accorded to?' He leant forward, all eager, a child awaiting a prize.

'To the . . . the, ah, mystery of faith?'

Inchin Ben had left her some luck for the parson was delighted by this guess.

'Ah! You appreciated my use of the Nicene and Athanasian formularies.'

'Yes . . .'

'I thought you might.' He nodded to himself. 'I knew you to be a clear-sighted man, Mr Williams.'

'One recognises a kindred spirit,' Anna said.

'Ah – you are too kind! And what are your plans now, on such a beautiful day as this the Lord has gifted us?'

'We had not thought, had we, my dear?'

I shook my head. ''Tis such a change to see Morwenstow in the sun, and after the dreadful dirty weather we've had.'

'You are quite correct, Mrs Williams. It has been *foul* along this coast. Quite, quite foul.'

'The night Joseph Ians likely met his death was the worst of it, I think. That was a rough night to die.'

'Indeed, though we are sadly used to such weather here.'

'When did it start, the storm?'

'I'm not certain . . . By the time I left here after evensong it was blowing strongly.'

'Did you see anyone else when you left?' I said. 'Anyone in the churchyard you weren't expecting?'

'I don't think so, though I will admit I didn't tarry on my way back to the vicarage, the weather being so bad.'

'You didn't have to go out in it again, I hope, once you were home?'

My Most Righteous Cat jumped onto the seat next to him, and the parson scratched him beneath his chin.

'Heavens, no, and I pity any who did. I had much to occupy me at the vicarage that night. I had heard, you see, that some of my parishioners in Coombe were unwell – dangerously so. The typhoid came there last year and I feared it might have returned.'

'Gracious!' Anna said.

I had been right to fear entering the Sanders' cottage. Well, it was too late now. Perhaps we'd die in Morwenstow and the parson would bury us next to the dead sailors.

'The family I feared for,' the parson said, 'the typhoid took the mother, you see, and I know the father finds it difficult. Eight children, no – six now, the two littlest taken. None of those the Lord saw fit to spare are well enough to work.' He shook his head. 'I did what I could, scoured the vicarage for supplies. I must confide in you, my good Mr and Mrs Williams, that Mrs Hawker fears I give too much away. She does, doesn't she, my sweet?' And he kissed the top of My Most Righteous Cat's head. 'But she was early to bed that night, so Nancy and I could empty the cupboards without my beloved fretting.'

'This parish keeps you busy,' Anna said. 'It's a wonder you have such strength, Parson, you being so late to bed seeing that your flock don't go cold and hungry.'

He grasped her hand. 'You are right, sir! Right! But what choice do I have when the poor would suffer even worse hardships? That is my duty.'

'And Nancy's too?' I said. 'She stayed with you until late that night? What a godly soul she is.'

'Ah no, you must not think so bad of me as that. I kept Nancy only a little while. The storm blowing so hard, she feared for her father's cows so near to calving. She was anxious to get home, so I granted her that. I sought out the socks alone.'

'And what time was this, Parson?' Anna asked.

He stopped scratching the cat's chin and frowned at her. 'I don't know that I can recall . . .'

'I only ask for Nancy's sake,' Anna said. 'She has made a request of us, you see.'

'A request? Whatever for?'

'She has some relation – what was it, my dear?'

Anna turned to me, and as if her quickness of lying was catching like the typhoid, I heard myself say, 'A second cousin. On her father's side. An orphan. With a bad eye. And her leg is—'

'That was it.' Anna turned back to the parson. 'Nancy has asked if my wife and I will consider taking into our household this cousin who is without a friend in the world, it seems. Nancy tells me the girl is a hard worker, and godly, too. But before we commit ourselves, we would know of Nancy's character, to better gauge the recommendation.'

'Can we trust her?' I said.

'Oh, without a doubt!' the parson said, and took My Most Righteous Cat into his lap where the creature rolled about. 'If Nancy says the girl is worth having then she will be, despite her afflictions. Nancy herself would have stayed longer with me the night of the storm, sorting the things for the Sanders, but I could see she was distracted by the weather. So I sent her home not long after the clock chimed ten, I think it was. Or was it eleven?'

'You didn't keep Nancy with you until the day was ended, then,' Anna asked, 'until midnight?'

'Heavens no! I might have been up that late myself. I can't now remember. Once I have a notion to do something, I can think of little else. Mrs Hawker says it is like a fever. Much of my poetry is written in this way. I have been meaning to share some of my lines over supper. Tonight shall be the night.'

Then the bells rang again and saved us. The cats stretched, jumped to the floor, began to march towards the door as if the bells were their sign to leave.

The parson took a watch from his pocket, looked at it, then put it back. 'Mr Seldon always rings on time. Now, you must excuse me. I have something I must attend to at the vicarage.'

'Of course,' Anna said.

Was he going to his secret room again? We stayed where we were, and when the door was shut behind him, Anna spoke her thoughts aloud.

'How interesting. It would seem all three who were in the vicarage on the night before Joseph Ians was found have time that cannot be accounted for.'

'Nancy left the vicarage before the parson had finished with his socks and all that business, though we can't be sure when. He wasn't certain, was he?'

'No, but the effect is the same even without the exact time – Nancy's departure meant the parson was alone and so could have gone out to the cliff. Mrs Hawker, too, is without anyone to speak to her movements.'

'We know that both the Hawkers have reason to want Joseph Ians dead,' I said. 'Both would gain.'

'And Nancy? What would she gain?'

'Nothing that I can see.'

We made our way outside. There was the vicarage to the left, the deadhouse to the right. Between them the graves spread before us, all their leaning stones and slates.

'Let's go back a stage,' Anna said, 'to the figure seen fleeing the church just before dusk. Two people have now told us of this figure – Inchin Ben and Mr Seldon.'

'Could the figure have been Joseph Ians?'

'It's a distinct possibility. Was he waiting to meet someone here, but found Inchin Ben instead?'

'Meeting who?' I said.

'That I don't know. Let's put that to one side for a moment. Put it in your pocket in your head, Shilly.'

'All right. Let's say Joseph Ians was meeting *someone*, but it was Inchin came out of the church. Joseph ran away, towards the vicarage at first.'

'That fits with what Mr Seldon told us,' Anna said.

'When Inchin was gone, on his way back to Coombe, Joseph set off in the same direction.'

'Mr Seldon saw the stranger go to the stile, so that works too.'

'But what if Joseph didn't go so far as Coombe?' I said.

We looked at each other, but it was Anna who put the thoughts into words.

'The hut is the only structure on the cliffs between here and Coombe.'

'You think Joseph went as far as the parson's hut and there saw something he wasn't meant to?' I said.

'It's possible. What if Joseph saw the parson himself, readying a false light at the hut to draw a ship to its end on Morwenstow's cliffs in the hope the cargo would end his money troubles?'

242

'But the parson suffers for those who die here. Why would he seek more bodies for the deadhouse?'

'Money, Shilly. It can make a man do anything.'

And a woman too, I thought, remembering the argument with Mathilda, the way Anna had made us practise thrift in our spending. Remembering the letters.

'If Joseph Ians *did* stumble across someone setting a false light,' Anna said, 'that could be a motive to murder him. The description of the stranger would seem to support this reasoning. Inchin Ben and Mr Seldon said the person's face was covered.' Her false teeth began to tap. 'Which must mean that whoever it was feared being recognised, that they *weren't* a stranger in these parts. It could have been Joseph. Even after all the years he'd been gone, he might have feared some would know his face.'

'And we know he had a reason to return to Morwenstow,' I said. 'He had his earnings from *The Eliza* to collect.'

'Speaking of which, there is someone we have yet to speak to on the matter of the ship shares. Mrs Grey, the widow at Coombe. Captain Ians' mention of her having had the pox hasn't encouraged me to call. However . . .'

'What makes you keener now?' I said.

'Because of what's on the way to Coombe, if we go along the cliff, that is.'

My stomach pitched at the thought of being so near the cliff again, and I had to lean against the church wall. 'I think I can guess.'

THIRTY-NINE

We passed no one else on the cliff path, for which I was grateful. My spirits were low, being so close to the sea again, fearing a voice calling me, and I didn't think I should be good at lying if we were to meet a soul who called for such a thing. I made Anna go between me and the cliff edge, and she held fast my hand against my destruction.

By the time we reached the hut the wind had risen. Not a lee wind that would drive a ship onto land. This wind was rushing *off* the cliff, blowing hard out to sea. Wanting to blow us away. Anna went first down the steps, and I went after on my hands and knees, my face turned from the water. Keep low, Shilly, I said to myself. Make yourself low and hunkering as this hut the parson has built into the cliff and which has stood heaven knows how long, and you'll not be lost today.

'You know, Shilly, walking backwards means you're more likely to end up going over.'

'I'd like to hope you'd catch me first.'

'This wind might make that difficult.'

She held open the door of the hut and was using all her

not-very-much weight against it to stop the wind tearing it off. I scuttled inside and then she nipped in, fastening the door tight. It was gloomy in the hut. The only light came from round the door, where the planks didn't fit the jamb snug. We had to stand close together for it was narrow, and the roof was low. A place only large enough for one fat parson to sit and write his poems.

'We should have brought the means to make a light,' I said. 'We'll never see anything in here.'

'A sad irony when a light is what we're looking for.'

'Well, at least there's not too many places *to* look.' I made out I was peering close at the hut, turning to each wooden wall and saying oh yes, I see, oh yes.

'You'd never do on the stage, Shilly. I know you want to get away from here. From the edge.'

'Can you blame me?'

'Of course not. The way you've felt since we got here . . . I can see the toll it's taken. You look like you've barely slept since we left Boscastle.'

And with her words I felt it then, my weariness. Bone-deep and heavy as a ship washed onto its side, washing in. I sat down on the bench that ran around the edge of the hut, where the parson must sit likewise. I wondered if I'd ever get up again.

'You do the looking, Anna. I must just rest my eyes.'

I lay down, best as I was able, the bench being so narrow. The wood was cold and damp beneath my face. Anna was searching the hut, noisy as if she was charging about some huge place, when really she was only turning around and poking the walls. Her voice swung in and out of my hearing.

'No sign of it . . . hardly surprising. An open fire? No, the weather was too poor . . .'

And between her words, the waves. I gripped the bench beneath me, for we had begun to pitch.

'A flare. No – too quick.'

My hands at the mast. Holding tight, but I knew soon I'd have to let go for she was bent too low in the water. The wood wet beneath my fingers.

'Some sort of brazier?'

My fingers were stiff, were claws. They were pressing into the wood when I should have been letting go, making ready to jump. The rocks were coming. But my fingers were locked now, pressing the wood, which gave way.

There was a hole in the bench. No – a *line*. Carved in it. My finger was following it. And another line joined to it. This second had a curved tail.

I sat up and crashed straight into Anna's elbow. When I had shook myself back to thoughts, I shouted that she must give me her hand.

'Shilly, whatever's the matter? Did you hear her again, calling you?'

Anna spun round, as if about to charge out of the hut and over the cliff, to swim out to find this woman.

'No, here!' I said. 'Come here!'

I laid her hand against the part of the bench where mine had been, set her thumb in the carved line I had felt. She did not understand so I moved her hand for her, as if I were helping her to write as she had helped me. Or doing something else. Something we did together with each other's hands.

She looked at me, with the same startle she did when we *were* doing that thing, when we lay together.

'J,' she said. 'Carved into the wood. A letter J.'

'J for Joseph,' I said. It was no bigger than a sixpence, and set right at the edge of the bench. So easy to miss it, as we had missed it the first time we'd come to the hut.

She tore her hand from mine and ran her palm across the bench. After only a heartbeat her hand stopped.

'There's another letter. A different one.' She ran her finger over the shadowy tracks in the bench. 'A sea.'

'The sea? I don't—'

Now it was her turn to take my hand and help me find the shape in the gloom of the hut. She set my fingers in the carving and then I knew – the letter C.

'C for Charlotte,' Anna said.

'You think Mrs Hawker carved this?'

'Well, who else in these parts is C? And remember the letters of the tattoo. That was a J and a C as well.'

I sat down on the bench again, this time next to the letters rather than on top of them. 'But why?'

'A means of remembering her brother, gone from home for many years? She's not allowed to mention him to her husband. Perhaps she comes here when he's off doing the Lord's work.'

I ran my hand over the letters. J and C. 'She's done them very small, hasn't she?'

'So that the parson wouldn't see them, presumably.'

'Then why make them here at all? Mrs Hawker could carve any old bit of wood she liked. Why choose the place her husband has for himself?'

Anna shrugged. 'Some need to go against his wishes, to rebel, but not in such a way that would cause her lasting problems. Or perhaps . . .' Her false teeth clacked. 'J and C. Could it not be the parson's own work, for Jesus Christ? We need more light.' And she was opening the door. She pinned it with a rock and the wind raced inside and I felt all a whirl in it.

The clouds had cleared and the sun streamed in so I could see, but I couldn't stand.

'Anna, please – can we go? I don't like it here. I don't feel safe.'

But she didn't seem to hear me, was staring past me to the bench where the letters were.

'Well, would you look at that.'

I did look, for there was such wonder on her face, such as I had previous seen on other faces at chapel. The sun shone full on the plank where the letters were carved. It was a short plank, shorter than all the others. And the gaps between it and the other planks was larger than anywhere else on the bench. Almost as if—

'It's a lid,' Anna said.

We took one end each. The plank lifted.

That was when we found our light. Hidden inside the bench. A lantern, fixed on a long metal pole that had at its end a wicked-looking stake.

Together we lifted out the lantern. It wasn't as heavy as the parson's, the one he used to keep the devils away.

'It's been used recently,' Anna said. 'See the mud on the stake. It's been driven into the ground.'

'Don't touch it – it's sharp!'

'We need to take it outside,' Anna said. 'There's too little room to see properly in here.'

'Anna – wait. There's something else.'

I reached around her and grabbed the scrap I had seen at the bottom of the box. 'It's paper. But thickened. Can you move? You're in my light.'

'This is hopeless. Let's get outside.'

She took the glass end, I took the stake, but wrapped my skirt over it to be sure I didn't cut myself. The lantern was like a rope, keeping us joined as the wind raged. Together we carried it back up to the cliff path and set it down by the thickety bush that grew around the hut.

'Anna, look – the glass is dirty. I don't think it can have been used for a goodly time, even with the mud.'

We crouched beside the glass. I lifted the lantern's box into my lap so Anna could see it better. She opened the door and poked her fingers inside, then gave a crow.

'That's not dirt, Shilly. It's paint.'

'Well, that's a waste. No use to anyone, a painted lantern.'

'Ah, but it's useful if you only paint three sides. Look.'

She turned the lantern's box over, and I saw that one pane of glass was clearer than the others. Much clearer. It shone.

'Whoever used this wanted to direct the light to a specific place. Where's that paper you found? I have a feeling it's—Yes. Just as I thought. It's been painted. The same black as that used on the glass.'

'But why?'

'We need to find where it was used.' She stood and looked about her.

'It's too heavy to move easily,' I said, and she helped me to my feet. 'I don't see how this could have been a moving light.'

'I agree, and it's likely that whoever used it, they must have done so close by. Who would want to be dragging this around the cliffs in a storm?'

Who indeed? That was still a question to answer.

Now that we knew what we were looking for, we found the hole easily enough. It was on the first step down to the hut, looked like the hole of a rabbit until we knew better. Together we lowered the stake in, but the lantern wouldn't stand up, kept pitching forward. I thought of the mast of a wrecked ship, leaning down to the rocks. I shook the thought away. You are on land, Shilly. No one's ever going to make *you* go out to sea.'

'Strange,' Anna said. 'The hole is the right size, it's in the right place to be the light that Mr Seldon saw.'

She gave the pole a shake, and as she did so it turned, and the stake seemed to find purchase in the ground. The lantern stood straight. We took our hands away.

'It's like a lock and key,' I said. 'It'll only face one way, and that's towards . . . Oh.'

We stood either side of the lantern and looked in the direction the clear pane looked. And there before us was the vicarage, and the Seldons' farm.

FORTY

'We've been thinking of the light the wrong way,' Anna said, 'assuming it faced out to sea, and all the time it was pointing in land. Whoever used this lantern, their aim wasn't to draw a ship onto the cliffs.'

'I'd say it was the last thing they wanted, the glass painted like it is.'

'The light might not have been moving along the cliff path, but I'd warrant it was flashing on and off, with this card the doing of it.'

She held the painted card against the clear pane, then took it away. Did the same again. I thought of the light showing, not showing. 'This light was used as a signal, Shilly, but for what?'

'Calling to someone at the vicarage or the farm.'

'It seems likely. And who was that, I wonder?'

We put the lantern back where we had found it, and the plank to hide it. No sense letting anyone know what we'd discovered. Then the bench was a bench again. No one would know there was anything beneath it. Did the parson know? Was the lantern his? J and C for Jesus Christ. J and C for Joseph and Charlotte. Either seemed likely.

Anna led the way back to the cliff path. 'Even if the light wasn't used to draw a ship, it's still possible that Joseph Ians was killed because he saw something here that he wasn't supposed to. He might simply have been an innocent casualty of some greater plan.'

'And on a night when he just *happened* to be back in Morwenstow after all those years away?' I said. 'And the captain just *happened* to have a dream in which he saw his brother's death? There must be some join between all these things, Anna. Whatever took place here, Joseph was part of it.'

'But what *was* his part? Setting a light? Finding one? Or did lights play no part and it really was just the Lord's plan all along?'

'You don't believe that for one moment,' I said.

She laughed. 'You're right. I don't. But I *do* believe we're right in going to see Mrs Grey. She has a stake in *The Eliza*. For that reason alone, we need to speak to her.'

'And then?'

She took my arm. 'Then we might need to pray.'

We had passed Mrs Grey's house the day before, when we went to see Inchin Ben, but hadn't known it. She lived in a fine house at the start of the straggle of cottages that was Coombe, the end nearer to Morwenstow, so we didn't have to pass the coughing Sanders again. As Anna knocked on Mrs Grey's door, I thought I heard the coughs on the wind. I would rather have heard the mermaid's call than that.

There was the sound of bolts drawn back, a few of them, and then a key turning. Mrs Grey's door had been fastened tight against the world. The door opened, but only a crack. It was a girl standing there, and her apron told us that she did for Mrs Grey, that Mrs Grey was moneyed enough to have other people open her door.

Anna gave our names and said we would like to make the acquaintance of the lady of the house. The girl turned back to the hall, as if there was someone else there, someone we couldn't see. Then she turned to us again.

'My mistress isn't seeing callers today. She's not been well. I'm to say that to strangers. That she's not well enough to come down.'

'I'm sorry to hear this,' Anna said. 'But I would hope my wife and I wouldn't be thought strangers for too long, given that we are friends of Captain Ians. He has asked us to call on his dear friend Mrs Grey as he is indisposed at the present time. You may have heard—'

'About his brother? Him being dead?'

'A sad affair,' Anna said. 'But the captain—'

Captain Ians must have been talked of regular in this house for he was like a key – the door opened and the girl said we should come in and wait in the parlour. Her mistress would come shortly. I felt in my pocket for the other key I carried with me. The one found inside Joseph Ians. We still didn't know what door *that* opened.

The house was not so large as the parson's – not so many rooms, I guessed, and them smaller, the ceilings lower. But the rug in the parlour was deep enough for my boots to sink into it, and the covers on the chairs were very soft.

'Mrs Grey doesn't seem a poor widow,' I murmured to Anna.

She nodded and picked up a little creature with a long nose made of metal, a shiny yellow metal. 'I shouldn't wonder if this is gold.'

The door opened then, and she quickly set the creature back in its place.

'Good afternoon!' said the lady.

She was old in her bones but moved freely, with no stick to aid

253

her. She was likely still fair, with thick hair caught up in bright pins, and her eyes not so sunken that their blue was lost. Fair, were it not for the marks the pox had given her. All around her mouth they were, the red braggaty spots. But they were healing. I'd seen enough of the pox to know that.

'Forgive us for calling without a formal introduction,' Anna said, and held out her hand to Mrs Grey, as men do. I knew she wouldn't want to, for fear of catching the pox, but I guessed the pay owed us by Captain Ians gave her the strength. 'And when you have been so unwell.'

Mrs Grey was wearing gloves. Indoors. Had the pox attacked her hands?

'Any friend of dear Frederick's is a friend of mine.' Mrs Grey pressed my hand and the braggaty marks at her mouth moved with her smile. 'Please, sit.'

We did as she said, and there were a few heartbeats of silence, which were terrible sharp. I didn't know what to say, and Anna didn't seem to neither. Mrs Grey's face was so wretched and yet she'd let us in and so we had to speak of it. I wouldn't be the first, though.

In the end, Anna and Mrs Grey spoke together.

'You must forgive my appear—'

'I'm so sorry to see—'

And that did the job, for we all laughed a little and then I found that I could speak.

'You're not so bad as you were, I think?'

'You know this affliction well, Mrs Williams. In truth, I am much recovered. My appetite has returned and I can get up and down the stairs without needing to lie down. If only my skin would follow suit and return to its usual ways.' She fussed with the skirt of her dress – a lovely silk, still deep black. No browning crepe for her. 'But perhaps my skin won't go back to how it was,' she said quietly to her knees. 'This might be the way of things now.'

I didn't want to sadden her so I didn't say what I knew to be true, that though the redness would fade, her skin would be always marked. It had been a bad poxing. I'd seen plenty. Instead I told her that we were guests at the vicarage, and Anna added that we were helping Captain Ians find an answer to a *delicate matter*.

'It seems your household has heard the news about the man found dead beneath the parson's hut,' Anna said.

Mrs Grey nodded sadly. 'My little maid Sarah told me it was Joseph. I didn't want to believe it. Is it true?'

'I'm afraid so,' Anna said. 'That's why Captain Ians hasn't called on you since returning to Morwenstow. He is—'

'Devastated, I should imagine,' Mrs Grey said. 'Poor Frederick. And poor Joseph too.' She took a handkerchief from her sleeve and wiped her eyes. There were real tears there. I saw the shine of them.

'Frederick sends you his very best wishes,' Anna said. 'He will call on you soon, but in the meantime he has asked us to convey his apologies.'

She waved this away with her handkerchief. 'There is no need for him to think of me at a time like this. He thinks too much of others. Always has. But that is his nature, and if you are helping him, then your souls must be as good as Frederick's.'

Or being paid.

'You know the Ians family well?' I said.

'Yes, or rather . . . I used to. James – Frederick's father – I knew since I was a girl, and his dear wife Suzanna became a good friend. We aren't many in these parts, as I'm sure you'll have gathered. To like one's neighbours is fortunate. To love them is a blessing.'

'James Ians remembered you in his will, I understand?' Anna said.

'He did, with *The Eliza* shares. Though he had no need. My

husband left me well provided for. Ah, Sarah – thank you.' The girl had brought in the tea things.

So Mrs Grey really didn't want for anything.

'And you knew the Ians children?' I said.

'The boys—' She laughed. 'The *men*, I should say. They were both so young when they left that I still think of them as wearing short trousers. Frederick would always call on me when he was back in Morwenstow, though not so much of late. And Joseph, well . . .' She took the cup Sarah held out to her. 'In some ways, he has been dead for years. I'm sure that sounds dreadfully cruel.'

'Not at all,' Anna said. 'He's been gone a very long time. But Mrs Hawker – Charlotte – has remained here, of course. Do you see her often?'

'Not as often as I'd like. The parson . . . You said you're staying at the vicarage?'

'We are,' I said, and it was my turn to take a cup from Sarah. So thin, the china! The light seemed to shine through it. 'He's a strange creature.'

Mrs Grey looked relieved by these words. 'I try to visit Charlotte when he's not at home. It makes things easier. One doesn't like to be pressed.'

'Pressed?' Anna said.

Mrs Grey shifted in her chair, as if all at once seeking to escape it. 'I wouldn't like to speak poorly of him. He's a good man at heart.' Sarah was heading for the door, was closing it behind her. Mrs Grey watched her go, then was all at once frank. 'It is the *money*.'

'Ah.' Anna set down her teacup. 'We have faced such entreaties ourselves.'

'It is most difficult, because the man will not let the matter rest, even when it's made clear to him that the subject is closed. I don't know how Charlotte can bear the embarrassment.'

'Because she loves him.' The words were out of my mouth before I could stop them. I quickly drank some tea but that didn't help for I slurped it with noise.

'My wife is something of a romantic,' Anna said, and I saw that she wasn't cross with me. She was trying not to laugh.

'Would that the world had more such people in it,' Mrs Grey said.

'Indeed!' Anna said. 'You've been to call on Mrs Hawker recently, I gather?'

This question surprised me, and I wasn't certain how Anna's thoughts were moving. Mrs Grey was likewise surprised.

'I've been too unwell to venture outside,' she said.

'Forgive me,' Anna said. 'I had heard that you were near the church, the night before Joseph Ians was discovered. I assumed that you were visiting the vicarage.'

At this, Mrs Grey's cup dropped from her gloved hand. It wasn't that *she* dropped it. It was as if her whole body shrank from Anna's words and the cup was left behind, in the air, and so it fell. The fine china smashed to pieces, the tea a puddle betwixt them.

FORTY-ONE

At once the girl Sarah was back in the room, as if she'd been waiting outside, expecting such a doing. She didn't speak, didn't ask her mistress if she was well, but fell straight to clearing up the broken cup. None of us said anything while this was happening. I felt, and I was sure Anna felt the same, that we should wait. That Mrs Grey needed this moment to find her words.

Sarah stood and asked Mrs Grey if she'd like a fresh cup, and Mrs Grey said no thank you, that would be all for now. But between the old woman and the girl, something else was said, without words. *Are you all right? Yes, for now. Don't go far.* And the girl left.

'Forgive me for causing you distress,' Anna said, 'but several people have told us they saw a hooded figure at the church late that afternoon. The person's face was covered. It was you, Mrs Grey, wasn't it? You were hiding the marks of the pox.'

She nodded but wouldn't meet Anna's eye.

'Why were you at the church that afternoon?' Anna asked.

'I . . . I don't know. Truly.'

'But that makes no sense,' Anna said. 'How can you not know why you had gone somewhere of your own volition?'

I could see the sense in it. The truth was there in Mrs Grey's pallor, in the many locks at her door, in the girl's care of her mistress. In the gloves.

'You went to the cliff path because your feet were not your own,' I said. Both turned to look at me, Mrs Grey's eyes wide with surprise. 'Because you were drawn from your chair, from your house. Set to walking when you didn't wish to. Because your name was called.'

'She calls you too?' Mrs Grey whispered.

I nodded and gripped the underside of my chair. Speaking of her now might bring her. Would she take us both?

I kept my gaze on Mrs Grey, but from the corner of my eye caught Anna looking between the pair of us. There was a time when she would have swiftly put an end to this kind of talk, or stopped me talking so in the first place. But not now. I had been right too often.

'Do you know who she is?' Mrs Grey said, her voice barely there. '*What* she is?'

'I have an idea,' I said.

My words were a charm I didn't know I'd cast, for they drew Mrs Grey flying towards me from across the room.

'Please, you must tell me! Why does she come? What does she want from me?' Mrs Grey clutched my shoulder and began to sob. 'I cannot bear it any longer!'

'My dear,' I said to Anna, 'I think it would be best if you left us ladies to talk.'

Anna looked pleased by this. She thought she was escaping to the safe quiet of the hall. But I had work for her to do.

'Come, kiss me before you leave.'

Her hand was on the door. 'I do not wish to intrude any further. I'll just be—'

259

'Kiss me!'

She did as she was bid, which was no end of difficult, for Mrs Grey was pressed into my other side, sobbing into my dress. With the widow thus blinded I gave Anna the key I had carried since we'd found it in the ruin of Joseph Ians' chest. As she bent to kiss me, I whispered to her.

'Try every lock you can find.'

Then I made Mrs Grey sit up for I had something she must hear. I told her to listen very carefully. I told her that my husband also knew of this woman who could draw people to her by calling their name, and that there were sometimes signs as to why some people were called, why some weren't. I told her that my husband was to be given the run of the house to search for these signs, that it would help us understand what was happening.

'Of course, of course,' Mrs Grey said, and wiped her face on her sleeve. 'Whatever you need, you must have it. I would do anything for answers.'

'You'll tell the girl to leave my husband be while he searches? And tell anyone else in the house too. He must not be watched.'

She called Sarah and told her this. Did the girl fear we were Gypsies, thieves? I would have thought such a thing, had I still been in service as she was, and had I cared about my mistress. But she could say nothing. Her mistress had told her what she must do. Anna nodded at me, then hurried from the room, leaving me and Mrs Grey alone.

I might have lied about the signs Anna was meant to find in the house, and about having answers too. But I didn't lie about what had happened to me. I told Mrs Grey of the first time I heard the voice, while still in Boscastle, and about the woman I had seen swimming there. I told her of the call that was on the wind, in the sea. I told her how my body was not my own after that, and she nodded at this.

'At first, I wondered if it was the Lord,' Mrs Grey said, 'if the feeling was what it meant to be called home, for I was rising – up up up! I was *glad*. But then I found myself close to falling over the cliff and I knew it wasn't the Lord's work, for why would He wish me to drown myself? It was then I had the new locks put on.'

'They've kept you safe?'

'Yes, but not without pain.'

She took off her gloves and her nails were as badly split as mine had been after I had tried to claw my way out of the bedroom at the vicarage. On her right hand, much of the skin across her knuckles was torn.

The ceiling creaked. Anna, I thought, going room to room with the key. Anna, what have you found?

'How is it that you hear her?' I asked Mrs Grey.

Her poor, hurt hands clutched one another. 'When I am close to sleep, I find I can hear the sea, but the house isn't close enough for that to be possible. The sea doesn't sound here. You cannot hear it now, can you, Mrs Williams?'

I shook my head. There was only the creak of boards above us.

'But when my eyes grow heavy the sea creeps closer, and I hear the waves breaking. In the pause between each one, she is calling. She calls my own name!'

She fell to weeping again, and there was salt water in the room, as if the sea really had come to Coombe.

'That's when my body rises from my bed,' Mrs Grey said, 'when I am not myself. My thoughts go dark, as if I am already in the water, and then my mind is empty until I wake. The terror of that moment – not knowing where I am, that is the worst of it.'

'Made so much worse by the nearness of the cliff,' I said.

'Ah, but it's not just the sea she calls me to. Sarah found me with my face pressed into a basin of water in the kitchen. Inches deep only, but she had a job pulling me free.'

'Enough to drown in.'

'Why does she wish that for us, Mrs Williams? I've tried to live a good life, a Christian life. To my knowledge I've never harmed anyone. Why is this happening?'

Her poor ragged face was drawn with pleading, and what answers had I truly?

'I don't think it's about sin, Mrs Grey. I think it's something else, something . . . stranger. Older.'

I told her of Captain Ians' dream, of his certainty that a woman had been part of his brother's death. I told her what I'd learnt from the barman at the Bush, too.

'You believe we're being plagued by a . . . a *mermaid*?'

'Yes,' I said.

'But why?'

'Because this one is a beast. She's full of rage for what the squire's nephew did, leaving her. It's only some of us wretches who can hear her, and fewer still driven to destroy themselves by her. It's those of us who've lost someone, someone we loved very much. Who is it that you've lost, Mrs Grey?' I asked gently.

She closed her eyes and sucked in her breath all at once, sharp. 'Jane – my daughter. Last year, it was. My only child. Just a little fall, they said – her horse took fright. But she hit her head and Thomas, her husband, he wrote that the sense was knocked clean out of her. Slurring she was, and she couldn't move herself. When I got up there, to Plymouth . . .' Mrs Grey wiped her eyes. 'Well, when the end came it was a mercy.'

I took her poor hurt hands in mine. 'I'm so sorry.'

'And you, Mrs Williams? Who have you lost?'

Mathilda said a voice loud in my head. A voice that was and wasn't my own. Was the here and now and the then and the still-to-come. Was the dreams of me hanging on a meat hook in a butcher's shop back in Boscastle, my poor girl weeping somewhere nearby.

Now it was Mrs Grey's turn to take my hands in hers.

'Don't upset yourself, my dear. There's no need to say. We're the same, you and I. We share a loss, and a curse too, it seems. Though I can't believe it's . . . well, a *mermaid*.'

'You don't believe me?'

'I have a better notion,' Mrs Grey said, her voice hardening. 'I know why *I* can hear the voice.'

'Really? Why?'

'Because she's ill-wished me.'

'The mermaid?' I said.

'No, no. The one who works at the vicarage. The older of the two. I don't know her name, but I see her there when I call on Charlotte.'

'You mean Mrs Seldon?'

'That's her. She's done this.' Mrs Grey stood up, purposeful now. Her wailing uncertainty gone. 'I'll have her blood drawn. They say that's how to do it, don't they? How to end a curse.'

'Mrs Grey, what are you talking about? Why do you think Mrs Seldon's ill-wished you?'

She looked at me as if I was mazed. 'Because she was there that night. When I was on the cliff.'

She was opening the door, calling to Sarah, and I had to get her to tell me. I rushed to her side.

'When was this, Mrs Grey? It's important.'

'After I saw Inchin outside the church. I was going to go home. I wanted to, but—'

'Start from the beginning.'

'You're right, dear Mrs Williams. I must. I'd fallen asleep, late afternoon it must have been. The voice drew me from my chair and set me walking, and the door wasn't bolted so I went as far as the church stile before I woke properly. I felt so weary, I thought I'd go into the church for a little rest, but Inchin was there, and I couldn't bear for him to see my face. I hid from him, and when I saw he'd started for Coombe I planned to do the same myself, letting him get far enough ahead of me before I set off. But she'd taken all my strength and I couldn't walk.' As if the weariness had returned now, Mrs Grey leant against the door jamb. 'Then the weather turned.'

'You were out in the storm?'

'Dreadful it was, but I couldn't get myself home. That's when I saw her, near the parson's hut in the dark. Mrs Seldon. Why else would she be out there if not for ill-wishing?'

'Why indeed?' Anna said, now in the hall.

'Sarah found me, thank the Lord, and helped me home. I've not been out since.'

At the sound of her name, the girl was back, hovering at her mistress's elbow.

'Ah, good girl,' Mrs Grey said, and reached for her. 'Help me now, up the stairs. I must rest.'

'Mrs Grey – wait,' I called. 'When you saw Mrs Seldon at the hut, was there a light? Did she have a lantern?'

'No, no light. That was how she crept up on me, for the ill-wishing. You'll know someone who can help me put a stop to that, Sarah, won't you? You'll get her blood drawn for me.' And then to us, over her shoulder she said, 'Forgive me. Give dear Frederick my love, won't you?'

We saw ourselves out.

'Well, well,' Anna said, 'it seems Mrs Seldon hasn't been

completely honest with us. Telling us she didn't go out that night and yet now we have a witness who saw her, and at the parson's hut!'

'A witness we can trust?' I said.

'I think so, for all her recent . . . wanderings.'

'I been wandering likewise, Anna, and you're trusting me.'

'I am, and I see no reason not to put the same faith in one who suffers alongside you. Added to which, Mrs Grey has no motive to kill Joseph Ians that I can see.'

'And Mrs Seldon?'

'Let's see what she has to say for herself. Oh, and you'd better have this back.' She handed me the key. 'It had no home at Mrs Grey's.'

'The farm seems more likely now, doesn't it?'

And so we made our way back there. Mrs Seldon would have to let us in the door this time.

FORTY-TWO

Mrs Seldon was surprised to see us back so soon. All was changed since we'd last been there, for she showed no caution when she opened the front door and led us into a big downstairs room. There was no sign there had been a gathering earlier that day. No teapot on the table, no cups with dregs to speak of the drinkers, the singers. No piles of plates bearing crumbs. No sign that the fire had been lit, even. Nothing. But we knew.

Anna and I took the settle by the hearth and I got straight to the matter at hand for it was time we were leaving Morwenstow. There was Mathilda to think of, and the woman standing before us, making out she was polishing a spotless milk jug, she'd led us a merry dance.

'Why did you lie to us, Mrs Seldon?'

The milk jug slipped but she caught it before it fell. 'Lie to you, Mrs Williams? I don't understand.'

'You told us that on the night before Joseph Ians' body was discovered, you didn't go out to the cliff. The weather was too bad, you said. You were glad to be at home.'

'And who's been telling you otherwise?'

'Mrs Sally Grey of Coombe,' Anna said. 'She saw you out there that night, at the parson's hut. What were you doing, Mrs Seldon?'

She set the jug down on the table, purposeful, like she wouldn't be rushed. When she looked at Anna her chin was tucked in, her shoulders straight. She was the most certain woman in all of Cornwall as she stood in her farmhouse on that April day.

'Who are you, truly?' she said. We gave no answer. 'You might have fooled the parson into taking you in, letting you poke about in other people's business, but I don't owe you anything.'

'How funny that you should mention making a fool of your employer,' Anna said. 'Given that said employer is, after all, a minister of the established church.'

'I don't see what's funny about that.'

'No,' Anna said, 'I don't suppose you would, given that your family are dissenters.'

She didn't move an inch, but she was shaken by this. Her gaze was not so haughty now.

'You've made your home a meeting place, and in sight of the church!' I said.

Anna turned to me. 'What was it that Parson Hawker called John Wesley, my dear, can you remember?'

'The great *for nick ay tor*,' I said, but slow, for the word was a tricksy one. Much like the parson thought Wesley, leader of Mrs Seldon and her singers.

'Indeed.' Anna turned back to Mrs Seldon. 'Such a colourful turn of phrase. We have been minded to tell the parson of the outrage occurring on his doorstep. It seems only fair, given his position, that he should know of vipers in his nest. For that's how he'll see your family, Mrs Seldon. You know I'm right.'

'You wouldn't,' Mrs Seldon said, and leant against a chair. Her knuckles were white.

'We would,' Anna said. 'Unless you tell us what you were doing out on the cliff that night. A small price to pay, I'm sure you'll agree.'

We let her sit down and sort her thoughts. There was no sense rushing her now that we were so close, for we were, weren't we? Mrs Seldon was about to confess to killing Joseph Ians, then we could tell the captain, collect the pay and be gone, back to Boscastle and Mathilda by nightfall.

'I was on the cliff that night,' she said. 'I'll grant you that. I saw Mrs Grey out there too. Thought she'd lost her wits, the way she was shouting into the wind. Just being out there in that weather was madness.'

'And yet you were out there,' Anna said. 'Did you see Joseph Ians?'

Mrs Seldon shook her head.

'What about a light near the hut?'

Another shake.

'Why *were* you out there?'

'I was looking for Nancy,' Mrs Seldon said quietly.

Nancy?

'But she was with the parson,' I said, 'helping him sort things for that poor family in Coombe. Wasn't she?'

'She was, but . . .'

Anna drummed her fingers against the side of the settle.

'But she was so late coming back,' Mrs Seldon said, with a great sigh like a wave falling. 'And with the weather so dirty I was fretting. My husband said perhaps she'd gone for one of her walks on the cliff, like she does sometimes, but I couldn't believe that. The wind so bad. I couldn't sleep for wondering if something had happened. So I went down there myself.'

'To the vicarage?' I said. 'What time was this?'

'Coming on to midnight. The parson was still awake. He said she'd left hours ago.' There was fear in Mrs Seldon's voice. Was it the memory of how frightened she must have been then, hearing that news from the parson? Fearing her daughter might have been hurt in the storm? Or fear now, as we sat together before her hearth, at what these words meant?

'Then your daughter has lied to us too, Mrs Seldon,' Anna said. 'She told us she *was* at the vicarage until almost midnight. Just around the time you say you called there only to find she was hours gone. Now, why would she lie about her whereabouts on that night?'

'I . . . I don't know.'

'I think you might have an idea, Mrs Seldon,' Anna said. 'Not at first, perhaps. Once she came home, did she tell you where she'd been? No, I see that she didn't. But when news came of a man lying dead beneath the parson's hut, I think you began to wonder if Nancy had seen him, *done* something that night involving him.'

'She's never said anything about him.'

'But some of her clothes have gone missing, haven't they?' I said, thinking of the violence done to Joseph's body. The blood there must have been.

Mrs Seldon looked as if she'd lost a great deal of blood herself, so pale she was. 'I . . . I won't say no more. You asked me what I was doing on the cliff and I've told you.'

'You still don't know, do you?' Anna said. 'You don't know if she did do something wicked that night.'

'But you fear it,' I added.

Mrs Seldon covered her face with her hands and sobbed.

Anna was asking Mrs Seldon where Nancy was, saying that we had to speak with her. I was up and looking for the stairs. If Nancy was in the house and had heard any of our talk, she might be thinking to run, for it looked bad for her now.

269

There were only two rooms upstairs. The first I opened had a man's clothes hanging on the back of a chair – Mr Seldon's, I guessed – and the furrow of two bodies on the bed. I knew the other room had to be Nancy's. The door was shut. I pushed it open gently, ready to bar her way if she was there, if she'd try to get past me.

But the room was empty. A narrow bed, a narrow shelf above it. A narrow life – Nancy living in this corner of nowhere with her parents, emptying the Hawkers' slops. Thank God for Anna saving me from such a fate. I sat on the bed and stroked the cover, which was coarse but clean. A pale blue, the colour of a gentle sea. The kind of sea not seen at Morwenstow. The colour likely deeper once but faded, now, from washing. Time had taken its toll.

On the shelf was a worn Bible, some folded squares of linen, and a cup. The cup bore some letters. I picked it up to see better, for the lettering was faded as the bed cover. The first word was an easy one – *The*. But the second was harder. I mouthed the sounds. *Bee oo duh*. *Bude*. The next was made like *Heaven* was made, but missing something – *Haven* it read, which must be close to Heaven. And the last word I knew, for I'd seen it in Boscastle – *Hotel*. The Bude Haven Hotel said the cup.

It had rings of dirt inside. The rest of the room so clean and yet this cup stood proud unwashed on the shelf. *There* was a mystery, but then people were the most mysterious things in the world. Some could never be solved.

Anna appeared in the doorway. 'Mrs Seldon thinks Nancy is at the vicarage.' She sat beside me on the bed and the mattress dipped, sending our shoulders crashing together.

'I don't think this is meant for a second body, Anna.'

'No, only Nancy.'

She stroked the bed cover, as I had done. We were more the same than we were different.

'Mrs Seldon feared the worst when she couldn't find her daughter,' Anna said. 'But next morning Nancy was here, sleeping the sleep of the saved.'

'And she didn't say where she'd been?'

'Not according to Mrs Seldon.'

'Who has lied to us once already,' I said.

'She seemed genuine this time. She's very frightened, Shilly. I think we're finally nearing the truth.'

'We still don't have a reason for Nancy to kill Joseph.'

'Well, Nancy herself might be about to throw some light on that. Come on. We'd best get over to the vicarage.' She struggled to her feet, having to fight the sag of the mattress.

I did the same, shuffling forward, and felt a stab beneath my leg. There was something under the bed. Something pressing up through the mattress. I knelt on the floor and peered beneath the bed.

'What are you doing, Shilly?'

I reached under and my fingers met wood. I tried to pull it towards me but it was too heavy.

'You'll have to help me, Anna.'

She glanced onto the landing, then did as I asked.

Together we pulled it out, this heavy wooden thing. It was a box. And in the box was a lock. My hand was shaking as I took the key from my pocket. For the last time?

The key we had found in Joseph Ians' chest fit perfectly. I turned it, and the lock clicked open. Anna and I looked at one another.

I drew back the lid.

FORTY-THREE

All the letters in the world were in that box. We tipped them onto the floor and sat in the paper nest we had made.

Anna picked up a handful and flicked through them. 'These have been sent from all over – Sydney, Odessa, Istanbul.'

I didn't know these places but the wonder in Anna's voice told me they were far away. The letters themselves looked like they'd been on long journeys. The paper was yellowed and stained, often torn. And amongst them, something else yellow, but brighter. I fished it from the paper. A flower, pressed flat between the pages. I put it to my nose. There was still a hint of sweetness there, though the flower was dried and had likely been in the box many months.

Anna was flying through another clutch of the letters. 'Izmir, Naples.'

There were so many words, dancing across their paper in blue and black curves and lines and swoops. All of them crowding to be read. I put the flower back in the box, put my hands over my eyes to hide the silent clamour of the letters.

'All of them signed Joseph,' Anna said, 'addressed to his *beloved Crow*.'

'Crow like the bird? That's a funny kind of name.'

Anna checked a few more letters. 'It's the same in all of them. *Crow*. I don't think it's a real name. More of an endearment. A pet name.'

'A crow would make a poor pet. And everyone here has a better liking for cats.'

'It's not the bird, Shilly! There's no "w". Look.'

I did look, and I saw. *Cro* it was written. 'Is Nancy Cro?'

'I can only assume so. Why else would these letters be under her bed?' Anna began reading again. 'He tells her, he tells Cro, that in Odessa the stars shine bright as her eyes.' She let that paper slide to the floor and picked up another. 'And in Malta, all the rivers speak her name. He has found favour with the captain and hopes to make first mate, in time. Then he will have enough money to return and they—' Anna looked at me. 'They were engaged, Shilly. Joseph and Nancy were engaged.'

'It must have been a secret,' I said. 'Nobody here seems to know anything about it. Not Nancy's family or Joseph's.' I picked up a letter. I couldn't read it. But I wondered if the feeling it held might be there still. Surely such love would leave a scrap of itself? Some beat that went on? How could it fade to nothing but paper thin as a first frost?

Anna scrabbled on the floor. 'Some of these have been delivered by hand. The dates are from before he left. No more than notes. *Cro, I love you. Cro, we don't need them. Cro, you must wait for me.*'

'So they were engaged before he left,' I said.

'But Cro, Cro,' Anna was muttering. 'Why did he call Nancy that?'

My knees were beginning to ache from being on the floor, so I sat on the bed again. 'There might not be a W in how Joseph spells it, but there is a C, Anna. Just as there was on the tattoo, and carved into the bench in the hut.'

Anna dropped the letters she was holding. 'It isn't C for Charlotte, then. It's C for Cro, whatever that word means to the pair of them. It must have been Nancy that carved the letters in the hut.'

'Or the two of them together, before Joseph left Morwenstow,' I said. 'To mark them getting engaged?'

'You're forgetting that the hut isn't as old as that, Shilly. Parson Hawker built it, and he came to the parish after Joseph had left.'

'Nancy's way of remembering him?'

Anna spread the letters wide on the floor. 'Remembered *him*, when he'd forgotten *her*. The last date I can see is 1823. He stopped writing more than twenty years ago.' She looked at me. 'Joseph never came back for her.'

'And she never married anyone else,' I said. 'She believed him, believed he'd come back.'

Anna eyed the letters scattered on the floor. 'He told her often enough that he would, those first years after he left.'

'He lied, then.'

Anna sat next to me on the bed again. 'Perhaps he meant to come back for her, but as the years went by and he saw more of the world, Nancy faded from his thoughts.'

'But he didn't fade from hers.'

'The fact she's kept these letters so long suggests not.'

My eye strayed to the shelf above us, to the cup from the Bude Haven Hotel. The sad, dirty cup. Nancy had kept that, too. It must have some specialness for her.

Then I looked at the letters on the floor, these sad treasures. The only proof that Joseph had loved Nancy. And the proof that he'd forgotten her. It felt wrong for the letters to be on the floor, for us to have touched them, so I put them back in the box, on top of the yellow flower. It was then I saw the many fingermarks smudging the pages. How often had Nancy read them as the years passed? As no more letters came?

I locked the box and put it back under the bed. Anna's teeth were clacking – her thinking noise.

'What if their engagement wasn't a secret?' she said. 'Joseph left Morwenstow under a cloud. What if he and Nancy became engaged and the Ians family disapproved. It could hardly have been the desired match for them. What if Joseph's parents forbade him to marry Nancy, threatened to cut him off, and instead of giving in, he did what he had planned and went to sea, to earn his fortune? Everything we've heard about him suggests he was something of an idealist. Remember Mrs Hawker telling us he thought there was copper under Coombe? That he dug up the old wall?'

'And he wanted to grow flowers – Anna, that's it!'

She frowned. 'That's what?'

'Cro!'

'Slow down, Shilly. I don't follow your—'

I grabbed the box again and found the flower. 'I saw another of these in the grate in the kitchen. A fresher one. Mrs Hawker told us that Joseph wanted to grow flowers in Morwenstow to send to London.'

'My God, you're right. And the kind of flowers Mrs Hawker spoke of were crocuses. This kind!'

'*That's* why he called Nancy *Cro*,' I said.

Anna took the dried crocus from me and twirled it between her fingers. 'So Nancy was to be the endeavour that came good. And then he forgot her, and no one here even remembers they'd promised themselves to each other. Time has removed her from the story.'

'Surely she must have feared he'd died?' I said. 'All that time with no word. Death would have been easier to bear than him not keeping his promise to come back for her.'

'But then he did come back, Shilly, didn't he?'

'More than twenty years later, half Nancy's life gone.' I thought of that morning she and I had talked, on the landing of the vicarage. I'd told her of my learning to read, how I feared I'd never master it. And what was it she had said then? *This world can be cruel. Sometimes waiting isn't enough.* 'Nancy would be more likely raging than pleased to see Joseph when he did finally come back.'

'I think we have our motive, Shilly.'

'We have something else, too. Something that shows Nancy was there, with Joseph's dead body.'

I held out the key. The key that opened the box of letters beneath Nancy's bed.

The key to Joseph Ians' death.

FORTY-FOUR

Mrs Seldon was no longer in the room downstairs. There was no sign of her outside either. I feared we'd spent too long with the letters, working things out. Mrs Seldon had likely gone to the vicarage to warn her daughter that others were suspicious of her. We hurried past the graves, making for the vicarage.

Something was troubling me, some tail we hadn't caught. I spoke my fears quickly, as the front door of the vicarage came into sight.

'The lantern hidden in the hut, the light shone over this way – who did that?'

'Joseph – it must have been. He and Nancy could have arranged it between them beforehand, by letter. She left him the lantern, left the initials so he'd know where to find it. He flashed the light to let her know that he had finally returned.'

'Yes, but only after more than twenty years. Why would they need all that hidden business now, Anna? Joseph's parents are long dead. His brother is an old man himself. Joseph could have knocked at Nancy's front door and carried her away. No one would have minded.'

277

Her teeth clacked again. 'True. So what happened that night? We're missing something. But if we can just get Nancy to—What's this? Locked?'

She had made to open the door to the vicarage, which had never been locked since we'd arrived. But it was locked now.

'Something must have happened,' I said.

Anna banged on the door. I peered through the dusty squares of the porch window but could see only the shoes and boots. Nothing beyond. None of the cats or the dogs. And no sign of a person.

'We'll go round the back,' Anna said, setting off. 'The kitchen door.'

We passed Gyp the pig but he didn't come and ask us for food, or ask to be let in himself. He was lying half in, half under a flowery bush that he'd squashed to ruins. I had the feeling he was hiding. That was a bad sign.

Anna tried the kitchen door with care. It opened. The room was cold. The fire had been allowed to go out. The makings of supper were on the big table, and so were the cats. Two of them licked the joint of meat left there, while another had the butter.

'This doesn't bode well, Shilly.'

And then we heard it – crying.

We crept through to the hall and then to the dining room, following the sound. The door was shut. I pushed it open. Before we could see into the room, Mrs Hawker's voice rang out.

'I've nothing left! Nothing! Have mercy – please.'

'Do not fear, Mrs Hawker,' Anna said, opening the door wide. 'It is only my wife and I. Good heavens!'

Mrs Hawker was cowering in the corner of the room. 'Oh, Mr Williams, thank the Lord.'

Her right arm hung limp by her side, the sleeve darkened. We rushed to her, and something clattered under my foot. A little knife, the blade wet with blood.

Anna tried to tend the woman, pressing a napkin to the wound, but Mrs Hawker wouldn't stay still.

'You have to stop her,' Mrs Hawker said. 'She's taken it all. When Robert finds out . . . Please, go after her!'

'Mrs Hawker, don't upset yourself so,' Anna said. 'You are hurt. If you would let me see—'

She shook off Anna's care. 'It's nothing! The money's more important.'

'What money?' I said, and put the bloodied knife on the table. It stained the white cloth soon as it touched. The blood bloomed.

'Joseph's money! She's taken it – Nancy has taken it.'

'If she's here in the vicarage,' Anna said, 'rest assured we'll—'

'Of course she's not here. She's run away, hasn't she? With the *money*.'

'Mrs Hawker,' I said, nice and firm, 'if you want us to help you, you have to tell us everything. Now, this talk of your brother. You told us you'd not heard from him for many years.'

She wouldn't look at me, remembered then the cut on her arm and grabbed the napkin from Anna to staunch it.

'Did you lie to us?' Anna said. 'Have you been in touch with Joseph?'

She looked to each of us. 'If I tell you, you promise you'll go after Nancy?'

'It would be our pleasure,' Anna said.

She let me help her into a chair. 'Joseph wrote to me. Five years ago now. I'd heard nothing before then. Not since he'd gone. He needed money. I sent him some, the little I could save from the housekeeping, but then Robert found out and . . . I had to stop. All he'd heard of Joseph was bad. None of the good in him. Robert said there shouldn't be charity for a wastrel such as him. And we couldn't spare it anyway, what with Robert's . . .'

'Overspending?' Anna said.

'But if you had nothing to send Joseph,' I said, 'what's this money Nancy has now?'

'It's because of the shares! Those wretched shares. I wish *The Eliza* had been wrecked.' She covered her face and sobbed. Through that noise, some words came clear: *my fault. My fault.*

Anna eased Mrs Hawker's hands from her face, then crouched beside her. 'Mrs Hawker, what is it that you blame yourself for?'

'For Joseph's death! It's my fault he came back here.'

'You told him of the money owed him, didn't you?' Anna said.

Mrs Hawker nodded. 'A share of the money earned by *The Eliza* was his. I only wanted to do what was right.'

'But your actions weren't entirely selfless, were they?' Anna said. 'Because Joseph's earnings were a means to make him come back here. Did Joseph ask you to send the money instead?'

Her lack of answer was answer enough.

'So you refused him,' Anna said, 'told him he could have the money only if he returned to Morwenstow. It was your way to bargain with him.'

'And he did come back,' I said, 'only to die.'

At this Mrs Hawker sobbed again.

'But he couldn't come to the house,' Anna said, 'not with your husband so ill-disposed to him. And you couldn't risk him being seen by anyone else. I see it now. You arranged to meet him at your husband's hut, well into the evening. You had it all worked out beforehand, with the lantern stowed beneath the bench so he could signal to you when he'd arrived, the letters carved into the bench so he'd know where it would open. Did you agree a signal for the light, so that you would know for certain it was him?'

She blew her nose on the bloodied napkin, which I took for yes.

'You couldn't have known the weather would be so dirty on the day Joseph reached Morwenstow,' I said. 'That was bad luck.'

'That certainly didn't help.' Mrs Hawker sniffed. 'If Robert were to learn of what I'd planned, he'd say the Lord sent that weather on purpose to show me my sin.'

'But the Lord didn't send quite *enough* wind and rain to stop Joseph, did he?' Anna said. 'Your brother was able to send his signal, and from what we've heard from the others who saw a light at the hut that night, it would have been around ten.'

'I saw it from my bedroom window. I'd been looking out all that week, expecting him. When I saw the light I nearly fainted with relief.'

'And then you went out there to look for him,' I said, 'while the parson was sorting his socks.'

'I couldn't leave straightaway. Robert had gone downstairs for something and it seemed to take him an age to go back up. I had to wait. I couldn't risk him seeing me leave the house.'

'And when you finally did get out to the cliff,' Anna said, 'did you find your brother?'

'There was no sign of him, or the light. The lantern was back in the bench, as if it hadn't been used. I wondered if I'd dreamt it.'

'Or the parson's devils had come to play their tricks,' I said.

Mrs Hawker gave me such a look I stepped away from the table, thought of picking up Nancy's knife to guard myself.

'What happened then?' Anna said.

'I came out of the hut and I heard . . . I don't know if I can describe it.'

'Try!' Anna said, quite harsh, I thought.

Mrs Hawker closed her eyes, as if that would help her find her words. 'It was awful. As if the wind had somehow found a way to speak. A woman's voice.'

'What did you hear this woman say?' Anna asked.

'It was closer to a cry, or, what's the word? A keening. She was keening. I've never heard anything like it. The pain, the anger. And then one word. I heard her cry one word.'

'Which was?' Anna said. We were both of us leaning forward. I barely noticed as a cat came in and sat by Mrs Hawker's feet.

'His name. She called Joseph's name.'

The mermaid's call. I knew it. The hairs on the backs of my arms stood up and my belly pitched. Here was the truth of it. I opened my mouth to say so, but Mrs Hawker was speaking again.

'The sound was so evil that I ran straight home. When I was back inside, in bed, with the curtains drawn, it all felt so foolish. I thought it couldn't possibly be his name I'd heard. It was a trick of the storm. It *had* to be the storm. Joseph hadn't come back yet. It would still be all right.'

'But then in the morning you saw different,' I said. 'Inchin Ben came with news of a dead man beneath the hut.'

'You knew the dead man was Joseph all along, didn't you?' Anna said.

She picked up the cat and pressed her face against its fat stripy cheek. 'I suspected, but I hoped to God I was wrong. I didn't go and look at him. There was no cause to, it would have made Robert suspicious. I hoped and hoped it was some other wretch. But then Frederick arrived, quite suddenly, and him *knowing* it was Joseph.' She shook her head. 'I didn't know what that meant. His dream . . . Now I know it was Nancy. Nancy Seldon killed my brother!'

'Did Nancy tell you that herself?' I asked.

'She didn't need to! The way she went after me with that knife, taking the money – it's clear as day she's fleeing Morwenstow because she killed my brother and knows she'll be hanged!'

'Nancy's flight could have been prevented if you'd revealed that Joseph was the dead man,' Anna said. 'Why didn't you?'

'Because it was my fault he'd come back!' The tears came again and the cat jumped away from her. 'Robert would have been livid if he'd found out, and I feared for myself, too.'

'Feared the parson?' I said.

'Feared her, the woman I heard, whoever she was. The anger in that voice . . . And now I see that I was right to be afraid.' She waved the bloodied napkin at me by way of proof.

'But what made Nancy do this to you now?' I said. 'Joseph's been in the ground for days.'

'I don't know! Her mother rushed over from the farm and then Nancy was on me with the knife. She wasn't making any sense, but she feared she'd be hanged. I got that much clearly.' Mrs Hawker narrowed her eyes. '*You* pair. It's you who caused her to attack me – she feared you were close to the truth.'

'Well,' I said, 'she was right, and here we are. But saying it's our fault is a bit—'

'The money,' Anna said loudly. 'How did Nancy know you had it for Joseph?'

'He must have told her before he died. No one else knew I'd cashed the savings in advance of him coming. It wasn't a lie – I really would have given him the money once he'd come back.' She stood, with a shake in her legs, but her voice was firm. 'Now I've told you everything and you promised you would go after Nancy. You mustn't waste any more time!'

'But how are we to find her, Mrs Hawker?' I said.

'She said something about a ship, not meaning to, but she must plan to go to Bude and find passage from there. That's the best chance of getting clean away. The roads will be too slow. I don't think she cares where she's bound as long as she saves her neck. She has the money – she could go anywhere. Start again. You must—'

There was the sound of the porch door being tried. Then a knocking, for the caller had found he couldn't get in. Parson Hawker's voice came loud as if he was just outside the dining room.

'My dear?'

Mrs Hawker threw down her napkin and hurried us from the room. 'Quick – go out the kitchen. He mustn't see you. Go to Bude, stop her. I'll keep Robert here. Try to explain . . . Heaven preserve us.'

And we were back in the garden, the kitchen door shut and bolted on us.

FORTY-FIVE

'We'll ask at the Bush for a gig, a cart – anything,' Anna said, already rushing into the dusk.

I ran after her, but my thoughts were running likewise. They were scat all over the place by what we had learnt that day.

'Anna, wait! What do you think happened to Joseph?'

'We know what happened,' she called over her shoulder. 'Nancy Seldon killed him.'

'But Mrs Hawker didn't see her do it. All she heard was that voice, calling his name.'

'You think it was the mermaid?'

'It could have been, couldn't it?'

She grabbed my arm to make me go faster. 'Here's what I think happened. Joseph Ians was at the hut, signalling to his sister at the vicarage, just as they'd arranged. Nancy left the vicarage at ten, which is when Mrs Hawker thought she saw the light. Nancy could have seen it on the way home and gone to investigate. Did she fear a return to the past, when people *did* signal from this coast to lure ships to their end?'

'If that ever happened at all, Anna.'

'Yes, all right. *If.* Who knows why Nancy went to the hut, but she did. And there, to her complete shock, she finds her sweetheart, now an old man. She's overjoyed – at last, he's returned!'

'Until he tells her that he only came for the money promised by his sister. He'd forgotten all about Nancy.'

'And in her rage, Nancy pushes him over the cliff.'

'Or, Nancy doesn't see the light, doesn't go to the cliff, and it's the mermaid that calls Joseph Ians to throw himself from the cliff path. When she has him in her claws, she tears him to pieces, as she tore the squire's nephew who abandoned her.'

Anna looked at me in such astonishment that her steps slowed, stopped. 'Do you really believe that, Shilly, after everything else we've heard? Nancy being missing that night, lying to us about her movements. The fact she has fled Morwenstow after first stabbing her employer, then robbing her.' These crimes Anna counted on her fingers. 'Not to mention Nancy's motive as a forgotten fiancée who has wasted her life waiting for her lover to return.' Anna lifted her eyes to heaven as if she couldn't believe the Lord would couple her with such a simpleton. 'Nancy Seldon killed Joseph Ians. What else could it be?'

'But say Nancy did push him over the cliff. How did he end up the way he did, so torn . . . How did she do it?'

The Bush was in sight.

'With a rock, I expect.' Anna said this like she was speaking of her supper, or her hopes for the weather. 'An easy murder weapon to rid oneself of. She could just throw it in the sea afterwards and it would be washed clean.'

'I still don't—'

'Nancy was enraged. Mrs Hawker heard her screaming Joseph's name. She was sent mad by the shock of seeing him, her hopes raised and then just as quickly dashed. Most of her life she's spent waiting and she sees at once that it was for nought. That could unsettle even the most quiet of minds. I believe she pushed Joseph off the cliff, then, with no thought to her own safety during the storm, she went down the path to the shore below.'

'And there?'

'There she took a rock and carved him to pieces. It was anger that caused her to go down the cliff path, to carry out such violence. I don't believe she was thinking clearly, not at first.'

Nancy's anger was strong as the sea's. She was violent as the waves that dragged people over the rocks. And she did that with her *hands*. That made Nancy much like the mermaid of the story, even if she was a woman of the land.

'But then,' Anna said, 'when it was done, Nancy must have come back to herself, realised what she'd done. She couldn't easily hide the body on the shore, and she couldn't rely on the tide to take it out either. The sea might have just washed it straight back in again. So she did what she could and tried to erase Joseph's identity. She had already gouged away his face, but she had to take the tattoo as well.'

'Which left the gobbet.'

'There were two kinds of injuries on Joseph Ians' body – the random and the deliberate. Left by two different states of mind. But it's just one woman we're after. And we have a good idea of where she's gone.'

And Anna was away into the Bush to ask about a means for us to get to Bude.

The rain came then, and though I knew it was falling on my head, I couldn't feel it, for my thoughts were dark and sore. It seemed to me as I waited for Anna in the rain that Mrs Hawker was to blame for her brother's death just as Nancy was, for it was she who'd called him back to these shores. She'd given him a reason to return. But it was more than that, more than a letter, I was sure of it.

What if Mrs Hawker had been out here on the cliffs, calling Joseph's name into the wind many times since he'd left? Those who called at the Bush for drink to ease their fears on stormy nights, they had heard *someone* calling. So had Inchin Ben. Parson Hawker thought the noise the calls of the dead, but it could have been Mrs Hawker calling her brother.

Until the night the voice was Nancy's, screaming with rage. Or was it Nancy's voice all along, all these years, calling for the man who left her? I'd seen her, hadn't I, on the cliffs, her back straight, her head held high though the rain pounded her face. I could believe it of her.

Or both women calling, for both had lost him. Both had mourned.

But only one of them had been betrayed.

But then what of me and Mrs Grey? We had each heard our *own* name called, not that of Joseph. What if Mrs Hawker hadn't spent years calling Joseph home, nor Nancy either – what if they'd both been drawn to the cliffs to answer the mermaid's call instead, and it truly was the mermaid that Morwenstow people heard? There seemed only one way to know.

We had to catch Nancy.

Anna called me from the doorway. She'd found us a dog cart, she said, and a boy to drive it. I followed her round to the stables, the ground now puddled.

'Captain Ians has agreed to bear the cost,' she said once we were on our way. The boy had whipped the horse and we were racing along the lanes.

'You saw the captain inside?' I said.

'I did, and I told him we nearly had our man. Or woman. If we can get to Bude in time, that is. Can you go any faster?' she called to the boy driving us.

He flicked the reins and we lurched quicker still. I had to hold onto Mrs Williams' false hair to keep it from streaming away in the wind. The hair was a wet nest.

'I had a job to stop the captain coming with us,' Anna said. 'He's been so long without proper sleep, he's like a madman.'

'Let's hope we find Nancy before she sails away, then.'

'I'm told there's a constable at Bude, which is something at least. If we can get there in time . . .'

The dog cart tilted as we rushed a bend, and I had to grab Anna to stop her falling out. If anyone was driving towards us, or heaven forbid walking in the road, they'd be dashed to pieces, and us too!

'But *how* to find her?' Anna said once we were righted. And then to the boy, 'How big is Bude's harbour? Are there many ships that dock there?'

'Not usually, sir. Most passing this coast don't want to come in for they say the mouth was made by the Devil it's so tight. But when the weather's dirty—'

'They've no choice,' Anna said. 'With this wind, it'll be like looking for a needle in a haystack.'

A very wet haystack, I thought, as the rain came on worse.

The boy took us through the town to the water, and there we saw a forest of masts and ropes, the tangle I'd heard Boscastle people call 'rigging'. But there was more of it here, for Bude's harbour was bigger, busier. Voices came to me on the wind but they were men's voices. No women called.

The wind and the rain seemed to have eased, but was that only because of the cold? I was soaked all the way to my drawers. I couldn't feel the weather any more. But then I saw that it *must* be better at

Bude, for a ship was risking the harbour mouth to leave port. Her lights pitched as she swayed into the darkness of the open sea beyond.

Anna sprang from the dog cart and raced to where the ground dropped away to the harbour's water. The boats and the ships rocked in the strong swell, and all around us was the creak of wood, the smell of salt. The few lamps guttered and spat.

Anna was counting the boats. 'Fifteen, sixteen. And how many already gone, now the wind's dropped?' She shook her head. 'A fine detective agency we are, Shilly. Our third case and the murderer will once more evade justice. He was right.'

'Who? Who was right?'

'It doesn't matter. None of it does now. It's over.'

She looked so wretched that I didn't press her on what she meant, and she was wrong besides. There was still time, and I had a thought where Nancy Seldon might go in Bude.

I took Anna's hand. 'We'll find her.'

'How?'

She was almost blue with cold, and I wondered if that was the colour of a mermaid's flesh too, them living in such cold water.

'The cup, Anna – didn't you see it, on Nancy's shelf?'

'Cup? I don't understand.'

I pulled her from the harbour, but she was slow, her steps heavy. She had given up. Too soon, Anna. Too soon.

A shadow passed us on the other side of the road. I ran to it. It was an old man with a beard near as long as his stick. He cowered away, as if I was a danger, and I must have been, the way I grabbed at him with my hands so numb they felt to me like clubs to beat a person.

'Please – where is the Bude Haven Hotel?'

'Oh, that's long gone,' he said.

'Gone? How can it have gone?' I thought of Nancy – had she managed to vanish with a hotel?

'The Temperance,' the old man was saying. He spat. 'The Temperance has it now.'

As we ran through streets dark and narrow as dreams, I told Anna of the dirty cup on Nancy's shelf.

'She's kept it so long without washing, it must mean something to her. All she has in the world are things that speak of Joseph.'

Anna kept looking back, towards the harbour. 'But what if she's got on board? She might leave while we try to find the hotel. We shouldn't risk—'

'You have to trust me, Anna.'

'If you're wrong, Shilly, it's over.' She tripped on a drain and I ran back to help her. 'If we don't get paid by Captain Ians, I—I'm sorry, I'm so sorry!'

I had no breath to ask what she was talking about. And no courage either. For something wasn't right, but Nancy – we had to get to Nancy.

A light ahead – warm, glowing, big as my heart fit to burst at that moment. And a sign above it that made my heart beat faster still. Just enough to help me reach the door.

The Temperance Hotel.

Anna and I fell inside, and everyone there looked up, of course they did. Everyone but the woman seated in the far corner. The woman in an old, worn dress I knew, the woman slumped, her hands tight round the cup on the table before her. The same cup as the one she'd left behind in her room.

FORTY-SIX

Anna was all for rushing over and catching Nancy, to tie her to a chair, I supposed. Hit her over the head with the cup to see her senseless.

I held Anna back. 'Nancy's not going anywhere.'

Anna bucked against me with the last of her breath. 'How do you know? She's a murderess, Shilly – she could do anything!'

'Look at her. She's worn out with it. With waiting.'

Nancy hadn't moved. She gave no sign she was even alive.

'So what do you propose we do?' Anna's body softened. She was trembly with relief. Was it only because we'd found Nancy? I said to myself, don't think about it, Shilly. Don't let those fears come into your thoughts and dash everything about.

'You fetch the constable,' I said. 'I'll stay here. Make sure she doesn't leave.'

'I'm not sure—'

'Go, Anna! I can do this.'

With a last glance at Nancy, Anna took her leave, but not before speaking quietly to the man behind the long, wooden counter that wasn't a bar, couldn't be a bar, not in that place where no drink was poured. Anna spoke to the man and then both looked first to me, then to Nancy. The man who was not a barman nodded. Anna left. The man shut the door behind her. Then quietly locked it.

Nancy didn't look up as I came near, but I saw that her hands weren't fixed, as I'd thought. They twitched against the cup. Her fingers stroked it, gentle as if it was a baby's cheek, or a cat loved as much as a child.

'Hello, Cro,' I said, and the word was a charm. Her head jerked up, her back jerked too, and she was staring at me. And then she was even sadder than she'd been before, because I was not the person who had called her that name long ago. He who had forgotten her. He who was gone. And she had done it.

'Cro . . .' She went back to staring at the cup. 'You've seen them, then, the letters. You must think me a foolish creature, Mrs Williams.'

'There's nothing foolish about hope.' I sat next to her. 'Hope can keep a body alive more than bread and water does. Can hurt it too, though.'

'You sound as if you've known the same suffering,' she said, and lifted the cup as if to drink. It was tea in there by the look of it. But as the cup touched her lip, she set it down again, hard on the table, as if the smell made her want to purge her insides. Perhaps she needed something stronger. The Lord knew I did in that moment.

'Who hasn't known the price of hope?' I said.

'It's cost *me* dear, I know that much.' She patted her thin, lank hair as if to check it was well set. Oh, my sweet Nancy. What have you done? And what will you do, Shilly? I asked myself.

I had told Anna I would keep Nancy from running away, when in truth I wanted her to run, to get on a ship and sail away, all Joseph's money in her pocket. For she had been true to one who hadn't been true to her. She'd done what he'd asked and waited, and what had that got her? Nothing but sadness. How many others were there, like her, all along this coast, or the coast of the country, the coasts of other countries, the names of the places Anna had read out to me, in the letters? The world was full of the betrayed. Them that did the betraying, they deserved to have their heads staved for the crime. To be torn to pieces.

But the thought of Joseph Ians' wreck of a body made me think another way, of Anna's way of thinking. A crime had been done to Joseph. The woman seated before me, looking at me as if she saw something in me that was the same as her, she had killed a man.

'We've spoken to Mrs Hawker,' I said.

'Have you now?' Nancy pushed the cup further from her, as if she feared it was creeping.

'My husband,' I said, 'he thinks that you killed Joseph Ians. That you killed him because you learnt he'd only come back to Morwenstow for the money his sister had promised him.'

'And what do you think, Mrs Williams?'

'That's not my name.' Why did I tell her that? Because of the way she was looking at me. Because of the letters kept all these years.

'What is your name, then?' she said.

Could I tell her? Would she call me? Would I get up, tell the man at the counter to unlock the door, then walk back through the darkness to the harbour where I would gladly step into air, into water, into her arms?

I hadn't answered her, and she was looking at the door. I said to myself, you must make sure she keeps talking, Shilly. While you wait for Anna. While you decide what to do.

'You came here with Joseph, didn't you?' I said.

'Only once. The day he left. We made a promise, right here, in this very spot, before the Temperance bought the Bude Haven, of course. We promised to wait for each other. That no one would take the other's place. No matter how long it took. I was seventeen when Joseph left Morwenstow. I'd never been outside the parish, save coming here, to Bude. What did I know of the world, of men? We made our promise. We drank to it.' She laughed. 'As if *that* meant anything.'

'It meant enough that you kept the cup you drank from,' I said.

'I didn't have much of him. Had to keep safe the little pieces. The cup. The crocuses when they flowered each spring. I used to tell myself they were sent by him. They were signs he would still come back. I kept the notes too, the first ones. He used to leave them under the sacks in the barn. My mother could never fathom why I was so happy to fetch the turnips in.' Her fingers twitched, as if she was remembering how she drew the notes from beneath the sack. As if there could be one there now, a note that said all that had happened was nothing more than a way to judge her, to see if she really would wait for her lover. 'But that was before,' she said. 'Before *they* made him leave.'

'You mean the Ians family? They didn't like the match between you?'

'They didn't like anything Joseph did. None of his wonderful ideas. They never believed in him.' Her voice was shrill now, as if she was a girl again, and in truth she did look all at once younger. The love she had felt for him, this man who had forgotten her, made her tired face slip its lines. Made her eyes dance.

'But you believed in him, Nancy.'

'That's why he called me that name, the one you said. No one's called me that in . . . Oh, more years than I can bear to count!' She smiled at me through her tears. '*Crocus*. His crocus. Never to lose her bloom, no matter the wait.' She laughed again, but sad now, a cruel laugh at herself. 'And I waited. Most of my life I waited for him to come back.'

'And then he did,' I said quietly.

A wave of pain broke over her then, over her whole body. She was brought low by it, falling forward on the table with the agony. Her breath left her in a deep moan, as if the memory was squeezing all the air from her. I thought of the cry Mrs Hawker had heard on the cliff that night, how frightened she'd been by it, and I was frightened at that moment in the Temperance Hotel, for no living person should make a noise like that. It was the sound of misery.

There was another noise. It came from the door. Someone thumped it. Was it Anna, back with the constable?

Nancy's chest was still pressed against the table, as if she was pinned in place by her grief. 'They'll hang me, won't they?' she whispered into the wood.

The man from the counter was unlocking the door. I moved closer to her. There was hardly any time.

'I . . . I have to know,' I said, my tongue all at once thick in my mouth, as if it was someone else's. 'In the sea, is there someone . . . Some*thing* . . .'

With a struggle she forced herself to sit upright again. She was frowning at me. I swallowed.

'The sea?' she said.

'I mean, was it a creature of the sea that killed Joseph? Some . . . spirit, that speaks with the voice of a woman. That calls. A terrible call, it is.'

The door was open, and there was Anna, and a man came in behind her. A man in a dark coat with shiny buttons.

'Was it a mermaid who killed him?' I said quickly.

Nancy Seldon was looking at me as if I had cursed her. The man in the dark coat was striding over to us. A man who knew his purpose.

'I did it,' Nancy said, angry now. '*I* did it. I'd waited long enough. I thought the sea would take him, once I'd cut him, but it didn't. There was nothing in the sea wanted Joseph Ians.'

The constable was at my side. His coat stank from the rain getting in the wool. He bade me move, and then he had Nancy by the arm, was hauling her away. I had one last sight of her face, older now than it had ever looked before.

'Charlotte,' she said – my true name.

And the Temperance Hotel was washed away in darkness.

FORTY-SEVEN

Anna said we must eat before we went back to Morwenstow. She said that was why I had fainted, for when she asked me when I'd last eaten, I couldn't answer her. So perhaps she was right, and it wasn't because I had stood before the spirit that lived in the sea and called wretches to their ends, wasn't because I had been called by my true name. Perhaps it hadn't happened at all.

So we had stew and bread before the fire, for our clothes needed drying, and Anna told me the food was good, and I said yes, yes it was, though I could taste nothing. After the excitement of the constable coming and Nancy being taken away, the hotel had quietened. People had gone back to eating and drinking tea and wondering if tomorrow would be dryer than today.

'Where did he take Nancy?' I said. 'The constable?'

'The cell at his lodgings. Not much more than a room, I gather, but it's got a stout lock. They don't have many murderesses in Bude, he told me. Once I'd managed to convey the seriousness of the situation, he couldn't get into his boots quick enough.'

'But Nancy won't stay here long, will she?'

Anna pulled a strand of onion from her teeth and laid it gently on the table, as if it were a precious thing she'd need to keep. 'She'll be taken to Bodmin in the morning.'

'To the gaol?'

'You sound surprised by this, Shilly, which is itself surprising.' She set down her spoon and wiped her hands on her skirt. 'Tell me, what did you and Nancy speak of while I went for the constable?'

'Nancy told me herself what we had guessed.' My spoon was heavy in my hand. Too heavy to hold.

'Good.'

'And of her pain.'

Anna ran her tongue across her teeth. 'I see. But there was no danger she would have got away, was there, Shilly? I was right to trust you?'

I nodded quickly and made myself pick up my spoon again.

'Good,' she said again, but her voice said she didn't believe I was good. Not good at all.

'Was it Captain Ians you were talking of, Anna, when we were down by the water?'

Now it was her spoon that lolled. 'The captain?'

'You said, *he was right*. About not having an agency, not making it work. Who was right?'

'I think you're mistaken, Shilly. I don't believe I said any such thing.'

Was that true? I tried to remember, but Anna was speaking again.

'Captain Ians is the only part of this case that doesn't quite make sense.'

'You mean his dream,' I said.

'That he should see his brother's death before it happened. How to explain it?' She was frowning at me, as if thinking how to explain me likewise, for the captain's dream was much like the way I saw things sometimes. And what was the truth there? I didn't know.

'The captain was certainly right about one thing,' Anna said. 'It *was* a woman who lured his brother home, but it wasn't the dead man's lover, after all, and it wasn't his sister either.'

'What do you mean?'

'Captain Ians knew from the dream that a woman had a part to play in his brother's death. It was *The Eliza* he was thinking of. A ship with a woman's name. That was what brought Joseph back. The money he'd earned from her.'

'Yes,' I said, when in my head I said *no*. No, Anna, I can't believe it's as simple as that. Because Nancy called me Charlotte, I knew she did, and I had no sense how she knew my true name. I hadn't spoken it in Morwenstow, had no cause to, and I was certain Anna wouldn't have done. I often thought she'd forgotten my name *wasn't* Shilly. That I had been someone else before that.

But there was another way of looking at it. Charlotte wasn't just *my* name. It was Mrs Hawker's too. Was Nancy's last word a sign she blamed Mrs Hawker? A curse on her? After all, it was Mrs Hawker who'd brought Joseph back to Morwenstow. Face to face with him at the parson's hut, Nancy couldn't go on telling herself he was dead, that that was why he hadn't come back for her. Mrs Hawker had forced the truth on her, and it was wretched.

Or was Nancy telling me that it was Mrs Hawker all along, that *she* was of the mermaid? Some shared saltwater blood, their shared rage. The voice had been heard in Morwenstow all these years. It had to come from somewhere.

All of this thinking, and I had the words for only one question – bare and plain, and not the right one.

'And what of the mermaid?' I asked Anna.

'I think we can safely say that the vengeful women of Morwenstow are those on land. Now, eat up. We must get back to the vicarage tonight. The Hawkers and Captain Ians deserve to hear what's taken place here.'

'And then home?'

She stood and pulled on her coat. 'Home?'

'To Boscastle, and to Mathilda.'

'Of course,' she said. 'Where else?'

It was late when we reached the vicarage but all the lights were burning. The porch door was thrown open before we'd had chance to knock. The parson pulled us inside, helped us find a clear path through the dogs and the cats to reach the drawing room, where we had sat with him the first night we'd come to Morwenstow. And this was to be our last time under this fine roof. We had done what we came to do and now we had to get back, to Mathilda.

Mrs Hawker and Captain Ians were seated by the fire. The room was so hot and smoky, they'd surely been waiting hours for us.

Mrs Hawker rushed to us. 'You found her? You found Nancy before she could get away?'

'We did,' Anna said. 'She's in the charge of the Bude constable.'

'Oh, thank heavens!' Mrs Hawker threw her arms around her husband. Her dress was different to that she had worn that afternoon, and one sleeve was bulky. I guessed it must be a dressing on the wound Nancy had given her.

'Let them come in, my dear,' the parson said, for the four of us were crowded in the doorway. He took her by the elbow and steered her back to her chair.

Captain Ians hadn't risen. In truth, he didn't look as if he had the strength *to* rise. I hadn't thought he could become any paler and more ill-looking than when I had last seen him at the Bush, but he looked worse still that night in the drawing room. He was the drowned man again, but this time he'd been too long at the bottom of the sea. The fish had begun to eat him.

'It's done?' he murmured. 'The woman who killed Joseph is caught?'

'Yes,' I said, for I needed to say it out loud. I needed to start believing it myself. 'Your dream was right, Captain. It was—'

His eyes had closed, his mouth had fallen open and from it came a soft snore.

Mrs Hawker patted his shoulder. 'At last. We'll let him rest.'

My Most Righteous Cat was stretched out to claim a whole, wide chair, wide enough for me and Anna to sit together, not touching. Mrs Hawker lifted him gently onto the captain's lap, so that we could sit in the cat's stead. His blessed warmth was deep in the horsehair stuffing.

Anna took off her coat, but before she set it down she took something from the inside pocket. A thick wrap of paper. I thought for a moment it was letters, Joseph's letters to Nancy, or Anna's own letters, those I hadn't had chance to read. But she was giving the packet to Mrs Hawker.

'This belongs to the captain,' Anna said. 'I trust you will keep it safe for him this time.'

Mrs Hawker tore off the paper and gave a cry. It was the money. Joseph's earnings from *The Eliza*.

The parson's boyish blue eyes widened, and he sank back into his chair.

'After you left for Bude, I told my husband everything,' Mrs Hawker said to us, and then to the man himself, 'and he has had the grace to forgive me writing to Joseph, for summoning him home.'

The parson clutched her hand, and the money was a rustle between them. 'Your grief is punishment enough for the sin, my dear.'

There were worse sins in the world than what Mrs Hawker had done. Far worse.

'All is well,' the parson said. 'The law has been upheld, what was wrong has been made right.'

'Joseph Ians is still dead,' I said, for I couldn't help myself. The parson's happiness at such a bad business made me want to throw myself onto the fire. 'And his death brings another, for Nancy Seldon will surely hang.'

The parson looked uncertain, as if I was telling him a riddle, and a bad one at that. 'Nancy's fate is right and proper, Mrs Williams. She has committed the worst sin known to man and so she must pay the ultimate price. That is the natural justice of the world.' He looked to Anna, smiled nervously as if to ask my husband to see that I was made to understand.

'I would not deny that Nancy has committed a grave crime,' Anna said, 'an inexcusable one. But we must acknowledge the part others have played in bringing us to this point. Mrs Hawker, my understanding is that it was your family who forbade the match between Nancy and Joseph.'

Mrs Hawker gathered the money back into its paper packet. 'My parents were united in their disapproval, and Frederick and I felt this fair. The Seldons work their own land, for heavens' sake! They are very different people to ours. But this was all such a long time ago.' She squeezed her husband's hand. 'It hardly matters now.'

'On the contrary,' Anna said, 'it is the key to your brother's death. Nancy Seldon was a young girl, naive in the ways of the world and in love with a man who was her social superior in almost every way. He extracted a promise from her, and she kept it all her life. It was all she had in the world – her faith in him, her love. And yet he forgot her. The world was Joseph Ians' for the taking, while Nancy Seldon had only the wages you paid her to clean your floors.'

'There was no *fairness* between them,' I said, trying not to spit the words. 'No fairness at all. There never is for women like Nancy.'

'Ah, but it's not always so, is it, Mrs Williams?' Mrs Hawker said, and there was some slyness in her voice. 'For you've done well in your life, I think.' Her gaze flicked to Anna, to all the world *Mr Williams* – my husband who dressed well, spoke well, was of her standing. '*You* have done what Nancy couldn't.'

I felt my shame hot all up my back, my neck, my scalp. There was never any escape from people like the Hawkers, like the Ianses. All the wigs and paints in all the world couldn't hide who I was truly. As I was born into this world, so I would leave it. But I would rather be my own self, she with cows' dirt scored so deep in her hands that it would never come out, than be like these cruel souls.

And then I felt a hand grasp my own dirt-scored one. Anna's hand. She gripped it tight.

'Mrs Hawker, there you are mistaken, comparing two things that could not be more different.'

'I'm afraid I don't see it, sir.'

'Well, then I am delighted to explain it,' Anna said. 'My wife has been lifted from her start in life. Nancy Seldon was never offered such a chance, and that speaks more about those surrounding her than Nancy herself. It speaks of a want of Christian charity.'

No one spoke then. I looked Mrs Hawker in the eye and she had to look away. I held tight to Anna's hand.

Then the parson gave a nervous laugh. 'Come, come – we need not speak further of these matters. The world is set to rights, shown by this bounty sent us by the Lord.' He tapped the packet of money in Mrs Hawker's lap, then beamed at Anna and I. 'For this we owe you a debt of thanks. What would you ask of us by way of recompense?'

If Anna was going to ask for money besides that owed us by the captain, she didn't have the chance for I spoke first.

'We would see your room at the top of the stairs. The one you keep locked.'

The parson's face flushed and he looked to his wife. She in turn looked fretful. But this only made me more certain I was right in my asking. There was much about this man that had been strange and speaking of guilt. The room kept locked, his fear of what might be found on the dead man, him not wanting to see the coroner. How he'd fallen at the funeral. Wasn't this what guilt looked like? Nancy would go to the gallows but the parson still had something to hide. I couldn't leave Morwenstow without knowing what was behind that locked door. Would it have anything to do with the mermaid? I didn't know. But I had to see it for myself.

FORTY-EIGHT

'What the room holds . . . It is not pleasant,' the parson said. 'This is truly your desire, to see inside it?'

'It is,' I said.

'As you wish, then, Mrs Williams,' he said sadly.

Mrs Hawker clutched his arm. 'You don't have to do this, Robert. You know it's not good for—'

'Stay with Frederick, my dear. If he should wake, he will need you more, I fear.'

He gave Anna and I a candle each, which made three with the one he carried.

'You will need the light to see it properly,' he said, 'all that is there.'

We followed him up the stairs and our shadows were tall and hunched as they climbed the wall beside us. At the landing he stopped and took a key from deep inside his long brown gown. His hand was shaking.

'Mrs Williams, I ask you once more, do you truly wish to see that which is better locked away, undisturbed?'

'More than ever, Parson. Open the door and let me see.'

He nodded, and his shadow was a great shaking beast behind

him. Anna kept close to my side. We would go in together.

The parson fumbled the key into the lock, took a deep breath, turned it. He murmured to the Lord, then pushed open the door.

At once, the smell of the sea was with us again, as it had been when last we'd seen the parson open the door. It was so strong, we might have been standing on the beach beneath his hut. Before us was a deep bank of darkness.

The parson stepped back from the door. 'I have done as you ask. If you must touch that which is kept here, I beg you to leave it as you found it. The labels must be kept in order or my work will be undone.'

'Labels?' Anna said.

I held up my candle and went into the room.

It was full of things. The table set before me, the shelves that ran up every wall, all cluttered. Spectacles. Pocketbooks. Handkerchiefs. Pipes. Lockets on chains. Lockets without chains. Beads. Crosses, the kind that hung in churches. Buttons. A doll with red wool for hair, a dress of blue cloth. Another doll with no dress. A doll with no eyes. A knife with a bone handle – two notches at the hilt. A heap of shoes, each with a scrap of paper tied to the lace, or if there was no lace, threaded on string through an eyelet. Then I saw that everything in there, everything crammed into the parson's room, had a scrap of paper tied to it in some way.

'My word,' Anna murmured behind me.

I picked up a brooch. It was made of tin, a bird, with a hole pierced for an eye. The paper with it had writing on. I put my candle nearer to help me read. *The Cal e do ni a*, it said. And some numbers. One and eight and four and two.

I turned, looking for the parson, and found him still on the landing.

'This,' I said, 'all this. It's from the dead. Those who wash in to Morwenstow. Why do you keep it?'

'To help others find them, find what happened to them.' His voice was trembly with grief. 'When the dead appear, if there is something with them, or lies nearby, I bring it here and I keep a record. People write, you see. Sometimes they come in person. If they know where a ship was lost, there's a chance the bodies came ashore not too far away.'

I thought back to our talk with him after Mr Good had come, and saw that we had made a grave error. When the parson had asked if we had found anything on the dead man to name him, it wasn't because he feared such a discovery. It was because he wanted it for his room. To keep it safe.

Anna was looking at the labels. 'But these dates go back years.' She turned a circle in the small, crowded room. 'There are so many.'

'Because so many have been lost, Mr Williams. I never knew, when I started, how many . . . But I can't stop now.' He stumbled forward and I went to help him. He leant heavily on me and I could feel the shakes running through him. 'I can't stop. If someone should come asking, a father, a wife . . .'

'And these.' Anna was going through a pile of papers, each of which bore a drawing. Strange shapes, with colours flooding them – more birds, flowers, things that looked like waves, and writing too. Names. 'Tattoos,' she said. 'You record them.'

'I am no great artist,' the parson said, 'but they are the best way to identify the lost. More distinctive. Personal.'

He used the tattoos just as we had done, to find out the name of the dead man. He was his own kind of detective. And a sad one at that, for what a burden to bear, being the keeper of the dead. And every time the wind rose, knowing more would come, torn, as Joseph Ians was torn, and nameless. Parson Hawker had given his life, and his health, I feared, to tend the memory of strangers lost far from home. He buried them and cared for their belongings. He mourned them. It was no mystery he was as he was.

He was sobbing now. Anna put down the papers and took both our candles. I helped the parson back onto the landing, and Anna shut the door. The parson had been right in his warning to me. Better to keep the belongings of the dead hidden. It was the only way to keep living.

We had asked the man who drove us back from Bude to wait outside, for we would return to Boscastle that night. Though it was late, I was fretful to be home. To stay another night at the vicarage was a poor doing, now that our work was done. I felt that even more having seen the parson's room. I wanted to be away from the dead.

Anna and I packed the travelling case, and between us we carried it down to the hall. Captain Ians was awake. Even that little sleep had done him some good, for colour had come back into him. His eyes were easier. Not so darting and fearful.

He and Anna talked of the fee he owed us, and she was happy enough that he would call on us before the week was out, to pay it.

'Will you return to your ship?' Anna asked, pulling on her coat.

'I doubt the owner will welcome me, given my abandonment. And even if he is willing, I fear my days at sea might be over.'

'With your brother's earnings from *The Eliza*, life will be easier for you,' I said.

He nodded but would not meet my eye.

We took our leave of him, and of the parson and Mrs Hawker. We were all but out of the porch when Mrs Hawker said we must wait.

'Mrs Williams – forgive me. A letter came for you, this morning.' She had turned back into the hall and was sorting through the papers there. 'With all that happened, I quite forgot.'

The look that was on Anna's face, I had seen it before. Before we left Boscastle. She made to stumble after Mrs Hawker but I got there first. I would know what it was she was hiding.

'Ah – here it is.' Mrs Hawker held out the letter to me. 'To think you nearly went without it. Are you quite well, Mr Williams?'

Anna had caught the post at the bottom of the stairs and leant against it. 'Shilly – don't!'

'Shall I fetch you some water?' Mrs Hawker said, fussing Anna. 'Dear me. Robert – help the poor man!'

I let them fuss. I had to know what was in the letter. Some secret from her past. The man she'd spoken of at the harbour in Bude. It was from him, this letter. Her husband. The *real* Mr Williams. I tore open the letter and tried to read the words as quick as I could. They were a mess of lines, curls. Anna was standing, reaching out to me.

'Shilly – I'm sorry!'

She hadn't helped me with reading, though she'd promised she would. It was to keep me from finding her secrets and now I couldn't read this page though I wanted to, so bad my eyes were water with the trying of it. Dear God, I wanted to kill her!

And then a word came clear through the water.

Yeo. The letter was from Mrs Yeo.

I blinked my eyes clear and tried to make myself slow down. The voices of the Hawkers buzzed like bees, far away and not for me. The words I cared about were on the page in my hands. I could do it. I just had to try very hard.

Mrs Yeo was writing to tell me she was so *ve ry so rry*. That we must come back to Boscastle at once.

Mathilda was dead.

The paper fell from my hand. There were more words on it but

I couldn't read them. I had forgotten how. I stared at Anna. I could not speak to tell her.

She was reaching for me. I could see her hands were scrabbling at my dress, but I couldn't feel them there. Her voice was a babble, not her own.

'I'm sorry, Shilly! He made impossible demands. All would be ruined if I didn't pay what he asked, and we had the money. Mathilda's money.'

Mathilda's *money*? Why was Anna talking about that now? She took my face in her hands and she was afraid. But there was only one thing that mattered now. I gave her the letter. She snatched it up but before her eyes had even turned to look at the terrible words it bore she was gabbling again.

'He made me do it, Shilly. I had no choice. You have to understand that. Mathilda found out that the money was gone and then she—'

'Read it, Anna!'

She seemed uncertain, her mouth all a-quiver, her wig more askew that she would ever allow usually. But this was not a usual day. This was the end of the world.

'It's not what you think it is,' I said.

What *that* was, I couldn't bear to guess. The argument with Mathilda – it was about the money, about Anna giving it away, for something I didn't understand. But Mathilda was dead.

The Hawkers were staring at us. I had forgot them. Had forgot where we were. A cat ambled past, as if all was well.

Anna read the letter. She looked at me. 'Mathilda – dead?'

From some clear, sharp place in my thoughts, I saw that she did not know Mathilda was dead before this moment, and that was a good thing, but . . .

Mathilda. Gone.

311

'How?' I managed to say. 'How did she die?'

Anna's gaze fell to the letter again. 'Mrs Yeo says Mathilda didn't recover from the chill. That she worsened and then . . . Then there was sickness.' Anna looked at me. 'Mrs Yeo fears Mathilda was poisoned.'

I lay down on the cold slate and called Mathilda's name. Called it with every bit of strength I had, as if that could bring her to me, there in the vicarage in Morwenstow. Not far, we had never been far from her left behind in Boscastle. But it had been far enough for someone to take her life while we were gone. My poor girl. My poor, poor girl.

AUTHOR'S NOTE

The Mermaid's Call is a work of fiction though it is set in a real place and some of the characters are based on real individuals. Chief amongst these is Parson Robert Stephen Hawker, vicar of Morwenstow from 1834 until his death in 1875.

Hawker is a fascinating person: poet, antiquarian, mystic, devotee of animals, bibliophile, a believer in mermaids. I have long wanted to write about him, and when Shilly and Anna were bound for a new case, it seemed the right time to introduce them to Parson Hawker. He has already featured in their lives, of course, though they didn't know it: Hawker's poetry lies behind the story of *The Magpie Tree*, the second book in this series.

Today, Hawker is perhaps more well known for his reputed eccentricities than for his poetry or religious acts. He was a complicated and mercurial man whose life in a remote coastal parish in north Cornwall was at times quiet and lonely, and at others rich in incident, not least due to the many shipwrecks that took place on his doorstep. Patrick Hutton, in his excellent study of Hawker's life and poetry, *I Would Not Be Forgotten* (2004), provides this sobering statistic concerning wrecks: between 1824 and 1874, over eighty ships were carried ashore between Bude and Morwenstow. Hawker's efforts in tending to the bodies of the dead who washed up in his parish, often horrifically damaged by rocks and in advanced states of decay, were Herculean. I have always felt that this work deserves greater recognition, rather than the tall tales that still swirl around his memory.

It must be acknowledged that, during his lifetime, Hawker had a hand in his own myth-making, to some degree enjoying and feeding his reputation as an eccentric. That aside, the chief architect in creating the legend of Hawker that persists today must surely be the Reverend Sabine Baring-Gould – another fascinating individual who deserves to be the subject of a novel in his own right.

The two men were contemporaries, both ministers of the established church in the same part of the world – the border between Devon and Cornwall – and with shared interests that included the saints of the early church. On Hawker's death in 1875, Baring-Gould rushed to produce a biography. His book *The Vicar of Morwenstow* was published within six months of its subject's passing and was hugely successful, with a new edition appearing almost immediately in 1876. It remains a controversial work for a variety of reasons, not least the fact that some of Baring-Gould's text was Hawker's own published work, used without proper attribution: see C. E. Byles' introduction to *The Life and Letters of R. S. Hawker* (1906), which he edited – Byles was Hawker's son-in-law. And yet, *The Vicar of Morwenstow* has, and continues to have, a huge influence on contemporary imaginings of Hawker. Mindful of this, as well as the caveats against the work, I have drawn on Baring-Gould's work for my fictional Hawker, but as part of wider research. It should be noted that the sermon that features in the novel is based on that reproduced as an appendix to the 1913 edition of *The Vicar of Morwenstow*.

In addition to the works already mentioned, Piers Brendon's *Hawker of Morwenstow: Portrait of a Victorian Eccentric* (1975: 2002) has been a key source for this novel, as has Jeremy Seal's *The Wreck at Sharpnose Point* (2003). I have also drawn on *In the Footsteps of Robert Stephen Hawker* by H. L. Lewis (2009), *Morwenstow Church* by Philip Docton Martyn (n.d., fifth edition), and *The Church of St. Morwenna and St. John the Baptist, Morwenstow: A Guide and History* by E. W. F. Tomlin (1982: 2003). Hawker's own words, too, have helped shape the parson of *The Mermaid's Call*. I have drawn on the *Life and Letters*, as mentioned above, as well as Hawker's book *Footprints of Former Men in Far Cornwall* (1870: 1948).

The man who appears in these pages is in many ways as fictional as the legends Hawker spun from his imagination, and the man part-fictionalized by Baring-Gould. This novel is in no way an attempt to present a biographical subject and the same is true for his companion. Little is known about Hawker's first wife, Charlotte I'ans (whose family name has been changed to Ians in this book) and no image of her is known to exist. We *do* know she had three sisters, and these I have replaced for the purposes of this fiction. The only other character with a real-life starting point is Mr Good. Readers of the first book in the series may remember Mr Good's previous appearance as the coroner in the case of Charlotte Dymond's murder in *Falling Creatures*. Hawker was in regular contact with a coroner of this name and I have no reason to believe they are not one and the same.

Hawker's antiquarian interests were widely shared during the mid to late nineteenth century in Cornwall when there was a concerted effort to record the county's folk stories. The two leading lights in this movement were Robert Hunt and William Bottrell, and it's their tales that Shilly and Anna often experience in this series. In *The Mermaid's Call*, the story of the titular fishy creature is based on the folk tale 'The Mermaid's Vengeance', which appears in Hunt's *Popular Romances of the West of England: The Drolls, Traditions, and Superstitions of Old Cornwall* (first series, first published 1865). Also playing a part is a tale of star-crossed lovers that features in many British folk traditions. I have drawn on Hunt's version 'The Lovers of Porthangwartha' and Bottrell's retelling of the same story 'A Legend of Pargwarra' from *Traditions and Hearthside Stories of West Cornwall* (first published 1870).

Another important source to mention concerns a real-life mystery: a sea captain's prophetic dream reputed to foretell a murder. In 1840, as Edmund Norway's ship drew near St Helena, he dreamt that his brother Nevell was set upon by two men on the road, back home in north Cornwall. In the dream, Nevell was beaten to death, his body left in a ditch. Shortly afterwards, Nevell was murdered in the manner dreamt by his brother. The resulting investigation led to the arrest and trial of another pair of brothers, the Lightfoots, who were found guilty and executed at Bodmin Gaol. My source for this strange story was *Cornish Murders* by John Van der Kiste and Nicola Sly (2007: 2013).

Other stories have loomed over this novel and were part of the motivation to write it. Whenever the subject of Cornish shipwrecks arises, so too does the charge that vessels were deliberately wrecked by the inhabitants of coastal communities. Morwenstow is no exception to this suspicion, and the sheer number of wrecks there has given the parish a certain notoriety, to which Hawker's eccentricities have contributed. This has meant that the trauma Hawker and his parishioners experienced when the dead washed up in Morwenstow has often been overlooked in favour of wild stories about false lights and shipwreck survivors being slaughtered. And though Captain Ians is right when he says there has never been proof of deliberate wrecking by the Cornish, this myth persists. There's an important difference between impoverished communities making use of the bounty offered them by wrecks, and intentionally causing those wrecks to happen. For more on this, see Bella Bathurst's excellent book *The Wreckers*.

For those wishing to see the real Morwenstow, there's no better place to stay than Hawker's vicarage, which is now a fantastic B&B owned by Jill Welby. The Old Vicarage provides a wonderfully evocative experience of Hawker's home, filled with period furniture and images of the parson and his family. Jill welcomed me so warmly and shared with me her extensive knowledge of Hawker, as well as useful texts for this book. I hope she will forgive a novelist's liberties.

A short walk from the vicarage is Hawker's hut, the National Trust's smallest property, which is open to the public. It's quite something. The buildings that appear in the novel as the Seldons' farm are now the Rectory Tea Rooms – a place that sustained the research trip for this novel, as did the nearby Bush Inn.

ACKNOWLEDGEMENTS

Thanks to all at Allison & Busby who have kept Williams and Williams Investigations in business, especially my editor Kelly Smith. Thanks, too, to my stellar agent Sam Copeland at Rogers, Coleridge and White.

Thanks to Dave for listening to my endless Hawker facts, for spending his Easter holiday braving the heights of the coastal path around Morwenstow, and sorting me out when I dreamt Hawker's ghost was wandering the vicarage (Shilly and I share a capacity for vivid dreams).

Thanks to my mum and dad, John and Veronica, and my sister, Lil, who, along with Dave, walked with me to Hawker's hut on a very cold and wet Christmas Eve through thick mud. Thanks for always saying yes to these trips, whatever the weather.

Thanks to my readers, whose insights made all the difference: Katy Birch, Carole Burns, Katie Munnik, Kate Wright, and Dave again.

Thanks to the Royal Literary Fund for awarding me a Fellowship during the writing of this book, which gave me much-needed time.

KATHERINE STANSFIELD is a novelist and poet whose first Cornish Mystery, *Falling Creatures*, was published to great acclaim in 2017 and whose sequel, *The Magpie Tree*, won the Holyer an Gof Award. She grew up in the wilds of Bodmin Moor in Cornwall and now lives in Cardiff.

@K_Stansfield
katherinestansfield.blogspot.co.uk